[handwritten inscription] Janice
Read & en
Clarence Hc
1/12/2002

The

Whipmaker's

Son

by
Clarence Hotchkiss

CeShore

Pittsburgh, PA

ISBN 1-58501-072-3

Trade Paperback
© Copyright 2001 Clarence Hotchkiss
All rights reserved
First Printing—2001
Library of Congress #00-107583

Request for information should be addressed to:

CeShore Publishing Company
The Sterling Building
440 Friday Road
Pittsburgh, PA 15209
www.ceshore.com

Cover Design: Michelle Lenkner - SterlingHouse Publisher
Typesetting: N.J. McBeth
CeShore is an imprint of SterlingHouse Publisher, Inc.

Printed in the United States of America

Table of Contents

GIDEON + HIS SON DAVID HOTCHKISS' IMMEDIATE FAMILY MEMBERS IN 1773

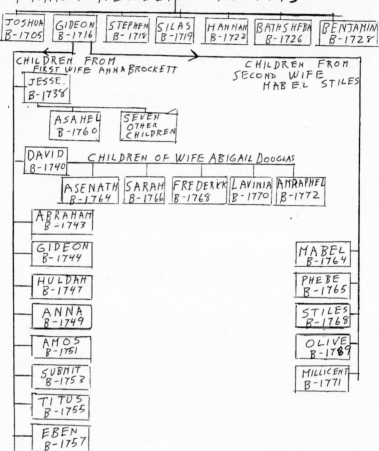

Chapter 1
The Wedding

It was the spring of 1773 in Waterbury Township, Connecticut, and the early morning was cool and brisk. As farmer Isaac Judd and his eleven-year-old son Chauncey came out of their house and began trudging toward their barn, Chauncey glanced at the road and saw a group of five runners heading east alongside the foggy Longmeadow Brook. He watched these neighbors dodge the puddles as they jogged toward the Naugatuck River and the town of Judd's Meadow. They were laughing and talking while they ran. Chauncey waved and continued walking toward the barn.

The runners ran through the town and began the long trek up the hill leading to the little town of Columbia. At the center of Columbia, they made a right turn and jogged on the road that led toward their father's house, the home they'd been brought up in.

The runners' father, Gideon Hotchkiss, formerly a captain in The French and Indian War, had ten living children by his first wife, Anna Brockett, and five more by his second, and on this day his oldest daughter, Huldah, was getting married. One of the runners, Jesse, was at 34 the oldest and tallest of Gideon's offspring. The curly-haired Jesse turned his head toward David, the next oldest, and said, "Well, are you going to go into that five-mile foot-race in Hartford or not?"

Before Dave, a handsome young man with sparkling blue eyes, could answer, their pretty, unmarried sister Anna spoke up, "I'd go in it, if Pa would let me."

She was petite with beautiful deep-set eyes and a small turned-up nose. Long dark braided hair bounced on her back while she ran with long strides to keep up with two of her brothers. Two other brothers, Titus and Eben, the two youngest in the group and still single, ran a few rods up ahead.

"Yeah, I may just go," David replied. "I want to take a wagonload of Pa's whips to Providence anyway. Anna, don't get your hopes up. The Captain won't let you go." He turned to look at her, noticing how attractive his sister was getting.

David, his shoulder-length hair in a queue, enjoyed these group runs with his sister and brothers. They all tried to run together at least once a week. Only a few people were sighted from the road this early in the day, and the Hotchkisses ran along easily with only the mud-holes causing them occasionally to break stride.

Anna, not to be deterred by her brother's remark, said, "I'd be safe with you, Dave. I never get to go anywhere. I'll wait till Pa's in good spirits and ask him."

Jesse, breathing hard, said, "Let's stop for a moment. Let Titus and Eben go on." The three of them stopped, and Jesse stretched his calves by leaning forward against a large maple alongside the road. "My knees are hurting some again."

Anna stretched too and said, "Aren't you fellows excited about Hulley's wedding? Do you think Joe Payne will make her a good husband?" and she looked at her oldest brother for a reply.

"Hah!" Jesse said grinning, as they started out running again. "He'd better be, or I'll wring his neck! Hulley's the most lovable person I've ever known; Joe does seem like a worthy fellow, though."

"He's certainly better than Clyde," Anna replied.

"Clyde is not suitable at all," Dave said. "Anyone could see Hulley wasn't interested in him. Why he kept after her so long I don't know. Hellfire, he's still only an apprentice!"

"Yeah, and not a good one either," Jesse added. "I wish the Captain would let me get rid of him. He's disruptive in the leather shop and often surly."

Dave was thinking how great it would be if his wife, Abby, ran too, when they heard the sound of a cart approaching behind them. As Dave looked around he saw man in a two-wheeled cart approaching at a rapid pace. "Get off the road!" David yelled. "It's Squire Everett, the varmint!" They all jumped to the sides of the road, but as the cart drew close it slowed down.

The heavy-set grey-haired driver yelled, his fat face turning red, "I might know! It's you damn fool Hotchkiss runners out here blocking the road! Get out of my way!" He cracked a long whip over his horse, which burst forward, almost hitting Anna.

Jesse shouted, "Watch it, Squire! You touch a hair on Anna's head, and we'll take the lash to your back!"

After Mr. Everett growled and passed by, they continued running.

"What are Pa and Mabel gonna to do with all the children during the ceremony?" Jesse asked. They halted now in front of Captain Gideon's home, a large white house, set fairly close to the road. Mabel Stiles was Captain Gideon's second wife, whom he had married shortly after his first wife died in childbirth eleven years before.

Anna said with a grin, "Mabel's agreed to watch them."

"Then she'll be watching about eighteen little ones, counting her own, mine, and Dave's," Jesse said.

"Before we go in," Jesse said, "I'd better see how things are going in the shop. You others go in the back door, or Mabel will have a conniption about the mud on your shoes."

While the little shop made shoes and other leather products, the main item was whips, which they made on a special machine that Captain Gideon had invented. This machine allowed them to make excellent whips with whalebone centers at a reasonable price. These whips were taken to major cities, where they were very popular.

"I'll come with you," Dave said, and the two men walked around the corner of the house and proceeded toward a decrepit-looking building about fifty feet away. A faded sign over the door painted in red proclaimed, "Hotchkiss Leather Shop." Here five apprentices worked under Jesse's supervision.

As they approached the shop, they could hear the crack of a whip hitting something over and over. Jesse ran to the door and opened it. Dave was surprised to see a man stripped to the waist, his body covered with sweat. He was using a long coach whip to lash out at an old saddle he'd mounted on a cross beam about three feet off the ground. His face was red, and with damp black hair hanging down in his face he swore and lashed out again, not even noticing the approach of Jesse. The other apprentices cowered over in one corner of the building.

"Joe Payne, you villain! Take that you bastard!" He yelled. He pulled the whip back to give the saddle another lash, but as his hand came back Jesse grabbed it.

"Clyde!" Jesse shouted, "what in hell are you doing? Have you lost your mind?"

Clyde turned and, seeing his supervisor holding his wrist, brought his arm down. With the danger over, the other workers returned to their benches.

Clyde said, "I know Hulley really favors me, Jesse. That Joe Payne, with his fancy ways, 'cause he went to Yale College in New Haven, ain't fittin' to kiss her boots."

Clyde then pulled the loose hair away from his face and tied it in a queue.

"Look, Clyde!" Jesse admonished. "Get a hold of yourself! She's made her decision. Joe Payne seems like a decent fellow. Give him the opportunity to prove it."

"He seems like a varmint to me, sir," Clyde replied, and his lip curled up as he sat down reluctantly at his bench.

Jesse went around to each man to see how he was doing and checked the supply of leather. Then Jesse said, "Look Clyde, if you want to go to the wedding with the other workmen here, you've got to calm down and behave. You're not a child! Do you understand?"

"Yes, yes, I want to go," Clyde replied. "I'll be all right."

"Come, Dave," Jesse said, "we ought to go in for Pa's meeting before they're all finished with breakfast."

The two brothers walked to the back door of the house, and when they opened the door, a young lady rushed forward and hugged Dave. The tall, blue-eyed bride-to-be was blessed with long, straight, flaxen hair.

"Hi, Hulley," David said, smiling. "You look beautiful enough to be a bride." They both laughed at his little joke.

Huldah gushed, "Today's the day. Hey, you better get in there for breakfast before your brothers eat everything. Mabel and I can't keep the victuals coming fast enough. Such fun. All my brothers and sisters are here now." She gave Jesse a kiss on the cheek, and then ran laughing into the kitchen.

Jesse and Dave went into the dining area where they greeted their father, a small but brawny-looking, bald man, who sat at the head of a long oak table with benches on each side. Dave yelled over the din of excited voices to his other brothers, "Hey there, Abram, Amos, Gideon! You fellows gonna save any victuals for a couple of old soldiers?"

"Old?" Jesse answered. "Speak for yourself, though my legs feel kind of old now."

"Hey, it ain't us that's eating it all," Amos replied. "Eben and Titus worked up a big appetite. Look at them!"

Amos, the smallest of the Hotchkiss men, often seemed to Dave to be over-whelmed by the large family, as if he was somehow still trying to find his place in the hierarchy. Eben and Titus, the youngest men at the table, Dave noticed, both ate like they were starving.

The seven brothers and their father all seemed to be talking at the same time, and Dave loved it. They were all eating and yelling to the kitchen for the ladies to bring them more. He remembered what it was like when he was a child, where it had been like this at almost every meal.

Gideon put his powdered wig on his bald head and announced, "All right, now the meeting can commence."

"So what's the purpose of the meeting, Captain?" young Gideon Jr., a carpenter, asked, straightening the knit cap on his head.

"Well," Pa said, as the others stopped talking to hear his reply. "As you know, Jesse and Abram are the only ones of you boys that are still working in the leather shop. I just thought now would be a good time to tell you how we're doing."

"Are you having trouble with the leather business, Pa?" Dave asked. "Jesse didn't say anything to me about any problems. I want to take a load of whips to Providence for you."

"No, no, it's not that," Gideon replied. "In point of fact, we're doing right well lately. As you know, I keep a separate account book for the leather shop. I've decided to sell the leather business to Jesse and Abram. I'll keep the building itself. David, if you or Amos, Eben, or Titus want to participate that's agreeable to me."

Dave stood up, put one foot up on the bench and said, grinning broadly, "Hey, this is exciting, though I don't care for a share for myself. I think I'd like to buy some land some day in New York when I save enough money. In the meantime I'd like to continue hauling wagonloads sometimes. You three fellows, though, you ought to be part of this."

"There's too many Indians in New York State, Dave," Captain Gideon said, "Can't see how you'd get title to any land to say nothing of what the savages could do to your family."

"I don't want to join the business either," the eighteen-year- old Titus said, as he ran his hand through his hair. "Don't think I can take orders from big brother the rest of my life. That's not your fault, Jesse. It's just me. You know the way I am. Maybe like Dave I'll move off to New York some day, if I can ever get some land."

Eben, the frail-looking teenager, said, "Pa, I appreciate the offer, but like Titus I don't think the shop is for me, at least not for now. I want to get some more schooling."

Abram then spoke up for the first time. The 30-year-old father of two was a chubby red-haired man with a deformed leg who normally let his older brothers speak for him. "Hey, what's wrong with you fellows? This is a good little business."

Amos, 21, then stood up, as if because of his small height he wouldn't be heard if he was seated, and said, "When I was single, Pa, I didn't think I'd ever go into the shop, but now that I've been married a few months and my Abigail is in a family way, I think I'll take up your offer. I'm not sure I can support my family on just wood chopping."

"Huzzah," Jesse cheered. "I'd love to have you in the business with us. You are as good a cordwainer as any young man I know."

"How about my taking a load of whips to Providence?" Dave asked. "What I'd like to do, Pa, if it's to your liking, is go through New Haven and New London on the way. I'd take Eben and Titus with me so we can go in the Hartford five-mile footrace on the way back. They're also having a whip accuracy contest at their fair. We ought to sell some there, too."

"Sounds good to me," Pa said, "but you should ask your brothers. They'll be the new owners as soon as we can write up a contract. But, do you need to take both Titus and Eben?"

"I'd prefer it, Pa. It's still mud season, and I may need all the help I can get trying to get through some of the swampy places."

Just then, the meeting was disrupted by the entrance of four of Captain Gideon's small, red-headed children. They greeted their half brothers, who made a big fuss over them.

Little freckled-faced, nine-year-old Mabel twirled in front of her father, giggling, "Pa, Pa, look at my new red dress."

Pa laughed and said, "Ooooh, what a dress!" and then gleefully picked up one of his young daughters and put her on his lap.

Olive said, "I'm want to see Hulley get married."

Another child came in from the kitchen and said, "A wagon is coming."

The family all got up and went outside. Dave looked off north and shouted out, "Jesse, here comes Charity now."

In the distance he could see Jesse's wagon coming up the hill loaded with little ones, with three children walking alongside. As they came closer, Gideon's little children ran down the road to greet their nieces and nephews, their red hair flying in all directions.

This commotion no sooner subsided than another wagon was spotted, and Dave's wife, Abby, arrived with their five children. "Dave, here's your clean clothes," Abby yelled. Dave noticed how pretty Abby looked with her dark brown, straight hair flowing down her back over her bright blue dress.

"Children, children, oh, so many," Mabel said, holding up her hands in exasperation.

The next few hours were filled with laughter as preparations were made for the wedding. Dave washed up and changed to the clothes Abby brought him. Huldah put on her wedding dress and came down the stairs to show the others.

Mabel spoke up, saying, "You look lovely, Huldah, but what's that on your dress?" Then she shrieked, "Ah, it's a spider!"

"That's very good luck," said Captain Gideon.

Mabel said, "No time to talk now; you'd better get going to the meeting house."

Huldah flicked the spider off and said, "Yes, everyone, let's go. And we'll take the three oldest children, too."

The large family all climbed into the wagons and began the three-mile trip to the new Salem meeting house. When they were all seated, Joe Payne joined Huldah at the front, and Reverend Fowler performed the ceremony. Joe, a tall, handsome, muscular man, looked to Dave like the ideal husband for the beautiful Huldah. The room was crowded with friends and neighbors, like the Judds and Williamses and some of the Brockett relatives as well.

After the vows were said the newly joined couple started down the aisle. Suddenly a foot shot out from one row, tripping the bridegroom and sending him flying forward on his face.

"My God!" David yelled out. "It's Clyde. Get him!"

"Damn you, Joe Payne!" Clyde shouted as he stood up and turned toward Joe. Clyde pulled the handle of a six-foot whip out of his belt. The specially made whip had a one-foot wooden handle and was flexible enough to wrap around his waist. His red face reflected the anger in his voice, and he shouted, "I'm gonna make you sorry you ever met Hulley, you bastard!" and he raised his whip to lash Joe, who was just turning over to see who tripped him.

Everyone froze up at this unbelievable turn of events except Dave and Jesse. Dave leaped over several benches and knocked Clyde down, but not before the whip came forward, catching Huldah's left leg at the calf. Clyde and Dave fell together on top of Joe. Jesse joined the fray and helped in trying to hold the furious Clyde down. Joe slid out from under the others and attended to Huldah, who was holding her leg in obvious pain.

Jesse shouted, "Damn you, Clyde, you idiot! What's got into you?"

Clyde swore and struggled to rise, but the other Hotchkiss brothers all held him down for a few minutes while the guests crowded around Huldah to comfort her.

Dave's brothers grabbed Clyde, picked him up, and dragged him out of the church. He then fell backwards down the steps to the ground.

Jesse yelled after him, "You're no longer working for us!"

As Clyde lay there with Jesse and Dave glaring at him, he propped himself up on one elbow, wiped the blood off his lip, and shouted out, "This ain't the end, you Hotchkisses! Nobody pushes Clyde Barrow around!" He stood up with a snarl on his face and a fist in the air. Then he turned around and ambled slowly down the road.

Dave said to Jesse, "Good riddance!"

Inside, Joe said, "Hulley, this fellow Clyde, was he sweet on you?"

"Maybe, Joe," Huldah said. "He's one of Pa's apprentices. Because I tried to be kind to him, he thinks I care for him."

The Captain asked, "Hulley, are you all right?" and he bent down beside his daughter who was seated on the floor next to Joe.

"Yes, Pa, my injury isn't serious. I guess this destroys the spider-on-the-dress superstition."

When Huldah stood up and appeared to be cheerful, the guests all crowded around some tables in the back of the meeting house to partake of the rum, cider, and victuals that were provided. A small musical group played, and Anna sang with them while some of the guests danced.

Abby said to her husband, "Who is the little boy playing with little Mable? He's a fragile but personable youth."

Dave looked around at the boy, "One of the Judds. I believe his name is Chauncey, one of Isaac's boys. His older brother Roswell is here, too, someplace."

"And who's the young fellow dancing with Anna, Dave?" Abby asked.

"You don't recognize him? That's that Williams fellow, Reuben. I think Anna fancies him, though he's a few years younger than her."

After a few hours of partying, the family returned to Captain Gideon's home.

After a time Gideon went into the parlor and took a little nap, but awoke when Dave's daughter, Asey, tiptoed into the room and said, "Honorable grandfather, would you tell us a story?"

When the children all gathered Gideon told them a true story about his first wife, where she had had a strange vision during the time he was away in the French and Indian war.

"Now, enough of stories; it's still nice out," Gideon said. "Go out and play," and he smiled and waved at them for dismissal.

An observer in the thick hedgerow nearby, shielding the sun with one hand, looked out at the family members emerging from the house to see Gideon's new foal. *How many are they?* he wondered. He continued to stare at the group looking for someone.

Bide your time, bide your time, Brutis. He shouldered his gun and slunk away through the hedgerow behind him.

Chapter 2

The Hartford Contest

Two weeks later on a sunny morning David left the shop with his big wagon full of whips and a couple of saddles. Up on the wagon with him were Titus, Eben, and Anna, who had convinced her father she'd be safe and that she could help her brothers. They made the thirteen-mile trip to New Haven without event to deliver to a store an order for wagon whips. A few days later they picked up some whalebone at Providence and then headed west toward Hartford.

Eben turned to Dave and said, "What's the contest at the Hartford fair going to be like?"

Dave, remembering the previous pleasant times at the fair, said, "It's not the same every year, but it's usually made up of three parts: a cutting contest, a pulling contest, and then there's blowing out candles."

They reached the fair on the outskirts of Hartford early in the morning before the public had arrived. Dave found the manager and paid the fee for a space for the wagon and the whip contest. The Hotchkisses were all kept busy setting up the wagon in the space allotted for them and putting up their sign. The fairgrounds were decorated with ribbons and signs. Rum and apple cider were served from one wagon, and music filled the air from a small band.

When the people started coming in, Eben said, "What do we do now, Dave?"

"Watch this, Eben."

Dave took out a twelve-foot, short-handled coach whip and with a casual thrust forward cracked the heavy whip several times in the air. When the people nearby looked around for the source of the loud report, Dave cried out, "Step up and get yourself a good whip! Hotchkiss whips are the highest quality. We have cutting whips, wagon whips, riding crops, horse quirts, express whips, bank up express whips. Step right up here! We even have holly driver whips. See this one!" He held up a whip with a three-foot long holly-wood handle.

"It's working, Dave," Eben said smiling; "here they come."

People approached cautiously to look over the variety of whips.

"Do you have an ivory-handled coach whip?" one gentleman asked.

"Not, here," Dave replied, "but I can get one for you and have it delivered."

"How about a cat-o'-nine-tails?" an old farmer asked.

"Sorry," Dave answered, "don't have much call for them. You want to punish someone? How about this cattle whip?"

And on and on it went. Anna smiled sweetly and handled the money while Titus and Eben held up different whips. They wore a whip coiled around each shoulder, answered questions, and sold a good number of whips.

Eben began to shout out a similar sales pitch to passers going by.

After a few hours Titus took a break to look around the fair. He soon came back, but breathing hard, and said, "Dave, you won't believe who's here. It's Clyde. He's demonstrating whips for old man Everett. They got a wagon over on the other side of the fair."

"He is? He's working for Everett, huh?" Dave replied. "Jesse won't like that. Clyde knows how to make Pa's whip winding machine."

Then he said to Titus, "See if you can find out what time the whip contest starts."

"I need a new lasher for my wagon whip," a farmer said to Dave. "You got any?"

Dave said, "Yes, they're right here. Take your pick," and he held up about a dozen of the foot-long lashers, designed to be fastened to the end of the thong of the whip. They were about one eighth of an inch in thickness and braided tightly.

During a lull in the interest by the crowd, Anna said, "Dave why don't you try the wrap around? That ought to draw a crowd."

"Are you sure you're up to it?" Dave asked.

"Certainly. We've done it before," Anna replied.

"All right, I'll get over here, and you stand at the other end of the wagon." Dave then cracked the whip a few times to get peoples' attention. "Are you ready?"

"Yes, lash away," Anna answered, smiling.

With that, David took a wide sidearm swing, and, letting the whip crack just the other side of Anna, he pulled back slightly on the handle, allowing the whip to wrap around Anna's waist without hurting her in the least. Dave then yanked the whip toward him, pulling his sister right up to him. The people watching were amazed at how skillfully this was done and came over and looked at the Hotchkiss wares.

When she had a chance, Anna said in a low voice to Dave, "Don't look, but an Indian over there by the oak tree has been watching us for about an hour. Why would he do that?"

"Hmm," Dave said as he glanced over Anna's shoulder at the Indian who was dressed like a white man. "I suppose I could ask him what his interest is. Odd-looking soul, isn't he?" Just then, several customers approached, and when Dave looked up again the Indian was gone.

Titus soon came back and said, "The whip contest is coming up right after the chicken judging, probably about one o'clock."

"Oh, no," David said, "I hate that."

"Why?" Eben asked.

"Chicken droppings, what else!" and he made a face of disgust.

Shortly before one o'clock David, Anna, and Eben showed up at the outdoor arena where many of the events were held.

"Why do you want to go into this contest, anyway?" Eben asked.

"Cause there's a cash prize. I want to win the money so I can buy a new wheel to replace the damaged one on my wagon; also I want to buy some pretty imported cloth for Abby to make a dress from. Then too, if I win, I think I'll get that book by Jonathon Edwards I saw."

The chicken judging was just finishing, and an official shouted, "Don't go away, folks! The whip competition is next!"

Anna said to Dave, "I wonder if Clyde will enter?"

"Oh, he'll be here all right," Dave replied, "and he's good."

Dave brought out the whips he intended to use and was doing some preliminary lashing when a voice from behind him said, "Dave Hotchkiss, I'm surprised you're here. Do you seriously believe you can beat me?"

"Hello, Clyde," Dave said. "What surprises me is that you're working for that fat scoundrel, old man Everett."

Clyde looked as disheveled as ever, and Dave thought he probably hadn't shaved in about a week. "Jesse showed me the door," Clyde said. "Where'd you think I'd go?"

The official shouted out, "First, we'll have the nail pulling contest."

"How does this contest go?" Eben asked Dave.

"See those boards over there, Eben? Well, they each have ten nails driven in them just a short distance so they're fairly loose. The object is to pull all ten nails out with as few lashes as possible. I use a longer lasher for this pulling work."

The crowd was getting larger now at the arena, and some were making wagers on the outcome. Each contestant in turn, using his whip, made his attempt, and it ended with Clyde winning and Dave getting second.

The official, after announcing the winners, said, "We'll now have the candle blowing contest. Bring out the candles and light 'em up."

Dave said to Eben, "The way this contest works is they put the ten lighted candles on a board and set it on that rail there. The object is to put out all the flames of the candles with just the breath of the lash and without hitting the candles. The one who does it in the fewest lashes wins."

The first contestant took a big sidearm swing with his whip, but it was too low and knocked five of the candles over. Of the other men who went before Dave, only one managed to blow them all out, but it took five cracks. When it was Dave's turn, he used a wide sidearm motion, and the crack of his whip blew out five candles. Once more his mighty whip was brought back and given a sidearm throw, and the rest of the candles were blown out, but still left standing.

The crowd applauded. The other men did not do as well, and now Clyde took his turn. After two lashes, however, there was still one candle lit.

"Congratulations, Dave, you won!" an excited Anna gushed.

"We now have two men tied for the overall whip championship," the announcer said. "This last contest, the cutting contest, will determine the overall winner."

"How does the cutting competition work?" Anna asked Dave, "and why did you pick me instead of Titus or Eben for your assistant?"

Dave explained that each man had an assistant hold a sheet of paper and that the whipper lashed out and cut it in half. Then one half was thrown away, and the whipper tried to cut the remaining half again, and so on as far as one could go. "As to picking you, Anna, I know I won't hurt you. People will remember seeing a pretty lady too so we may sell more whips."

"Which whip you gonna use?" Anna asked.

"I always use this long-handled coach whip with a short lasher. It's got a loaded thong."

"Look Dave, over by that booth! That vicious looking Indian is watching us again," Anna whispered.

"Yeah, I see. Got to put him out of my mind now." Dave noticed the Indian had a crock with him.

The competition was set so that the whipper had to be behind a line twelve feet from where the paper was held. In the first round, all the competitors were able to cut the paper in half. On the second round, when the helper just held one of the remaining halves, the first five men cut it cleanly, but the sixth man, lashed his assistant on the left hand, causing him to scream and eliminating him from the competition.

"All right, Dave, I'm ready," Anna said, gritting her teeth and holding the paper firmly.

Dave brought the whip slowly back over his right shoulder and, after carefully lining up his target, made an overhead swing, coming straight down on the paper, with the lasher cracking beyond the paper with a loud report only a few inches from Anna's body. The leather-covered thong sliced through the paper, cutting it cleanly in half. The other whippers were also successful with their second cut, including Clyde, who was last.

For the third round, the crowd watching the competition was getting more excited, and they yelled encouragement to their favorites or friends. The first five men all missed the paper or don't cut it cleanly and were eliminated; some of their helpers showed considerable pain on their faces.

When it's Dave's turn, he said to Anna, "Just hold it tight and don't move."

Dave again brought the whip back and then snapped it with a loud report to cut the paper through smoothly. The crowd yelled their approval.

Anna opened her eyes and said, "You did it Dave! Huzzah!"

The competitors after Dave all failed to cut the paper until Clyde, and he managed to cut his cleanly. This left Dave and Clyde to face each other.

Before Dave's next turn he said to Anna, "You better put these heavy gloves on, Anna, just in case." The half that was now left was barely enough to hang on to, but Dave brought the whip back, and as he did so, said to himself, *Just concentrate and relax, David!*

Just then Clyde cleared his throat loudly. Anna closed her eyes again, and at the sound of the cracking whip, opened her eyes and, feeling no pain, sighed and said, "You did it again, Dave!"

The crowd cheered even louder now, as much for the brave young lady as for Dave.

Now it was Clyde's turn. "I'm gonna drink a crock of rum after I win this contest, Hotchkiss," and with that the surly man cracked his whip with a wide sidearm motion, only to hear his assistant give out a loud yelp.

The official announced, "The overall winner of the whip contest is David Hotchkiss, representing the Hotchkiss Leather Shop of Columbia!" The crowd again yelled huzzahs.

Clyde yelled, "Damn the luck! It's your fault," and he clouted his assistant on the head with the butt of the whip and stomped off.

Dave was called up to receive his prize, and the official counted out the ten pieces of eight.

Several people, including a few of the competitors, came up and shook hands with Dave congratulating him. After Dave returned to his wagon and sold one of these men a whip, he noticed that the same Indian was approaching. He stopped about six feet away and said, "Hotchkiss, you at battle at Ticonderoga?"

"Yes, I was," Dave replied, and he suddenly shivered at the memory.

He was about to ask the Indian his business, when an old man stepped up to the wagon and said, "That's the best whipping I ever saw, son. I want to buy a whip just like the one you just used."

"Be glad to sell you one, sir," Dave replied, and when he looked past the man, the Indian was gone.

"Come, Dave," an excited Anna cried out. "Ten pieces of eight. You can get some beautiful cloth with that. Let me help you pick it out." She took Dave by the elbow and marched him off to a wagon nearby displaying all kinds of cloth. They picked out a very pretty piece of taffeta.

Chapter 3

An Accident?

In a nearby Hartford tavern that evening an excited nine-year-old Pres Redway sat at the supper table with his thirteen-year-old brother, Comfort, his nineteen-year-old brother, James, and his young cousin, Polly Hall.

"Jim," Pres asked, "can I come to the dance tonight too?"

"Yes," James replied, "but you and Polly and Comfort will have to bed down early 'cause of the race in the morning. Now, Pres, since this is your first footrace, you better stay right with Polly during the race."

"Ah, no," the young boy, Pres said, "I know I can't beat you or Comfort, but I think I can best Polly."

"Don't be so sure," Comfort said, "Don't know as I can best her myself."

Polly, just fourteen, her dimples somehow accenting her light brown hair, grinned and said, "Tell you what, Pres, why don't we run together for the first half of the race, and then we'll go on our own after that."

"Good," Pres replied, smiling, as he brushed lose strands of his blond hair out of his blue eyes. "Then we'll see who's really the fastest."

James said, "See that young lady with the dark hair over at that table in the back?"

Comfort looked to where James indicated. "Oh, isn't she the girl who was in the whip contest with her brother?"

"Yes, a brave young lady," James answered. "I found out she's going in the race tomorrow too, along with her three brothers over there; so I asked her to go with me to the dance."

A while later at the dance Pres met the Hotchkisses. Anna, now with her best dress on, seemed pleased to be dancing with the handsome James. When he was playing his fiddle in the band, though, Anna gave Pres some dancing lessons.

"Tell me Pres, does James favor any young lady? He's certainly manly-looking."

"Well, he has courted a few young ladies back in Killingly," Pres responded.

Pres noticed that both Comfort and Eben enjoyed dancing with Polly.

"You seem awfully young to go in this race, Pres," Anna said.

"Well, as James told me, if I'm gonna go in distance races, I got to start sometime. Polly isn't too much older than me."

At the conclusion of the dance the Hotchkisses and Redways along with Polly went to their separate quarters.

Early in the morning when Anna awoke, she threw cold water on her face and put on her buckskin pants, a white hunting shirt, and her moccasins. Looking in the mirror while combing her hair, she thought, *When will Anna's admirers appear? Then pinching her cheeks, Have I not sufficient charms to pierce the heart of James Redway? But still I won't despair. Who knows what mischief I yet may do?*

She went with her three brothers to the fairgrounds where the race was to start. She did her stretches while talking with James about the night before. *He's surely the handsomest young man I've ever met, Anna thought. Too bad he lives so far away. I wonder if I'll ever see him again?*

The race was soon underway, and about ten minutes later Anna found herself way behind her brothers and the other men, who had all disappeared up ahead. Looking behind, she saw Polly and Pres and slowed down a bit to let them catch up.

Anna chatted with the two young runners as they left the road and began running on the forest trail around the lake. She noted how the narrow path twisted and turned, going up and down sharply, forcing them to run single file to avoid the huge pines and white oaks.

"Watch out for the roots," Anna said.

The path around the lake was close to the water, giving them a pleasant view.

An observer in the woods, looking out from behind a large pine tree, had a good view of a short section of the path around the lake, which was about fifty yards away. *Where is she, damn it? What's's that noise? There she is. Aim carefully Brutis.* He slapped the stock of his long gun, and carefully aimed at the moving target. *Put a hole right through her. What happened? Where is she now? There, I see her now. Do your work. Squeeze!*

Anna, forgetting her own admonition, had just tripped on a tree root and dropped behind Pres and Polly about ten yards when there was a gunshot, and Polly screamed.

"Pres, Anna, help me! I've been shot!"

Anna found Polly on the ground writhing in pain and clutching her thigh. Blood was soaking her breeches around a hole in the cloth.

"My God! You are shot," Anna cried out. "Pres, get down low!"

"Who could have done such a thing?" Polly cried, grimacing through her tears.

Pres, crouching low, looked at Anna and whispered, "I heard someone run through the woods, the dirty coward."

"Must be some hunter thought you were a deer," Anna said, bending over Polly and trying to calm their fears. "Pres, rip off the bottom of your shirt."

Pres quickly took off his shirt and ripped the bottom off. After Anna tore part of Polly's breeches away, she bandaged the wound.

"What'll we do now?" the young boy asked.

"Pres, Polly and I will try and walk at least around the rest of the lake. You run ahead and get help at the fairgrounds."

When Dave finished the race, somewhat back from the leaders, he discovered Titus had won while James Redway was second, but Comfort and Eben were quite a ways back. After congratulating Titus and chatting with the other finishers for about ten minutes, James said to Dave, "Shouldn't Anna, Polly and Pres be here by now?"

"Yeah, you're right," Dave said. "I wonder what happened?" and he looked off into the distance. "Here comes someone now."

When Pres ran up he was exhausted and gasping for air, "The girls…"

"What, what is it?" Dave cried out. "Is Anna all right?"

"It's Polly," Pres said, as he bent over at the waist to catch his breath. "She's been shot."

"Shot? What? – Who shot her?" Dave shouted.

"It was an accident, I guess," the boy replied. "Anna's with her…It's her leg. They're walking slow."

Dave immediately sprang into action. "Titus, Eben, come with me in the wagon!"

James shouted, "Dave, let me go with you, too. Polly's my responsibility. Comfort, get a doctor to treat her!"

"All right," Dave replied. "Hey, Pres, just where are the ladies?"

"They should be back out on the road now," Pres replied.

After a mile or so, they saw Anna and Polly up ahead. Polly was limping badly, and Anna was supporting her on one side. Dave noticed on the white bandage, wound around Polly's leg just above the knee, that there was a considerable amount of blood.

As James and Dave jumped off the wagon, Polly wailed, "Oh, James, James, I'm so glad to see you," and she cried a little.

"What happened Polly?" James asked, and he gave the helpless girl a hug. Just then, Polly, who was very pale, collapsed unconscious, going limp in James' arms.

"Oh, my God!" James cried out, as he eased her down flat on the ground. "What'll we do?"

"Stay calm, James," Dave said. "I believe she just fainted. We'll put her in the wagon and take her to town so the doctor can patch her up. Anna, what happened?"

On the way back in the wagon, while Anna attended to Polly, she explained what occurred.

"Do you think she'll recover?" James asked. "Polly means a great deal to us."

Dave said, "I think she'll be all right, James. I saw a number of men in the last war with more severe injuries than this come around."

When they drove up to where the crowd was in the fairgrounds, a doctor stepped forward. Polly regained consciousness, and the doctor started examining her while the local constable fired questions. "What happened anyway? The boy here says she's been shot. Does she know who the varmint is that shot her?"

Dave said, "I understand, Constable, that Polly never saw the person who shot her; the pine woods are very dense there. My sister Anna was with her and the Redway boy. Anna thinks it was a hunter."

After the doctor attended to Polly, he turned to a group of young men that included James, Comfort, Pres, Dave and his brothers, and said, "She's lost some blood. I got the musketball out, though, so I believe she'll recover all right."

The organizer of the race approached and said, "Everyone in town knew we were having this race today. I wonder what some ignorant blackguard was doing out there hunting on this day? Maybe it was one of the Benson gang, but I don't see why they'd be shooting a girl."

As soon as Polly felt a little better, James and Comfort prepared to drive Polly and Pres off to her home in Voluntown.

Chapter 4

The Reaper

At about three o'clock, after selling most of the remaining whips, the traveling Hotchkisses began the 25-mile trip south to Columbia.

"Dave," Eben said, "why do you suppose that Indian asked you if you were at the Ticonderoga battle in the French and Indian War fifteen years ago?"

"I don't know; it puzzles me."

Eben replied, "Tell us, Dave, what happened at the battle at Ticonderoga? You and Pa were there, but I was just a baby when that happened."

Dave said, "All right."

"I never heard the story either," Titus said. "Hell, I was only three when you were at the Ti. Were you with Pa all the time?"

"No, though because I was a runner, Pa made me his messenger. The fort there was occupied by about 3,000 French soldiers while we had about 15,000 men. The fort is located near the lower end of Lake Champlain.

"All of our forces were bivouacked in the forest just a slight distance west of Fort Carillon, which now they call Fort Ticonderoga. Upon arriving, we prepared for a few days for the attack.

"On the morning of the eighth we received word that our own regiment was to be held in reserve, but Pa came to me and said, 'Rogers' messenger was wounded. I'd like you to go over there and serve Rogers. He's a great man, but if you don't want to go Dave, I'll understand. You'd be volunteering.'

"'Yeah, sure, I'll do it, Pa,' I said.

"'All right, but here take this,' Pa said, and he handed me a Long Distance Reaper."

"He gave you a Reaper? Ain't that the most expensive whip the Captain makes?" Eben asked.

"Yeah, it sure enough is. It's well balanced too, since the handle is loaded. This one was about twelve feet long with a good lasher on the end. I stuck it in my belt and wrapped the core around my waist about four times and was on my way."

"When I reported to Rogers, he said, 'Aren't you Lieutenant Hotchkiss' son?'

"'Yes, sir,' I said. 'My father thought I could be useful to you to replace your messenger.'

"'What's the whip for, son?' Rogers asked. 'Seems like you'd be carrying a pistol.'

"'My Pa just gave me this whip this morning. It's his business making whips. I don't own a pistol.'

"Just then Major Putnam rode up, and as he dismounted, he said to Rogers, 'Robert, I've been assigned to assist you in the attack. We're to lead off and start now.'

"'Aren't they bringing up the artillery?' Rogers asked.

"'No,' Putnam said. 'With this forest and the hill, they figure it would delay the attack too much to bring the big guns up. With our superior numbers, our British friends believe we can just overrun the barriers the enemy put up.'

"Rogers said, 'If we weren't going to use artillery, then we should have attacked yesterday before they'd finished this outer rampart. Now, our attack will be much more difficult. Israel, meet my new messenger, David Hotchkiss. He's Gideon's son.'

"'Good to meet you, son,' Putnam said, and he shook my hand. 'Yes, I know Gideon. Makes good whips. That must be one you're carrying.'

"I assured him it was and showed him the Reaper. Rogers began shouting orders, preparing for the attack. Then he turned to me and said, 'Stay with me, Hotchkiss, when we move forward.'

"It was about seven in the morning when we started out. Rogers' four hundred Rangers led the way. We worked our way forward, crawling and running from one stump or bush to the next. Some other American troops were behind us, including DeLancey's New Yorkers. Off to one side we could hear some Scottish bagpipes blaring and squealing.

"The French were using their artillery from behind the huge log wall they'd built, where they could see us much better than we could see them, and, of course, we had no artillery.

"Putnam, Rogers, and I were down in a gully behind a log on the ground along with some other Rangers. The Rangers' assignment was to keep firing at the heads of the French at the barrier to allow the British to attack. The three of us were close to the barrier wall but in such a position that the enemy could not fire on us directly. The two majors and I stayed there for a long time observing the battle. Off to our right we could see row upon row of the British infantry march forward in close formation. What a sight it was!

"But with the enemy's position so strong and with all their artillery, even though we had the French and their Indians outnumbered by about four-to-one, the British redcoats couldn't get through the ten-foot high barrier. By noon, bodies were littered all over the field, but they continued to make attacks. We could hear the screams of men in pain. The air was full of gun smoke, and the sulfurous stench of black powder stung my nose.

"All day the exhausted redcoats attacked. They didn't hide behind stumps and logs like the Rangers, but stayed in straight lines, looking neither to the right or left. I saw a few climb up through the huge barrier, but they were run through by bayonets."

"My God!" Titus cried out. "You mean we outnumbered the French four-to-one and still couldn't climb the wall. What happened then?"

"At six o'clock one more last attack was called, and the furious redcoats and Black Watch, as well as some Jersey men, charged again, but it was to no avail. The angry soldiers no longer had any strength left. When the retreat was sounded, they stumbled back exhausted.

"Our Rangers now held their ground and fired at the few hats that we could see at the barrier to help our British ranks retreat. One British officer fell dead from a bullet right on top of the log I was behind. He fell backward so that his head hung down over the log upside down, and he stared blankly at me."

Eben gulped and said, "I pray I'll never have to go to war."

Dave continued, "We could see the French now standing up and cheering, and some of the hostile Indians advanced beyond the barrier to chase us. Probably looking for scalps, I thought. I was watching them, when I suddenly saw that Putnam and Rogers had retreated. I looked around. No one but me was in the gully.

"I started to follow them, but when I looked up at the top of the steep gully I saw an Indian looking down at me. He let out a whoop, and threw his tomahawk at me, hitting me in my left arm."

"Is that how you got that scar?" Eben asked.

"Yeah. I fell to the ground. The Indian was a bare-chested, middle-aged, ugly-looking warrior. He pulled out a knife and charged down into the gully. But before he reached me, I got back up and let loose with a lash of the Reaper. Got him right around the neck, and he fell, clutching his throat. Blood spurted out. Just then I looked behind me and saw three more Indians coming down the other side of the gully. They were holding tomahawks, but having seen their companion fall, they were more cautious in their approach. I then cracked the whip at the one on the right. I cracked at one and then another as fast as I could. The one in the center was rather fat, and I got him once in the belly, and he let out a yell. They had never seen this long a whip cracked. It scared them so much they clambered back up the gully and ran back toward their barrier. So then I ran the other way.

"As I reached the top of the gully, I heard a noise and looked back and was surprised by a strange sight for a battlefield. Next to the Indian I'd killed was a young Indian boy, maybe ten years old. He was kneeling over the dead man and was crying with a loud wail.

"After pausing a moment, I turned around and continued running till I finally caught up to Rogers and Putnam.

"The next day General Abercromby had us withdraw from the area. It was all over."

"What were your losses?" Titus asked.

"I understand we lost about 2,000 men, most of them British. We figured the French only lost about 400."

The travelers arrived in Columbia after dark, and after letting his younger siblings off at Pa's, Dave headed for home. Abby and his children welcomed him with hugs. Even one-year old "Raiphe" crawled over to his father and hugged his leg.

Abby was thrilled with the pink taffeta Dave took from his pack. "I missed you so, Dave."

"I missed you, too. Maybe next year I can take you and all the children to the fair."

"Did you bring us any toys, Papa?" seven-year old Sarah asked.

"Yes, here's a little something for you," and Dave handed her a small doll. He then passed out small gifts to the other children.

"This doll is pretty," Sarah said, and she hugged the doll to her chest.

Chapter 5

A Murder

About a year later, in March, 1774, it was sugaring time, and Dave and Jesse were collecting the sap from the maples they had previously tapped, using spouts formed from sumac bark. From these spouts the maple sap dripped into troughs of linden and basswood. With six inches of snow on the ground, the sleigh was pulled by a pair of Jesse's horses through a gully of mature maples.

Some of the younger children were riding on the sleigh. Occasionally they dipped their fingers in the watery liquid and tasted the sap. They smiled and said, "Good, good!"

Jesse and Dave were driving the horses. "Well, who's going to have the next baby," Dave said at one point, "your Charity or my Abby? Abby must be awfully close to the time."

Eben and Asahel were taking the troughs from the base of the trees and dumping them into the large bucket on the sleigh.

When the last bucket was poured, they drove the team out of the gully and back toward Dave's house where a large pan over a big fire was waiting the arrival of the sap. Charity, Anna, and Abby, their backs to the fire, chatted and tried to stay warm.

After several hours, another sleigh appeared, and a pregnant Huldah and Joe joined the group around the fire. Anna and the pregnant ladies all greeted each other with hugs and giggles as they compared their protruding bellies.

Dave thought Huldah seemed a little upset, and when he was alone with her husband, asked, "Joe, is everything going normally with Hulley's pregnancy?"

Joe, looking concerned, said, "Her pregnancy seems fine, but she's been a little nervous since we've seen strange footprints in the snow lately in our yard."

"You mean some strange animal is on your farm?" Dave asked.

"No, no, they're human footprints," Joe replied. "Recently we've seen these footprints, but we've never seen the man. I don't know if it's just some curious fellow or what."

"Hmm, seems odd," Dave said.

He was hunched over, seated on a log, his gun in his lap in the woods, peering out at the Hotchkisses. *There they are, all the women together. Why are there always so many, hey Brutis? Hmm, must wait.*

A few weeks later, on March 28th, Anna shouted from Dave's yard, "Dave, come run with me. You've got to get fit. Let's run over to Hulley's and back." Anna had jogged over from her father's house to David's and was stretching her legs at the hitching rail. The snow had all melted.

Dave and Anna began running together on this sunny morning. The buds were just appearing on the trees.

The observer had just arrived in the woods across the road from Hulley's, where he could clearly see the front door. The newly sprouting leaves on the bushes and trees gave him enough concealment from the road. He sat down on a large boulder and, still holding his gun, removed the coiled whip from his shoulder, putting it down beside him. *Wonder if this will be the day, Brutis. It's a nice day for it. Brutis, now is the time!*

When Dave and Anna arrived at Hulley's, she came out on the front steps, her face beautiful in her pregnant condition. Smiling broadly she said, "Dave, Anna, am I pleased to see you! Joe's gone to Waterbury Center, so I'm all alone. Come on in."

"We'll come in for a few minutes Hulley, but I want to use your outhouse first," Dave said. Anna started up the steps and was about to embrace her older sister, when there was a loud report like the noise of a gun being fired. Dave had begun walking around the corner of the house, but upon hearing the shot he looked back and saw Huldah slump down from where she stood. Not fully realizing what happened, Dave ducked down, thinking, *What's going on?* He yelled, "Get down, get down!"

Anna screamed, " Oh my God, Dave! Hulley's been shot!"

Dave shouted, "Oh, no! Anna, keep down!"

"But Dave, Hulley's shot," Anna cried out, as she got down on her knees to examine Huldah.

Dave quickly stood up and sprinted over to where Hulley fell at the top of the steps. Anna was crying while holding Huldah's head in her hands. Dave saw the blood on her chest and felt for her pulse. "Hulley, wake up!" he cried. He looked into her beautiful staring eyes, and a cold chill went up his back.

"Oh God! She's dead, Anna. Someone shot her all right. Who the hell would shoot her?" Then he stood up, cupped his hands, and yelled out, "You bastard you, Clyde! I'll get you, you cowardly murderer!"

Anna began crying, "Dave, can't we do anything? Who would want to hurt Hulley? Everyone loved her. I can't believe she's gone."

"Anna, we should get in the house quickly before the varmint reloads his musket," Dave said, and he took her hand to raise her up.

Dave then picked Huldah up, carried her in, and put her down on a bed. "Anna, there's nothing we can do now for her." Then, looking at Hulley one more time, he closed her eyes.

"Pray with me Anna." Dave fell to his knees as did Anna beside him. While they looked at their sister with tears in their eyes, Dave put his arm around Anna's shoulder. He prayed, "Lord, Lord, please be with our sister's soul; and please help us to endure this burden and give us the strength to go on. And Lord, help us to find the murderer who committed this horrible crime." ·

When he stood up he said, "Anna, I wish there was more we could do for poor Hulley. You stay here. I'll take Joe's musket and look around."

"Be careful," Anna said. She watched Dave take down the Brown Bess musket from over the fireplace and load it.

He stuck a whip in his belt and went out the back door to explore the immediate area. He circled around, hoping to intercept the murderer. He was thinking, *Who could have done this? Could it be Clyde?*

When Dave returned to the house, he said to Anna, "I didn't hear or see anything. Can't understand who'd do this."

Anna, her eyes all red from crying, was seated next to the bed where Hulley lay. She said, "When Polly Hall was shot, we thought it was an accident, but this certainly was no accident. What'll we do now, Dave?"

Dave thought for a moment and said, "We can't just leave Hulley here for Joe to find. I'll see if he has a wagon here."

Dave found Joe's cart in the barn, and he hitched it up to the horse while Anna wrote a note for Joe and quickly wiped up the blood on the steps. They then drove to their father's house with Hulley's body in the back.

The Captain was walking back from the shop toward the house when Dave drove up. "Pa, a terrible thing has happened," Dave shouted out, and his voice cracked as his eyes watered. "Hulley's been shot and killed."

As Pa came over to the cart, his face turned white, and his eyes widened. Dave and Anna explained what happened. "Oh, God, not Hulley!" Pa yelled, his voice breaking. He looked down at Hulley's body in the wagon. Then he pounded his fist on the side of the wagon, after which he sank down on his knees and prayed silently.

Suddenly Mabel rushed out of the house, followed by Submit and Eben.

"What happened? Is it Hulley?" Eben asked.

Then from the shop Jesse emerged, followed by his workers.

Jesse hollered, "Pa, Dave, what's going on?"

"It's Hulley, Jesse. She's been shot." Dave replied.

Again Dave explained the strange events. The women were all crying. Jesse and his brothers looked shocked.

His face full of rage, Eben shouted, "Pa, we got to get the villain!"

Captain Gideon, his experience as a military officer taking over, with a crack in his voice, said, "This is horrible! Here, cover her body with the blanket so the little ones won't see her, and bring her body into the parlor. Dave, as you suggested, you go to Waterbury Center and inform the Constable. Eben, Amos, Abram, Jesse, get your horses! We'll go over to Hulley's house to see what we can find."

By now the ladies and children were all in tears. After laying out the body, Gideon said a prayer out loud, asking the Lord for strength and for Him to be with Hulley. Then the men mounted up and galloped off.

Dave rode north to Waterbury Center and finally found Constable Radcliff, whom Dave had not previously met. He was a young man. *He's younger than me,* Dave thought, as he looked at the blond thin Radcliff. I wonder if he can find the murderer?

"I'll come out there with a few deputies as soon as I can round them up," Radcliff said.

Dave then left and rode to Hulley's house. He had just arrived and dismounted when Joe Payne rode up. Eben came out of the house, and the two of them walked up to Joe.

Sensing something was wrong, Joe said, "Where's Hulley? Did she have the baby? Is she all right? What's happened?"

"Joe, something terrible has occurred," Dave said. "Your mysterious stranger fired a shot and killed Hulley. Anna and I were right here when it happened."

Joe, his face suddenly contorted with grief and anger, wailed, "Oh God, No! Why did I leave her alone? … Who was it, Dave?" Anna went up to Joe and instinctively reached for his hand to comfort him.

Then Dave explained the circumstances of the crime. Joe's face became white; he sighed and flopped down on the steps. With his head in his hands, he began sobbing. "The filthy bastard! I should have gone to the constable before. Oh, God!"

After a few moments, he wiped the tears from his eyes. "I'll get cleaned up and go over to Gideon's. I have to see her once more." He stood up and went into the house.

Dave and Eben looked around, and, after calling Gideon's name a few times, they found him and their brothers searching the woods across the road from Joe and Hulley's front door.

"Did you find anything?" Dave asked.

"We found a few tracks," Pa said, "but whether they're fresh or not I can't say. Also, Jesse found this," and he held up a piece of a lasher only about six inches long that must have broken off from a whip.

Dave stared at the lasher and rolled it back and forth between his fingers. "Clyde, mayhap?"

"I don't know," Pa replied. "It's not my construction, though."

"Constable Radcliff is coming later," Dave said. "Maybe he'll have better fortune, but the murderer may be far away now. I'm going home. I have to tell Abby and my children."

Two days later the funeral was held at the meeting house. The murderer had not been found. The same family members and friends who had attended Huldah's wedding just the year before were all there.

After the burial at the cemetery, most of the family returned to Gideon's house.

When David and his brothers, along with Joe Payne, sat down around the dining table with their father, the Captain said, "How can we find this menace and rid ourselves of him before he kills someone else?"

Jesse said, "I'm wondering, Pa, if we can find out who has the whip that would match the lasher we found. It's not one of our making. Could it belong to Clyde?"

Dave said, "It doesn't look like the lasher he was using last year at the Hartford fair, but it could be a different one he got. Perhaps the Constable can question Everett about it. In fact, he could ask Everett if Clyde was on the job or not at the time of the murder."

Titus spoke up. "I can't believe you all are so calm. Damn it all!" He stood up, his face now red, ran his hand through his black hair, and began walking back and forth, talking rapidly. "Hulley practically raised me after Ma died. Let's all go and find Clyde and take some coach whips and lash the truth out of him, the bastard! It's got to be him! Who else would do it?"

"I agree," Joe Payne said, "I'd like to hang Clyde from the nearest tree."

Gideon looked at Titus and said, "I understand your anger, Titus and Joe. I'm mighty vexed myself, but we don't know if it was Clyde or not. Tell you what, why don't you boys get Radcliff and go and challenge Clyde? Who knows, mayhap he'll just confess."

"All right," Jesse said, "I'll get Radcliff, and we'll meet back here and all go see Clyde."

In about an hour Jesse and Constable Radcliff came back, and Dave, his brothers, and Joe Payne, mounted up and trotted off toward Clyde's cabin.

When they arrived, while still on their horses, Radcliff called out, "Clyde Barrow, come out of there!"

"What do you want, Constable?" Clyde yelled from inside, as he peeked out the front window.

"Clyde," Radcliff shouted, "it's about Mrs. Huldah Payne; come on out."

"Hah," Clyde replied, as he opened up the door, "I see all the Hotchkiss men out there. Well, I didn't do it." He stepped outside, holding a rifle across his chest. Two of his brothers came out, also carrying muskets.

Joe Payne yelled, "We want to see all your whips," and he got off his horse and approached the cabin.

"Stay out of here, Joe, you bastard!" Clyde said. "Hey, Amos, you can come in and look. I heard, though, she was shot, not whipped to death."

"Where were you, Clyde, on the day of the murder?" Radcliff asked.

"I was in New Haven delivering whips," Clyde answered. "Hell, I wouldn't hurt her; I was mighty fond of her."

Amos brought out some whips, and Dave and Amos looked them over carefully. However, they could not find a broken lasher on any of them which matched the piece at the crime scene.

Titus dismounted now and, while approaching Clyde, exclaimed, "You misbegotten varmint, Clyde! I know you did it. Admit it, you killed her!"

"No, I did not!" Clyde shouted. "Hell, if you can find the villain who shot her, I'll help you hang him."

Titus came right up to Clyde and shouted, "Damn you Clyde, don't lie to me." He punched Clyde on the chin, knocking him to the ground. With that, Clyde's brothers pointed their muskets at Titus.

Radcliff then quickly grabbed Titus around the waist, dragged him away from Clyde, and shouted out, "Titus, damn it, calm down! We have no evidence Clyde did it."

"It's true," Dave said, "Amos and I can't find a lasher that matches the piece we found at the scene."

Titus yelled out, "All right. We'll leave, but I know you did it, and you know you did it. Somehow we'll prove it, Clyde!"

Joe Payne said, "I believe the same."

About a month later, on April fifteenth, Abby yelled up the stairs to her husband, who was still in bed, "Today's the day; Dave, get Mrs. Mollyhouse, now!"

"Are you sure?" Dave shouted back.

"After having had five babies, I ought to know when the time has come."

Dave dressed hastily and went for the midwife, stopping at the Captain's house to tell the family. By the time he returned with Mrs. Mollyhouse, Anna, Submit, and Charity were there along with Mabel and Dave's father. The ladies were all talking and preparing for the birth.

Now relieved that his job was done as far as the birth was concerned, Dave sat down with the Captain at the table and had a mug of rum. "Pa, did Radcliff ever find out where that lasher came from?"

Gideon thought for a moment and said, "I just talked to young Radcliff. He said old man Everett claims Clyde was in New Haven the day of the murder, just as Clyde said, delivering an order for him, and also that he didn't know who made that lasher. I guess we're at a stone wall on Hulley."

"Hmm," Dave said, "Clyde said he was fond of Hulley, but he didn't seem too bothered when his whip lashed Hulley's leg at the wedding."

"Oh, oh, help me! I'm gonna die!" screamed Abby from the other room.

Dave put Lavinia down and rushed to Abby's door. "Anna, is Abby all right?"

"Yes, yes, don't worry," Anna replied.

A few minutes later a baby cried out, and Anna came out of the bedroom, holding the baby and smiling, with the other ladies following. She walked up to Dave and said, "It's a boy, Dave, a beautiful boy."

"How's Abby now, Anna?" Dave asked, as he smiled and stared down at his new red-faced son who stared right back.

"Fine, she's just fine, thank God," Anna said. "What's his name gonna be?"

"We've decided on Cyrus," Dave responded, grinning.

"I like that," Pa said. "Has a nice ring to it, Cy Hotchkiss." Dave stood up and went in to see Abby.

Three weeks later, on May ninth, Charity had her baby. Jesse and Charity decided to name her Huldah.

Chapter 6
Another Wedding

Summer, fall, and winter came and left in the settlements along the Naugatuck River with no further clues turning up as to the identity of Huldah's killer. Whenever the Hotchkiss men or Joe Payne encountered Clyde at any occasion, harsh words were exchanged, but Clyde continued to declare his innocence.

On March first, 1775, early in the morning, Anna, Titus, and the muscular blacksmith, Ezra Hopkins, were all running together and stopped by Dave's house. While the men stretched at the hitching rail, Anna went in to get Dave to accompany them. Anna found Dave just finishing his breakfast while Abby was spinning flax and the children were taking turns operating the flax break and combing out the flax straw before the spinning.

After greeting the family, Anna said, "Come on, Dave, we're gonna run to Joe Payne's house."

While he was putting on his running moccasins, Dave said, "Anna, I see Ezra's running with you. Doesn't Reuben object to this, especially with your wedding only a few weeks away?"

"No, no," Anna replied, smiling as she threw her long dark brown braid over her shoulder. "I've told Reuben that Ezra's just an old school friend and not to be concerned, and he's amenable to this."

Dave answered, "I'm not sure if I was in Reuben's shoes that I could allow this. Plus, Ezra is such an odd fellow, with those peculiar eyes of his."

"Now, now," Anna said, "I feel safe running with him, plus Titus is with us anyway. Come out now while my muscles are still warm."

Abby looked up from her spinning and said, "Do you have your linens all finished, Anna?"

"Almost," Anna replied, "but I've finished the work on my bedding, the towels and the table covering."

Abby said, "Don't forget, Anna, we're having a quilting for you here next Tuesday in the afternoon; so invite all your young lady friends."

"I appreciate this," Anna replied. "I have a quilt partly done. I've got pieces from my mother's wedding gown and a large number of other pieces of all colors besides."

"It should be fun," Abby said. "And it wouldn't do any harm to let all the unmarried young men around here know that the girls will need escorts to take them home."

"Yes, yes," Anna laughed. "It'll be a frolic."

Dave went over and kissed Abby on the cheek. She smiled and said, "Hurry back, Dave. Winter's not over yet, and we're almost out of firewood. There are so many chores to do."

"Yeah, I know. I'll be back soon." Dave and Anna went out and joined the other runners. It was cold and windy with a few inches of snow on the ground, making the roads slippery.

As they ran along, taking short strides so as not to slip and fall, Dave said, "Titus, what do you think's gonna happen to the Colonies the way the British are behaving?"

"I don't know, Dave, but if our colony calls for volunteers, I'm going in."

"Not me," Ezra said, as he turned his head to look over at Dave. "My pa says we must be loyal to the King, or we could lose all our property."

Dave noticed that he couldn't really tell whether Ezra was actually looking at him or not.

Titus replied, "But the British are no longer treating us like British subjects. We can't even ship our whips to other countries. It's as if they just want us in order to obtain cheap raw materials to use for their own manufacture."

Dave decided to change the subject, "Now, what's the date of your wedding, Anna?"

"The sixteenth," Anna replied, "and Ezra, I want you to come, too."

Ezra looked around again and said, "Hey, I'll come, but I think you're making a big mistake, Anna. Reuben's not the man for you. By the by, can I bring someone?"

"Yes, surely," Anna said.

"Mayhaps I'll bring the widow, Penny Todd," Ezra replied.

"She's certainly a beautiful lady, Ezra," Dave said. "You should make a handsome pair."

Ezra paused a moment and said, "Perhaps you're right, though I doubt she favors me. Seems like women folk don't care for my damaged eye. Isn't that the truth, Anna?"

"Now Ezra," Anna replied, as she shook her finger, "stop feeling sorry for yourself. You'll find a suitable young lady some day."

Upon reaching Joe's house they found him outside splitting wood. With his powerful shoulders, he split the logs quickly and with what appeared to be little effort. "How are you doing these days?" Dave asked Joe, as the runners stopped and began stretching.

"I'm fair to middling," Joe said as he took another swing with his ax. "I like to think I'm splitting the head of that murderer, Clyde Barrow."

"After a year now, Joe, I see that, like me, you're still mourning," Anna said. "She's often in my dreams as well."

Joe stopped chopping a minute, "My grief is over, though I'll never forget her, but my anger at Clyde seems to grow every day."

"But Joe, we still don't know if it was Clyde," Dave said. He crossed his legs while leaning forward against a maple tree to stretch his hip muscles. "As you know, Radcliff said he talked to the merchant in New Haven, and Clyde did make a delivery that day."

"I know, but he could have made the delivery before or after the killing," Joe replied. "I'd kill him myself, if I thought I could get away with it, the dirty varmint!"

"Oh, Joe," Anna said, deciding to change the subject, "do you have anyone to bring to my wedding?"

"No, I was even wondering if I should come at all, Anna; I've been so out of sorts."

"Our cousin Hester Hotchkiss wants to come," Anna said. "Why don't you bring her?"

"I met her once, a pretty little lady," Joe said. "Do you think she'd allow me to escort her?"

"Yes," Anna replied. "I'm certain she'd welcome the invitation. I happen to know she has a mind to marry a Yale man."

"All right, I'll think about it." Joe smiled for the first time and resumed his wood splitting.

As the four runners began their return to Dave's, the sun came out and the trees showed pure white against the pale blue sky.

Two weeks later, on March 16th, the Hotchkiss family and their friends, just as they'd done for Huldah's wedding, gathered at the meeting house for Anna's wedding. Reverend Leavenworth performed the ceremony and preached a long sermon which put some of the people to sleep, including Uncle Stephen from New Haven.

Instead of having a frolic at the meeting house, Anna had arranged to have it at a tavern so that the guests wouldn't be saddened by the memory of Hulley's wedding two years before.

As they sat and looked around at the guests, Dave said to Abby, "My, that widow Penny Todd is certainly a lovely looking lady. It's a shame she had to come with that Ezra."

"Yes," Abby said, "I knew her in school. She's one of the more interesting persons I've ever met. She'll remarry, I'm certain, even with her having three children. Come let's dance, Dave." They danced to the lively music of the little Waterbury band in which Eben played. Anna sang a few songs with the band.

"Anna seems very happy, doesn't she?" Abby said.

"Yes, she does," Dave responded. "I'm only surprised she picked a man five years her junior, but I like Reuben."

Abby said, "I see Joe Payne brought Hester. This pleases me."

"Yes," Dave said, "I haven't seen Joe look this contented since before Hulley died."

Chapter 7

"Momma, Momma!"

Roughly three weeks later, on April fifth, Dave was lying on his side in bed at dawn, looking out the window at the stone wall and the field beyond which he'd have to plow soon. *Should I get up now or not? I feel so relaxed I could just lie here all day, and Abby, – her beautiful body.* He thought back to a time, just an hour before.

He remembered, Abby must have rolled over and hugged him, waking him slowly from a sound sleep. "Good morning, birthday fellow," she had said. "What would my big brawny man want for his thirty-fifth birthday?"

"Ah, hah," Dave had said grinning. "You know what I always want on the day of my birth."

They both had laughed and then made love, after which Abby had gotten up to do her early morning chores while Dave fell back asleep.

Now Dave thought, *I suppose I should get up. So many things to do.*

Just then his daughter, Asey, opened the bedroom door, and all the children ran in, yelled "Papa," and giggled.

"It's Papa's birthday. Get up Papa," Asey shouted, and she climbed on and straddled his chest and tickled his sides.

"Oh, Asey, you divil!" Dave said laughing, lifting her up and putting her on the floor beside him.

Immediately nine-year old Sarah jumped on him. "Hold Papa down," she screamed, and the children all piled on top of their father.

Dave laughed, "All right children, Papa has to get up now. Up you go." He heaved himself out of the bed, and the children all scrambled for the door, with three-year-old Raiphe bringing up the rear.

After working the farm all day, Dave came in for supper. He cleaned up, and as he and the children prepared to sit down, Anna arrived with Reuben. "Happy 35th, Dave," Anna said, hugging her brother.

"How's the bride?" Dave said. "You look radiant." He pushed her back a little so he could look at her. Anna blushed, and Reuben put his arm around her shoulder.

"The bride is doing just fine, thank you," Reuben replied. The laughter of the four of them filled the room, as Dave and Abby teased the newlyweds.

An observer noted Anna and Reuben's arrival while seated on a stump in a patch of woods where he could see the back door of Dave's house. *Just wait till they come out to go home, hey Brutis. Hmm, it's fairly dark now. No one should see us.*

Dave and his family sat down at the table and ate a delicious stew which Abby had cooked. Abby then brought out a cake she'd prepared for the occasion. Later, Reuben and Dave were enjoying a cup of flip at the table while the two ladies cleaned up the dishes. The children were playing in the living area.

Abby said, "Come Anna, come out with me." Abby lit the lamp, and the two of them proceeded out the back door.

Brutis, Brutis, there they are, the bitches! And with a lamp. Good! Now's the time, Brutis!

They only went about fifteen feet toward the outhouse when Dave heard a gunshot. A woman screamed. Dave grabbed his musket, and he and Reuben ran out the back and heard Anna shout, "Dave, Reuben, it's Abby! She's shot, Dave! It's happened again!"

Horrified, Dave thought, *My God! Not Abby! Not Abby!*

He ran up to her and found her lying on her back. The lamp had fallen to the ground. Dave grabbed it, lifted it up, and saw blood on Abby's dress where her belly was.

"Dave, oh Dave, help me! It hurts so," Abby cried. Then she coughed, which made her wince and cry out from the pain.

Dave jumped up and caught Rueben by the shoulder, "Go ride! Get Doc Jenkins! Go as fast as you can!

"Abby, be calm now. I'll carry you inside," and he picked her up and carried her into the house.

Reuben, in spite of his limp, ran to his horse, mounted up and galloped off.

"Anna, get some cloths and some water," Dave yelled.

Anna ran into the house ahead of Dave sobbing, "Who's doing this? Hulley, and now Abby."

When the children saw their father carrying their mother in, they began to cry too.

"What's happened, Papa?" Asey asked.

"Asey, Momma's been hurt bad. Be a good girl and watch the rest of the children. I'm taking Momma into the bedroom. Aunt Anna and I will tend to her."

"All right, Papa," Asey replied. "Momma, how are you?"

"I'll be all right, children; please do what Papa says." She tried to smile at her youngsters, who all crowded around her and their father.

Dave then carried Abby into the bedroom and laid her down on their bed.

At this point, Abby cried out in pain, "Dave, Dave, oh!" and she lost consciousness.

Anna and Dave cut off the front of Abby's dress, and put compresses on the wound. The doctor, who lived only a short distance away, arrived soon and attended to the patient.

"Reuben," Dave said, "would you go tell my pa what happened and then go tell Constable Radcliff?"

"I'll go now," Reuben replied, and he kissed Anna and hurried out the door. Dave then went in to put the children to bed.

Sarah said, "Is Momma gonna die like Aunt Hulley did?"

"I don't think so, Sarah. The doctor should make her well." he replied.

Asey said, "Papa, will you pray with us for Momma to recover?"

"Yes children, now bow your heads," Dave said. "Lord, please help Momma to recover. Heal her wound and make her well."

Dave had a difficult time getting the toddlers to settle down.

He tried to stay cheerful to diminish their fears, yet in his heart he knew he might very well lose his beloved wife of eleven years. Finally, having finished his task, Dave returned to his bedroom to find that Abby was unconscious.

The doctor said, "Come Dave," and the two men and Anna went into the kitchen.

"Will she live, Doctor?" Dave asked.

Doctor Jenkins sat down on the edge of a chair beside the kitchen fireplace and said in a low voice, "I can't do any more for her now. I'm sorry Dave. Her wound is so severe I don't believe she'll recover. Your sister and I dressed the wound as best we could, and I gave her some opium for the pain."

"David, Dave!" Abby called.

Dave, along with the doctor and Anna, went into the bedroom. "I'm shivering, Dave."

"Abby, we'll put more blankets on," Anna said.

Abby said, "Dave, what happened? Oh, Doctor, it hurts so. Can't you do something?"

The doctor bowed his head and nodded no.

Dave sat down on the side of the bed and said, "I think the same villain that shot Hulley fired his gun at you."

"Why, Dave, why?" Abby cried. "If I die, who will raise our children?"

"You're not going to die, Abby," Dave said, though he thought, *I'm probably lying.* "Here's Anna with more blankets. Now, you must sleep and rest to recover."

"All right, Dave," Abby replied weakly.

Again the three returned to the kitchen. Doctor Jenkins said, "I'll leave now. I can't do any more. When you change the dressings, put a milk and bread poultice on the wound."

"Thank you for coming, Doctor," Dave said.

"She's in God's hands now, Dave. It will be a miracle if she lives."

As soon as the doctor left, Dave slumped down in a chair, his head in his hands, and prayed silently. Anna put her hand on his shoulder; tears ran down his cheeks. Soon Captain Gideon arrived with Submit. Anna ran to her blond sister and her father and hugged each of them, trying to welcome them through her tears.

"How bad is it, Dave?" Pa asked.

"Alas, the doctor doesn't think she'll survive," Dave choked out. Anna took Submit into the bedroom to see Abby, and Dave and Pa looked in at the door. Abby was sleeping, so they soon moved back to the living area.

Gideon said, "Do you have any notion of who might have done this?"

"No," Dave replied. "It was dark out, but I can't help think it was Clyde, though if he was going to shoot someone, I'd think he'd shoot me rather than Abby. I was the one who knocked him down at Hulley's wedding."

After a while Abby woke up and called out for Dave. They all went in.

"I'll change your dressing, Abby," Anna said.

"No," Abby answered, "it's too painful. I want to see Dave alone."

The others left the room, and Dave sat down next to Abby's bed, noticing how pale she was. "Abby, you should let us tend to you. Here let me wipe your brow," and he took a wet cloth and dampened her forehead.

"That feels so cool," Abby said, and she sighed and closed her eyes for a moment.

"Abby, do you know of any reason why someone would want to shoot you? I can't for the life of me think of why anyone would."

"No, Dave. It puzzles me." She coughed and grimaced in pain. "Dave, I'm not going to recover; I can tell."

"No, no, Abby, you'll be better soon," he said, sobbing while holding her hand. ·

"Quiet Dave! With all our little children, you're going to have to marry again soon. They need a mother."

"No, Abby. You're their momma. I won't hear any more of this. I prayed with the children for you. The Lord will heal you, Abby; you'll see." He looked away from her for a moment, wiped away the tears with his sleeve, and prayed to himself. *Lord, please comfort her.*

"You should consider Penny Todd," Abby said. "I believe she'd be an excellent mother. Then there's Jane Campbell, though I don't know her very well."

"I won't hear anymore, Abby," Dave cried. "Anna, come in here and change the dressing."

Anna and Submit came in and changed Abby's dressing and wiped her forehead again. Then Abby went back to sleep. Dave stayed with her while the others were dozing in the living room.

Towards midnight something woke Dave up from dozing in the chair. *What is different?* he wondered. *Oh my God! she's motionless. She's not breathing,* he realized. He sat on her bed and clasped her in his arms. *It's over. Oh, oh, what'll I do?* He held her for some minutes, rocking back and forth. *In the prime of her life she's left me and our six children. Oh God, she's gone forever.*

Finally, he stood up slowly with his head bent and went into the other room. Tears were streaming down his face. He looked at those asleep. *Should I wake them all up?* he pondered for a moment.

Instead, he opened the back door and went outside and took a deep breath of the fresh air. He thought, *Why her, Lord? I don't even have an ache or pain, and she lies dead.* Just then Reuben and Constable Radcliff rode up.

As they dismounted, Dave said, "She just died a few minutes ago." He turned his head to wipe away his tears.

"Oh, no," Reuben said, "I'm so sorry. My God! We've got to get this dirty varmint. But what can we do?"

Dave said, "Come on in."

Radcliff asked a few questions, which Dave answered as best he could. Then Radcliff said, "Tomorrow we'll look around here, but I'm gonna see Clyde now to see what he has to say for himself."

Dave said, "I'll go with you, Constable."

"No, no!" Radcliff said emphatically, "You should stay here. I'll take Reuben with me, and we'll come back here after."

"All right," Dave said, "but don't let that stupid bastard get away with this!"

Dave went slowly back inside, and knowing he couldn't sleep, picked up his Bible and began reading in various chapters at random, trying to console himself, but as the hours passed he became more restless and angrier. Finally, he stood up and walked back into the bedroom, shut the door, and sat down next to his dead wife.

"Abby, I hope you're listening. I want you to know your death will be avenged." After a moment, he tightened his fist, held it up over his head, and said, "I swear before you and God that I'll get this murdering bastard; I don't care how long it takes." Then he stood up, his anger gradually subsiding, looked down at Abby's face once more and carefully pulled the blanket up over her.

Then he came out and went into the children's bedroom. *How am I going to tell them?* he wondered. He covered up Raiphe with his blanket. Just then he heard Radcliff and Reuben return. They opened the back door and came in as Dave came out of the children's bedroom, the commotion waking up the sleeping adults.

"What happened?" Dave asked.

Radcliff seemed more excited and nervous than Dave had seen him before. He said, "Well, when we got there, Clyde and his brothers were still asleep; so we woke them up.

"I said, 'Clyde, did you shoot Abby Hotchkiss?'

"'Abby,' he says; 'you mean Dave's wife got herself shot?'

"'Yeah,' I said, 'where were you this evening?'

"'I was right here all night; ain't that right fellows?'

"Then he said, 'I know Dave Hotchkiss and the rest of his clan will blame me. I ain't staying around here to get hanged. I'm leaving this town tonight.'

"I told him that was a mistake, but he's so scared of you and your family, he's leaving town now. Don't know how we'll ever capture him, even if we should find the necessary evidence."

Gideon, Anna, and Submit heard all this, and one by one they arose from the chairs they had been dozing in.

Asey suddenly appeared at the bedroom door in her nightclothes and, rubbing her eyes, said, "Papa, is Momma all well now?"

The other youngsters started getting up, too. Dave was tongue-tied briefly and then said, "Anna and Submit, will you please bring the children in here?"

While the ladies were rounding up the children and changing the baby, Dave said to Pa, "I wish I could remember the words that you used to try and comfort us when Ma died in '62. Course, most of us were older than my children."

"Just let it come from the heart, Dave," Gideon replied. "And, trust the Lord." He put his arm around Dave's shoulders. When the children were brought in, without answering their many questions, Dave hugged them each individually. Then he said in a soft, serious tone, "Children, do you remember last year when Aunt Hulley died?"

Sarah and Asey said, "Yes, Papa."

"Well, the good Lord last night took Momma to Heaven, too," he said in a breaking voice. "She'll be happy there, and some day we'll go and join her."

"No, no!" Asey shrieked.

Five-year-old Lavinia said, "But Papa, I don't want Momma to die."

Three-year-old Raiphe said, "Papa, I want to see Momma! I want to see Momma!"

The baby, Cy, looked bewildered and just cried, "Momma, Momma!"

Dave said, "Children, I know you all loved your momma, and I did too. We're going to miss her, all of us. My momma died too, thirteen years ago, and your grandfather here was able to take care of his young children, and I'll take care of you somehow."

Asey said, "Papa, I'm scared to go outside now."

"Don't be scared to go out, children. Whoever it was who shot Momma wants to shoot ladies, not children."

Dave continued to talk to the children to calm their fears and to help them accept the terrible loss of their mother. Anna and Submit held the two youngest on their laps.

Then Dave said, "Now your grandfather will give us a prayer. Please bow your heads."

Gideon said, "Lord, give us all strength to go on, and please be with our Abby. Help these poor children to accept their mother's passing. And Lord, let their momma be happy in Heaven."

"Where's Momma?" Raiphe said again, for about the tenth time.

After the children finally calmed down, Dave thanked Gideon for coming. Gideon said some words of comfort. Then he got up and left to go home.

Almost exhausted from lack of sleep and the emotional stress, Dave said, "Anna, I have to go out for a while. I'd like you and Submit to watch my youngsters while I'm gone." He put on his moccasins and stepped outside into a light rain.

It was shortly after dawn. As he ran along west through Judd's Meadow and southwest toward Derby, he kept thinking of Abby. *Here I am, moving along in the rain while my Abby, – – Oh, God! Why, why?* and he began sobbing again. Why has the Almighty mixed this bitter cup for me? After about an hour and a half of running, his toes began to hurt as well as the arch in his right foot.

When Dave arrived back home, after being gone for about four hours, he raced into the house. The children shouted, "Papa's back, Papa's back," and they ran to hug him, some in tears and some smiling.

"Papa, don't ever leave us," Frederick said.

"I won't, children; I just went for a long run."

Submit said, "Pa and our brothers, along with Radcliff searched around here, but they found nothing."

Submit then took the children outside. Anna and Dave sat down and began going over the details for the funeral, thinking about things Abby would want, and often sobbing when their recent memories tore at their emotions. Dave found himself still switching from emotions of sorrow and loss to those of extreme anger, at one point saying, "The hell with the funeral, Anna. Got to find Clyde!"

Anna said, "Dave, calm down. Clyde's gone, and we don't know if it's him anyway."

Chapter 8
The Widow

Submit came every morning from Gideon's and cooked and took care of the children, returning home at night. While Submit was cheerful Dave noticed he himself was getting more and more despondent. Immediately upon awakening in the morning he felt happy, only to suddenly realize that Abby was gone. He dragged himself out of bed and sighed often as he slowly and mechanically put on his clothes with no thought for his appearance.

One day, ten days after Abby's death, when Submit drove up, Dave noticed there was another lady with her in the wagon, a beautiful lady with long, yellow wavy hair, as well as three young children in the back.

"David," Submit said, smiling, "I'm not sure whether you ever met Mrs. Todd before." She made the introductions.

Dave was a little puzzled. He had seen this lovely lady before a few times, including at Anna's wedding. Submit was dressed in her usual clothes to work around the house, while Mrs. Todd was dressed in a blue gown with a low-cut bodice as if she were going to an important event.

Smiling, Mrs. Todd introduced her small children, Amos, Dan, and Rhoda.

"Well, come in Mrs. Todd," Dave said. "Your children can play outside with my brood if they wish."

While entering the house she turned serious and said, "I'm sorry to hear of your loss, Mr. Hotchkiss."

"Thank you, Mrs. Todd. I'm afraid I miss her very much."

Submit left them and went into the kitchen to fix some tea.

Dave noticed that Mrs. Todd had a soft smooth complexion with high cheek-bones, tinted pink.

Trying to think of something else to say to Mrs. Todd, he said, "With your children, Mrs. Todd, as a widow, I guess you must have some notion how it is for me now with six children and no mother for them. If it weren't for Submit, I don't know what I'd do. There's so much to do here on the farm. Also, I've been selling whips for my brothers' company, which I can't really do now."

Mrs. Todd smiled sweetly and said, "Well, this is why I asked Submit if I could come to see you."

"What do you mean?" Dave asked.

"You know that Submit is marrying Joe Payne's brother David in June. She needs to finish her linens and prepare for her wedding."

"Yes, I know, though I thought maybe she could continue for a while longer till I can find someone to come in and take care of the little ones."

"But that's why I'm here, Mr. Hotchkiss," Mrs. Todd said, with a smile that wrinkled the corners of her mouth. "I have only a few investments to live on since Mr. Todd died. I'd be willing to drive here each day from my home near Waterbury Center and do the cooking and mind the children, that is, if we can work out the amount of the wages."

"Hmm, this certainly sounds interesting," he replied, at the same time remembering Abby's dying words about Penny Todd. "I'm not certain, Mrs. Todd, I could afford a lady of your obvious considerable accomplishments."

"I've thought of that, Mr. Hotchkiss," she replied. "If you could work my farm for two days a week, I think the proceeds from the crops would pay for my labor."

Dave rubbed his stubbled chin. "That mayhaps would work out to both our liking."

Just then Submit came in with some tea.

"I'm afraid we only have Labrador tea to offer you, Mrs. Todd," Submit said.

"Mrs. Todd," Dave said, "your proposition sounds to me very reasonable. Do you think maybe we could try it for a week, and if it seems to be going satisfactorily, we could talk about continuing."

"Thank you Mr. Hotchkiss. I'll come every day except Sunday."

Dave, while looking at the bright, cheerful lady, suddenly became aware of his own slovenly appearance. He hadn't shaved or bathed since he took the children to the meeting house on Sunday. Also, his white hunting shirt was dirty and torn.

"I want to apologize for my appearance, Mrs. Todd. I didn't expect visitors."

"That's perfectly understandable, Mr. Hotchkiss. I know what you're going through. After all, I'm just applying for a position." She then stood up, and smiling, said, "Submit, your good brother must go to work. You can take me back now. Thank you, Mr. Hotchkiss, for hiring me. I'll be here early tomorrow morning."

And then she was gone. *Did I actually agree to hire her?* Dave wondered as he went out to feed some of his animals.

Chapter 9

A Widow's Thoughts

As the two ladies boarded the wagon and began the trip back, Penny Todd was elated.

She thought to herself, *I forgot what a handsome man David is. Even in his grief, making him neglect his appearance, he appears to be a likely suitor. I mustn't reveal my interest to his sister here, though.*

"So what do you think of my brother?" Submit asked.

"I think he'll be a good employer, though taking care of all of our children is a sizable job," she said, and thought, *He certainly seems to be more to my liking than Ezra, Joe Payne, William Macclure, or Squire Everett. Maybe I could somehow turn his head before Jane Campbell or one of the younger girls hereabouts fancies him.*

"Don't you think he's rather handsome?" Submit said, "though the death of his Abby has left him in a sad mood much of the time, and he has no regard now for shaving or his clothing."

"I want you to know, Submit, that I've only recently stopped mourning my dear Charles' passing. I'm interested only in providing additional income for my little family. I would not consider remarrying at this time."

"I understand," Submit said. "I'm sorry. It just seems that you are both, well, being the same age and in a similar situation, a possible match, don't you think?"

"Hmm," Penny said, knowing Submit was correct. "It is much too early to even think of such possibilities. Besides, I have other suitors to consider."

"You do?" Submit asked, rather surprised.

"Well, yes, there's Squire Everett, Joe Payne, both widowers, and of course Ezra. The school teacher has also called on me a few times, though he has now gone off somewhere to do some survey work."

"I see," Submit replied, as she flicked the whip to force her horses to move a little faster. "Then, with four suitors, you're not interested in David, is that right?"

Penny thought, *I must be careful how I express myself. I don't want to discourage this man, nor do I wish to imply my other suitors are unsuitable.*

"I didn't say that, my dear. It's just, well, maybe I'm not ready for a new hus-band. And as for David, his Abby's only been in the ground a few days. He'll have to overcome his grief before he can consider another spouse."

"Yes, I understand; you're correct of course."

Chapter 10

The Rout

When Submit returned to Dave's house to resume her chores, she said to her brother, "So Dave, what do you think of the pretty widow?"

"Well," he answered, "she certainly seems confident. With three children of her own, she should know how to mind my brood."

"I know it's very soon after poor Abby's passing, Dave, but do you not find Mrs. Todd the least bit attractive?"

"I'm a man, Submit. I could hardly ignore Mrs. Todd's physical attributes, and she's obviously an intelligent person, but I'm not about to start courting a lady. I will tell you, though, and I wish you to keep it secret, that one of the last things Abby said to me was that I should marry Penny Todd."

"She did?" Submit said, smiling. "How interesting that Mrs. Todd should appear on your doorstep, so to speak, already. By the by, Dave, when I asked her if she had any interest in you, she said she had four other suitors to consider."

"She did? Who, may I ask?"

Submit paused a moment and still grinning, said, "I thought you weren't interested."

"I'm not, just curious."

"Hmm," she replied, "Ezra, Squire Everett, Mr. Macclure, and Joe Payne."

Just then, Raiphe, Frederick, and Lavinia, who weren't at school, came in with some eggs which they had collected from the henhouse.

"Look, Aunt Submit, see how many we got!" Raiphe said.

"Yes, Raiphe," Submit replied; "good work. Now, your father has something important to tell you."

Dave explained to his children that Mrs. Todd would be replacing Submit, since she was getting married soon.

Late in the day, after Dave came in from the fields, Submit's betrothed, David Payne, stopped by and had supper with the family. The two Davids discussed the work they were doing on their respective farms.

Then David Payne said, "I'm pleased you're hiring Mrs. Todd, since I'll need Submit to help with the final preparations for our new house."

"Tell me," Dave Hotchkiss said, "While I think on it, is your brother, Joe, courting Mrs. Todd? If she's got a number of suitors, perhaps she won't have time to do justice to minding my children."

"I was just talking with Joe yesterday," Payne responded; "he said that while Mrs. Todd is a very handsome lady, he's set his mind to court your cousin, Hester."

Dave said, "That's good. I don't want the children to just get so they like Penny Todd and then have her marry some fellow and leave. Can't believe she'd marry Ezra, Squire Everett, or the school-teacher, though I suppose it's possible."

In the morning Dave was up early and went out to chop some firewood in his yard. He had already been at it for some time when Penny Todd drove up with her youngest child, Rhoda. "Good morning, Mr. Hotchkiss," Mrs. Todd said, beaming.

Dave stopped and after greeting her said, "The children haven't had breakfast yet, Mrs. Todd, so you can start off this morning feeding them."

When Dave came in an hour later to get some breakfast, three of the children, including the baby Cyrus, were in a tub of hot water, splashing and laughing.

"The children needed a bath," Mrs. Todd said. "The older children have finished and already dressed themselves."

Dave sat down and ate an excellent meal with eggs and bread. The cheerful Mrs. Todd tried to make conversation, and while Dave felt obligated to try and keep up his end of the talking in order to encourage her to stay in her new position, he found it difficult to have a stranger replacing his wife in the role of caretaker for his children.

When the older children left for school, Mrs. Todd asked many questions about Dave's little ones, and he answered them as best he could.

Although Dave appreciated having Mrs. Todd come over during the next few days, and though her cheerful disposition helped the children through the grief of their mother's death, Dave himself discovered that he still could not shake his despondency. *Nobody can replace you, Abby*, he often said silently.

Three days later, Dave asked Mrs. Todd if she'd stay at his house for about a week while he delivered a wagonload of whips to Boston, with stops along the way.

She agreed to this arrangement, and Dave left for Boston with Eben. After several days, they delivered a sizable whip order to a saddle store in Boston. They began the trip back by taking a different route, crossing the Charles River to Cambridge and heading northwest toward Concord where they were to make another delivery.

Dave asked Eben if he knew why the people along the way seemed so excited. "Don't know, Dave, let me ask this farmer."

A wagon was coming toward them with a load of hay, and Eben haled the driver. "Sir, we are strangers here. Why are the citizens here so agitated?"

"Surprised you're not aware, but the British just marched a few hours ahead of you west toward Lexington. They're trying to find our stores of arms. Be careful how you proceed."

When they arrived in Lexington, though, they were stopped at the edge of the town by some militia with muskets who asked their business. When Dave answered them, they said he could go ahead but that their militia had had a skirmish with the British. One said, "We were all lined up on the green, and when we did not disperse, the bastards fired on us without warning."

"Without warning? Were there casualties?" Eben asked.

"Yes, I fear we lost ten men."

"Where are the British now?" Dave asked.

"They were going west toward Concord," was the answer from a scruffy-looking young militiaman. Dave and Eben stopped at a Lexington tavern for their noon dinner and learned more details of the unprovoked attack.

"We had been warned about the approach of the British by a man named Paul Revere," a man in the inn told them.

The travelers then began going further west toward Concord, but after several miles they heard shots. Suddenly a sea of redcoats appeared ahead, coming directly toward them. They were approaching fast and appeared exhausted.

Dave said, "Look! They're not marching; they're being chased by our militia. We've got to get out of the way!"

"Dave, look, there's a break in the wall here."

Dave turned right off the road and drove his horses through an opening in the stone wall, putting the whip to them to get them clear of the rapidly approaching soldiers. When Dave thought that he'd gone far enough, he stopped, and he and Eben crawled under the wagon to watch the battle.

"Is this a battle?" Dave said. "Looks like a rout."

And it was; the British were being followed by militiamen, who called themselves minutemen, along with many other men in the area who had gathered when the word was spread ahead that the British were coming.

"Look, Eben! Our men are using Indian tactics. They're hiding behind trees and firing and then moving ahead to the next tree."

"Hey, look at that old man on the white horse." As they watched, the old man got off his horse, leveled his rifle on the saddle, and fired, killing a British soldier. Then he mounted up, moved forward, and repeated his action.

When they all passed by, Dave drove his wagon back to the road and headed west. "Finally we're at war now," Dave said to Eben. "This is more serious than any previous encounter."

"When they begin asking for volunteers for the service, I want to join," Eben said. "We can't let the British take our liberty."

At the Ephraim Jones tavern in Concord that evening Dave and Eben found themselves at a table with several other men they didn't know. Most of the people in the tavern were excited and joyous about the outcome of the day. One of the minutemen at their table said, "We sure gave it to the reg'lars today!"

"We surely did, Short Robert," a middle-aged man said. "Now, you know we'll be enlisting men in the army. I'd like you to enlist as a private."

The small man, Short Robert, said, "Colonel, I don't know much about why we're battling the British, except that they were trying to recover our arms and supplies, but I know you made my cousin, Long Robert, a captain. To improve my lot I want to be at least a lieutenant."

"Lieutenant, huh? But Short Robert, you're just an apprentice shoemaker," the colonel replied.

"Yes, I know, but you made my cousin a captain. I wish to raise myself up in the world. I may die, but if Long Robert dies, mayhap you'd promote me to captain."

Just then Dave noticed a familiar man approach them. "Hello, gentlemen. Tis good to see you here," the red-faced, rugged-looking man said.

"Yes, Mr. Macclure," Dave said, as he and Eben rose to greet the former school-teacher. "What are you doing up in this town?"

"I've been doing some surveying. How's your new school-teacher doing?"

"Our new teacher has left recently; so you may wish to come back. Let's move to a different table." They found another table where they could talk.

"Of course, we just got here, Mr. Macclure," Eben said. "We don't know much about what all this bickering and fighting is about between these good people and the King's men. We just held on to our muskets to defend ourselves."

"Well, as you know, the provincials hereabouts have not been too contented ever since the Boston Massacre. It appears the British were looking for arms and munitions, which were stored here by the patriots, as they call themselves. Also, I believe they wanted to capture their leaders: Mr. Samuel Adams, a man named Warren, and John Hancock. With this unprovoked killing of patriots in Lexington by the British and the atrocities I've heard of to boot — arson, pillage, raping, and murder — that even though we've driven them back to Charlestown, a general rebellion throughout America will be coming suddenly and swiftly."

When there was a pause in the conversation, Dave said, "What do you plan to do after this surveying job?"

"I don't rightly know," Macclure replied. "Perhaps I should come back to Judd's Meadow and teach again."

Dave thought to himself, *Macclure seems like such a clever fellow.* "Sir, you are probably the most learned man I've ever met; perhaps you're just the one to solve a mystery for us."

"Now what would this mystery be?" Macclure asked, smiling slyly. "I enjoy trying to solve a difficult puzzle."

Dave said, "We've had two killings in our town. One was my sister Hulley a year ago, and earlier this month my wife was shot too."

"Oh, no, I'm sorry to hear that," Macclure said.

"We suspect a certain man, but we have no evidence that he's the one, and now he's left town. Our constable is young and inexperienced. I think you might have success in discovering the murderer."

Macclure took another swig of ale and said, "Mayhaps I could give it a try."

"In any case," Dave said, "I'd like you to consider it, and I'd make it worth your time."

Macclure scratched his chin a moment while thinking and said, "Never attempted this before, but if your murderer is still in your town I might be fortunate enough to ferret him out. When I finish this surveying contract, I'll inform you of my decision. Shouldn't be too long. I have to run a line between west and upland."

When Dave and Eben arrived back home and stopped at Captain Gideon's house, the family was enjoying their noon dinner. Jesse, Amos, Abe, and Titus were there. They had heard of the defeat of the British at Lexington and Concord already, and listened intently to Dave and Eben describe what they'd seen.

The excited Captain said, "I must give the committee this information. We'll have to raise more funds to equip our troops." There was much discussion of what might happen in the near future, and Titus told them of his desire to join the army.

Eben said, "Titus, if you're going in, so am I."

Pa said, "I believe they're organizing a battalion in New Haven. I may want to start up a light horse militia company here."

Finally, Dave left and drove home. Upon arriving at his house, the children rushed out with joy to greet their father and began telling him all they had done while he was away. Mrs. Todd seemed pleased he was home as well.

"Did my children behave themselves while I was gone, Mrs. Todd?" Dave said as he picked up Lavinia and hugged her.

"Oh, no, they were horrible," she said and laughed.

"We were very good, Pa," Asey said. "What did you bring us?"

Dave brought out some trinkets he'd picked up in Boston and passed them out to the delighted children, and he had some for the Todd children as well.

Chapter 11

The Investigator

Two days later Titus rode off to New Haven to get information about joining the army.

Captain Gideon began organizing a company of light horse, which included Dave and most of his brothers. Gideon told them that they were to meet regularly to train for a few hours. The training consisted mostly of galloping around the countryside with their swords at the ready.

Over the next few weeks Mrs. Todd appeared each day, and the children, becoming accustomed to her joyful ways, gradually were getting over their grief. Dave, though, still found himself often tearful, especially in the evenings when Penny Todd had left and the children had gone to bed. Also, he often pondered about Penny Todd's loss of her husband. He thought, *How is it she is not sad, as I am?*

One day, in early May, at a noon dinner, when the children had finished their meal and gone off to play or do chores, Dave found himself alone at the table with Mrs. Todd. The grey cat, Bits, had climbed up on Dave's lap and was purring, waiting to have her neck scratched. Mrs. Todd was telling him a long story about how she and her husband first had met at a frolic in New Haven. When she finished, she laughed at the pleasant memory.

Dave smiled, but then turning thoughtful for a moment he said, "Mrs. Todd, you and I have undergone a similar experience, losing our spouses, but you seem so cheerful much of the time while I have this feeling of terrible sadness over my loss."

"Yes, it's obvious she was very dear to you," Penny said in a soft voice as she lowered her eyes.

David wiped a tear from his eye and said, "In the prime of her life she was taken from me. The wound is deep."

Bits continued to purr, unaware of Dave's grief. "Tell me, did you not grieve at the loss of Charles? And, if you did, which I don't doubt, how did you get over it?"

"Oh my, how did I get over my grief?" Penny said in a low voice, as if she was thinking to herself.

"When Charles died, of course, I thought it was the end of the world. I loved him deeply, and he loved me. He was attentive to my needs, and I did everything I could to make him happy. After he died, over a number of weeks I began to realize that Charles would not want me to be sad, but instead to celebrate living and be an inspiration to our children. Still, I was often sad, but I prayed frequently for guidance, and the Lord helped me. I guess the most important thing that helped me was..."

At this moment there was a knock at the door. "Just a minute, Mrs. Todd, I want you to finish," Dave said as he got up to answer the door while Bits made a loud squawk when she landed on the floor.

When the door opened, a cheerful voice said, "Hello there, Mr. Hotchkiss, your investigator is here, at your service," and the middle-aged man made a deep bow.

"Mr. Macclure, you came!" Dave said enthusiastically. "Come on in."

"Be glad to," Macclure replied, and he stepped in and took off his tri-cornered hat. "Oh, I didn't know you were here Mrs. Todd. It's pleasant to see you again," and he blushed, making his face almost crimson.

"It is? You know Mr. Macclure?" Dave asked, as Mrs. Todd stood up.

"Oh, yes, William came calling on me a while back," Mrs. Todd replied, and she also blushed. "It's a pleasure for me also to see you. I'll bring some cider."

When Penny returned and poured the cider, Macclure said, "When we were at Concord, Mr. Hotchkiss, you neglected to mention you have made an alliance with the lovely Mrs. Todd."

"But William, of course, I don't live here!" Penny said sternly. She tossed her blond hair back over her shoulder, raised her chin up, and said, "I still have my own home; just spend the day here taking care of the house and minding the children."

"I'm sorry, Mrs. Todd," Macclure said. "I didn't mean to imply there was anything improper."

"My fault, Mrs. Todd," Dave said. "I didn't make our arrangement clear. Mrs. Todd was about to tell me how she overcame the grief of her own husband's death. Please go on."

"Yes, I'd be interested in hearing this myself," Macclure said.

"Well William," Mrs. Todd said, "as I told Mr. Hotchkiss, I began to conclude that my husband would not want me to be sad; I often prayed; but as you've probably heard from others, I believe the most important thing is time. Over time, the soul and mind will heal."

"That's it? Time?" Dave said. "Hope you're right."

Macclure leaned forward from the chair he was sitting on and, after taking a sip of cider, said, "Now, Mr. Hotchkiss, tell me everything you know about the murders."

"Please call me Dave, and I'll call you William."

"Is your profession now that of an investigator?" Penny asked.

"Not officially," Dave said. "He's doing some investigating for me. I must find the murderer, Mrs. Todd, as I've often told you." Dave told Macclure everything he could remember about the two murders.

Macclure listened intently and then said, "Your sister Anna, isn't she the one who runs?

"Yes, that's right," Dave said. Dave then told him about the footrace in Hartford.

"Then she was at the scene of three shootings, not just two," Macclure said.

"Well, yes," Dave replied, "but Hartford is fairly far from here. You don't think there's any connection to the two murders here, do you?"

"Don't know, but for the same lady to be on the scene of three shootings in the past two years seems unusual. Maybe there's some connection, maybe not. Tell me, did she have any enemies?"

Dave pondered for a moment. "I can't think of any, except maybe Clyde, and I don't think he had anything against her. But William, she wasn't shot, she was just near those who were shot."

"I know. I'm not saying Anna had any part in these murders, but it's just so odd. I would like to talk to her."

"Well, we can stop in and see her now. She and her husband Reuben live only a short distance from here, right next to Isaac Judd's farm."

Dave and the older Macclure boarded Dave's wagon and drove to Anna's house. The young lady was just cleaning up after the noon meal with Reuben who was now out in the fields.

Anna seemed happy to see her brother and rushed to embrace him.

"Now, Anna, you remember Mr. Macclure who was our school-teacher, don't you?"

"Yes, he's not here for the Waterbury foot-race, is he?" Anna asked.

"No, I've asked Mr. Macclure to see if he can determine who the murderer is. However, we don't want anyone here to know his intention."

"Naturally, I understand."

"Anna," Macclure said, as he sat down in Anna's best chair near the fireplace, "do you know of anyone who would want to do you harm?"

"Do me harm?" Anna said with a puzzled look on her face. "Why would anyone want to do me harm? I don't have any enemies that I'm aware of. There's Clyde, of course, though I can't recall any animosity he's expressed toward me."

Macclure scratched his head a moment and said, "How about any rejected suitors, Anna?"

"Well, there was Ezra, of course, but he was always nice to me, and then I did turn down Squire Everett, though I doubt it was him."

"And why is that?" Macclure asked.

"Well, he hates my pa and my brothers because they're in the same business, whips; so I would think he'd shoot them to eliminate those who compete with him rather than some ladies."

"Are there any other enemies of you or your family, Anna?"

"Well, there is one thing that has me puzzled me for a time," Anna said. "An Indian who saw Dave in a whipping contest asked him if he was at the battle at Ticonderoga. He looked mean, as if he would like to hurt us."

"What's the point," Macclure said, "most Indians look at me that way, too."

"But Mr. Macclure, Dave killed an Indian with his whip in the battle at Fort Ticonderoga. Mayhap this Indian was a friend of the one Dave killed."

"I rather doubt it was that Indian," Dave said.

Just then the door opened, and Anna welcomed Titus, "What a surprise! Another brother visits me on the same day."

As Titus leaned forward at the fireplace with his hands on the mantle to stretch the back of his calves, he said, "I should tell you, I went to New Haven to see about enlisting in the army, but I'll probably wait and do it later this month."

"Really?" Dave said. "Tell me, what part of the army would you be in?"

"As you probably know, Massachusetts wants to put together a New England army of 30,000 men, with Massachusetts furnishing 13,600. They told Ezra and me, if we enlist, we'd probably be in Captain Wilmont's company in Colonel Ward's regiment."

"Ezra?" Macclure asked, "is Ezra Hopkins considering enlisting?"

"Yes, he is," Titus answered. "Like me, he wants to wait till after the Waterbury footrace.

"Before I forget, I stopped at the Whittemore Tavern on my way from New Haven and found that Clyde's back."

"Hmm, surprising," Dave said. "I thought we'd seen the last of that varmint. Well, this is good; now William, you can include him in the investigation."

Macclure scratched his chin and said, "It is astounding he'd return. Titus, outside of Clyde, Ezra, Squire Everett or the Indian, do you know of any other men, who for any reason might want to harm Anna?"

Titus, seeming to be confused at this question, said, "Ah, what a puzzling question. You don't think the shootings had anything to do with Anna, do you?"

Dave explained that Macclure felt there might be something to it, since Anna had been at all the shootings.

Macclure said, "Where do these gentlemen like to partake of their rum?"

Dave replied, "There's that tavern Titus stopped at. It's about five miles south of here in Chuse-town, Whittemore's Tavern. Ezra goes there sometimes, as well as Titus, Eben, and even Squire Everett."

Macclure said, "Dave, why don't you spread the word to Ezra and some of the other runners who are going in the race that you're organizing a card game Friday night at the tavern for the racers and that you'll buy the first round of grog?"

Dave said, "All right. That's three days from now."

"And Titus," Macclure continued, "could you see the constable and have him obtain that piece of lasher that was found at your sister's killing? You can tell the constable you suspect where it came from and want to see if you can match it up."

"I'll do it," Titus said.

Three days later in the early evening, Dave and some of his brothers ascended the bluff that was at one time known as Indian Hill, but now called Chuse-Town, and entered Whittemore's Tavern. They moved the large table over in front of the big stone fireplace, which had a roaring fire. Those who expressed an interest in playing cards, besides Dave, were Titus, Eben, Jesse, and Ezra Hopkins.

They had just begun playing when William Macclure came in and ordered a rum. He walked over to the table with his grog and said, "Card playing, and for money, gentlemen. 'Tis rather sinful, I say, but since your stakes appear to be within the limited earnings of a school-teacher, would you mind if I join you?"

"If you were to buy us all a drink, I believe we'd permit you to play," Eben said.

The schoolteacher sat down at the table.

Mr. Wooding, the bartender, came over and took a drink order for Macclure.

After about an hour of card playing, Squire Everett came in, and seeing the card players, he waddled over to the table, his large gut hanging over his belt. "Ah, ha," he said, "Ezra, Macclure, looks to me like you men are in with a bad crowd here."

"Don't fret, Squire," Ezra said, "I can handle myself in any card game. This one's for the runners in the Waterbury footrace tomorrow; so that lets you out."

"I wouldn't play cards with these Hotchkiss scoundrels no matter what the occasion," Everett said. He walked away to another table to sit down with his neighbor David Wooster.

"Damn Tory!" Jesse said, as he picked up his cards. "The Squire and that Wooster fellow ought to be run out of town."

"Why don't we just do it, Dave," Eben said smiling. "We could tar and feather them."

Dave said, "Ah, remember, we've got a flock of Tories around here."

A short time later Jesse, who is facing the door, said, "Well, I'll be damned! Look who just walked in!"

"Clyde Barrow, that murdering bastard!" Eben exclaimed. "He is back."

Jesse said loudly, "Fine place we came to for our card game — Tories and now a murderer." The Hotchkiss men all stood up and stared at Clyde.

Clyde, taken back somewhat at seeing so many in the family of his former employer, backed up to the door, but then, seeing they weren't attacking him, walked up to the card players.

"Where the hell have you been, Clyde?" Dave asked.

"Not that it's your business, but I was up in Boston."

"Not my business, you say?" Dave yelled, and he went up to Clyde and grabbed him by the front of his shirt. "You shot my wife, and you say it's not my business where you went to hide? You damn varmint!" He pushed Clyde, causing him to stagger backwards and fall down on the floor in a sitting position.

Clyde looked up from where he fell and said, "Look, Dave, I'm sorry about what happened to your wife and Hulley too, but I'm not the killer. Why would I do it? I went to Boston hoping to find work since I didn't like working for the Squire."

"So why'd you come back?" Dave asked, as he stood over Clyde with his hands on his hips.

"Hell, it's my home here," Clyde replied. "Besides, Boston was under siege. I had to get out of there; so I'm back working for the Squire. Now, leave me be," and he stood up and went over to the table where the Squire and Wooster were seated.

Dave started to go after him, but Jesse grabbed Dave and said, "Dave wait! We can't do anything to him here. Maybe he's not the killer. The fact that he came back makes him look less guilty to me."

"Yeah," Dave said, "I suppose you're right, though I think I'd feel better if I could just choke the bastard to death." Dave sat back down at the table, and the game continued. However, it was difficult for him to concentrate on his cards, finding himself often staring at Clyde.

Dave noticed that Macclure, who was sitting next to Ezra, was engaging Ezra in conversation, apparently to try and make friends with him.

Macclure said, "One thing I enjoy here in this tavern, there's no ladies here. Not like the one in Concord, where a lass tended bar so we had to control our language."

"Yeah, that suits me, too," Ezra said, "the bitches!"

Macclure continued, "As a matter of fact, I don't even like women. Most of them object to card playing and drinking, and they whine."

"Yeah, yeah," Ezra said, as he took a gulp of his rum, "I hate women. The damn ladies are always telling you what to do."

After about a half an hour Dave noticed Ezra was drawing on a piece of paper, working on it in between hands. "What are you drawing, Ezra?" Dave asked.

"Take a look," Ezra replied, and he turned the drawing around so Dave could look at it. The picture, very well drawn, showed Clyde sitting on the floor, his legs out straight and spread wide apart just as he'd fallen. It was a good likeness, but what really surprised Dave was that the picture showed Clyde completely nude.

An hour later most of the non-card players, including Clyde, had left the tavern. Dave said, "Well, gentlemen, since my coins are severely depleted, and we have the race tomorrow, I'm going on home." Dave's brothers agreed that it was a good time to quit, and they all departed together, leaving Macclure and Ezra alone at the table with a couple of mugs of rum.

Chapter 12

The Five-Mile Footrace

Early the next morning, as soon as Mrs. Todd arrived, looking very handsome as always, Dave mounted Old Buck. "May you have much luck in the race," Penny Todd yelled to him from the back steps.

After a four-mile ride with Eben and Jesse, going north together along the Naugatuck River, Dave met Titus and Anna on the outskirts of Waterbury Center. It was a really bright day with the sun reflecting off the dew on the new green oak and birch leaves.

All the runners lined up at the starting line. Mr. Scott said, "Now, we do have people out on the course to point out the turns; so you don't need to be concerned about getting lost. I'll fire this musket for the start."

Besides Titus, Eben, Anna, and Jesse, Ezra was there as well.

Suddenly the gun was fired, and the runners were off. A number of houses lined the road, and the residents and their children came out and yelled, "Huzzah!" for the runners and clapped their hands. Some little boys ran alongside the runners for a short distance before getting out of breath.

At about three miles into the race Dave was running in a small group with Jesse. Jesse, his hair bouncing on his forehead, turned to Dave and said, "Looks like Titus ought to take this race. His only competition up ahead is two Indians and Eben and Ezra. Titus always can out-sprint anyone at the end of a race."

After a sharp turn on the road, which headed west away from the Mill River, Dave could see someone up ahead standing in the middle of the road.

"Look, Jesse!" Dave said. "Looks like Macclure!"

"Yeah," Jesse said, "and Titus, Eben and Ezra have stopped, too."

When they caught up to the others, Dave could see Macclure was standing and nervously pointing what looked like a cannon-barrel pistol at Ezra, who was backing off to the other side of the road away from the schoolteacher. While the other runners were running by, all staring at those who had stopped, Dave said, "What's the story, William?"

"After talking to Ezra last night, I suspected he was the killer. So early this morning I waited till he left for the race and then searched his house and barn. In the barn I found this." He held up a whip with a lasher broken off.

"It matches perfect, Dave. Come look!"

Ezra started inching sideways on the road. Ezra wondered, *He suspects me of killing Hulley. What the hell's this crazy Macclure doing with a whip?*

Macclure said loudly, "Ezra, don't move any further, or I'll fire a ball right through you!"

Dave, Jesse, and Eben came over to Macclure, and Dave took the whip and compared the broken lasher on it with the piece of lasher found at Hulley's death. He said, "This is the whip all right."

Just then Anna arrived, and Dave told her about the match.

"Ezra," Anna cried out, "why did you shoot them? How could you do such a horrible thing?"

"I didn't do it," Ezra yelled back with a crack in his voice.

"We know you did it. You damn bastard!" Dave yelled, and his face turned red with anger. He was about to cross the road and approach Ezra when a wagon suddenly appeared, coming very fast toward them. Dave glanced up to see Penny Todd, driving the wagon with an excited smile on her face; the nine children were bouncing around in the back.

"Hi Papa," they yelled.

Dave looked back at Ezra and thought, *Where is he?*

Ezra said to himself, *Now's the time to get my ass out of here,* and he began sprinting.

"Where'd he go?" yelled Dave.

"There he is," Eben shouted. He pointed south, and there was Ezra sprinting all out on the road to New Haven.

"Get him!" Dave cried out, and they all ran after Ezra except Macclure, who untied his horse, mounted up, and began galloping toward Ezra.

Macclure had his pistol out, and as he came up to the sprinting Ezra, yelled, "Ezra, by all that's holy, halt right now, damn it, or I'll fire!"

Just then Ezra, who had reached the bridge over the Mill River, without stopping leaped over the stone railing into the fast-flowing spring water of the river.

In a matter of seconds the Hotchkisses arrived at the bridge. "There he is!" Dave shouted, pointing downstream. "I'm going in," and he immediately jumped in.

The cold water from melted snow took his breath away. *Now where is he?* Dave wondered, as he tried to look downstream. *Ah, I see him now,* and he attempted to swim and catch up with Ezra.

Oh, my God, he thought. *It's so cold, I can hardly move. Oh, oh! What's this? Damn!* and he found himself caught in some bushes and tree branches on a buried island. He stood up, but with the water up to his chest he was entangled; the rapidly moving water kept pushing him into the branches. After struggling for a while, he ducked down in the water low enough to escape the branches and continued downstream, but now he couldn't see Ezra.

I lost him, damn, damn! Dave said to himself as he swam toward the shore. Coming out of the water he noticed another bridge ahead down stream. Shivering almost uncontrollably, he climbed the river bank and half-walked half-ran toward the bridge. When he was still a good distance away, he could see someone looking over the rail. *Must be Macclure. Why didn't he tie Ezra up right away?*

Dave came up to Macclure, who was still looking over the rail, and said. "Did you see him, William?"

"No, no, we've lost him!" Macclure said. He spat on the ground in disgust. "Where does this damn river go anyway?"

"You can see up there about a half a mile. It goes into the Naugatuck. Then it runs right through Judd's Meadow. But where the hell is he? Did he drown? You didn't see him go by? Could he have gotten by you or got out of the water and walked in a different direction?"

"I'm sorry the varmint got away, Dave." Macclure said. "When he ran, I would have shot him if I was able to get off a good round, but just as I halted my horse to aim my pistol he jumped into the river. We need to spread the word that he's the killer. I'll ride ahead going south and let everyone know Ezra could be in the river or walking south. You better get those wet clothes off."

Macclure mounted up and started galloping south while Dave began running on the road going back toward town. He only went a short distance when he saw Penny Todd's wagon, which she had turned around; she was coming toward him rapidly, whipping her horse. When she came up to Dave, she stopped the wagon, climbed down, and hugged the wet runner, "Oh, my God! I thought I'd lost you."

Dave was surprised by her show of affection. In spite of how wet he was, she continued to cling to him, and he realized she was crying.

"Dave, I never told you. My Charles drowned trying to cross the Mad River."

"Oh, no," Dave said, "but I'm all right Penny," and he backed up and, holding her shoulders, smiled at her. She then quickly recovered her composure.

The children climbed down from the wagon to greet their father. Then Anna and Dave's brothers all arrived on foot and expressed their relief that Dave had not drowned.

"I fear we missed our chance to bring the killer to justice," Dave said. "Macclure is riding south, though, to tell people there's a killer on the loose and what he looks like."

Jesse said, "We should have tied him up immediately, but with so many of us I didn't think it was necessary. I'll go tell Constable Radcliff."

They all began walking back to where their horses were tethered near the finish line of the race, with the wagon following along behind them.

Dave said, "I want to run just to get warm," and he started jogging, his siblings trotting behind.

Though the Hotchkiss men along with Macclure and Radcliff, after mounting up, split up into two parties and rode on either side of the Naugatuck, no signs of Ezra were found.

"Mayhaps he drowned," Jesse said.

"I don't know. We didn't find a body," Dave responded. "He could be hiding with some relative. There's a number of the clan of Hopkins living around here."

Hours later at nightfall, when they reached Judd's Meadow, they all met on the bridge. Macclure said he would stay overnight in Porter's Tavern and then look into the schoolteacher position the next day. Dave paid Macclure his fee.

"William, how were you so sure that Ezra was the killer before you even searched his place?" Dave asked.

"Last night at the tavern I befriended him, as you noticed. After you left, when he drank more rum it became obvious to me he really did hate women, though I don't know why; so I decided to search his place as soon as he left for the race." Macclure and Dave said their good-byes, and Macclure trotted off.

Radcliff said, "I'll ride down to Whittemore's Tavern to warn them of our killer. Then we'll do some more searching tomorrow."

They then broke up and went to their respective homes. When Dave came into the kitchen, the children were having their supper. After they welcomed him, Dave said, "Why did you come to the race, Mrs. Todd?"

"I wanted to surprise you. I thought we could have a country dinner together alongside the river."

"Well," Dave said as he slumped down into a chair, "I think I would have enjoyed that. Right now, I'm so tired, I just want to go to bed."

"Don't you want any supper?" Penny asked.

"Well, yes, I am hungry. Let me put some dry clothes on," and he went off to change. When he came back to the kitchen, the younger children had been put to bed while the older ones were outside doing chores.

Candles lit the table, and a fire was burning in the large stone fireplace. "Mrs. Todd," Dave said, as he sat down to eat, "with this crazy man Ezra still on the loose I don't want you going home alone, and I'm too tired to take you. I think to be safe you should stay here tonight."

"Really, Mr. H, I appreciate your thoughts for my safety, but I'm concerned that your good neighbors will think I've compromised my principles."

"If anyone notices, I'll set them straight. By the by, I don't think we need to be so formal anymore. I'd like to call you Penny from now on, and I want you to call me Dave."

"Thank you," Penny replied sweetly. "I was hoping this day would come soon." Pausing, she smiled coyly and said, "Does this mean you wish to court me?"

"Ah, hah," Dave said, "does this mean that you favor me?" and he smiled at his cleverness.

"Oh, ah," Penny stammered, "I think I care for you just as you're concerned for my safety. If you're not going to court me, I'll understand."

"Well, neither of us are in our teens now," Dave said. She stood up and turned and looked out the window. Dave continued, "I would think the normal formalities of a courtship, as we are familiar with, would not be necessary. Having said that, Penny, in spite of my grief, I find myself drawn to you more and more each day. Please be patient and do not commit yourself to another man."

Penny turned around and looked at Dave, saying, "I can be patient, Dave, but shouldn't I be kind to other men who may desire me as a suitable wife?"

Dave took the last bite of supper and said, "Do what you must, but I must go to bed before I fall asleep at the table," and he yawned and got up from the table.

Penny said, "Well, if you're just going to leave me here, with no place to sleep, I'll take my wagon and drive home," and she headed for the door.

"No, no," Dave said, as he turned and walked up behind her. "It's too dangerous." With that he reached her. As she paused to open the door, he grabbed her shoulders, turned her around and embraced her.

"I'm sorry, Penny, for what I said. This day has been terrible, and I'm exhausted. When I'm ready to court someone, it'll be you. Please be patient."

As he was embracing her his loins began to stir, and he thought, *My God, she's so warm and soft. But what am I saying. Oh, Abby, no one can replace you,* and with that he pulled back from the embrace.

Penny was smiling and appeared to enjoy their hug. She said, "Yes, yes, I understand. It takes time. We shouldn't even be considering courtship so soon."

"You can sleep in my bed, Penny, and I'll make a pallet on the floor here in the kitchen."

As Dave settled down for the night, he thought to himself, *Perhaps I shouldn't wait too long to start courting her. What a beautiful lady she is...But where the hell is Ezra?*

The next morning, right after Dave's breakfast, Constable Radcliff rode up.

"Have you found him?" Dave asked.

"No," Radcliff said, "I've got men searching some Hopkins' homes in the neighborhood."

Chapter 13

Submit's Quilting

About a week later, on May nineteenth, Titus stopped by to say that he was joining the army. There was still no word about Ezra's whereabouts.

Titus said, "I'm wondering if Ezra went to Boston and joined the British army. His sympathies seemed to be with the Tories, though he did go with me when we inquired about joining the Connecticut Army."

"Take care, Titus," Penny said. Dave and his children, their faces turning sober, all waved to their Uncle Titus as he mounted his horse and rode off. As his young vibrant brother rode out of sight, Dave said a prayer for his safety.

"Now, Dave," Penny said, "you remember this afternoon is Submit's quilting, and, of course, I'm going. Do you wish to escort me home after the frolic, or should I ask someone else?"

"Yes, yes, I'd like that," Dave replied. "I haven't been to a quilting in ten years."

When Dave arrived in the early evening at the quilting, all the young single men in the vicinity had already arrived in order to enjoy the festivities. Upon seeing her brother, Submit rushed up to him and said, "Oh, Dave, we finished the most wonderful quilt. Come and see," and she led him into another room and held up the quilt which was white with exquisite birds and flowers sewn into it.

"I like it, Submit. I'm pleased you seem so happy."

"My Dave Payne is a wonderful man," Submit replied. "Are things between you and Penny Todd working out?"

"She's quite a lady and to my liking. It's only been about six weeks since we buried Abby, though."

Submit said, "But come now and enjoy yourself. Joe is here with cousin Hester. He seems quite taken with her, though she's not the lady Hulley was. And, of course, Mrs. Todd's here." They returned to the large room where Eben was now playing the fiddle.

They danced and played some games, including, "Roll the Trenches," "Button Button," and "Running Around the Chimney."

Later in the evening, shortly before the party was to break up, when Dave and Penny were dancing, Penny said, "You know, Dave, so many of these people are so much younger, except Will Macclure. They seem like children to me."

The two of them left the frolic, walking out into a breeze blowing through the big oak trees. They climbed up on the wagon, noticing the fluffy clouds fleeing by the full moon. Dave said, "You certainly look beautiful in the moonlight, Penny."

"Why thank you, David," and she took his hand. "Everything's beautiful out tonight, even my old horse."

"I feel the same," Dave said. "Perhaps it's the warm spring air. I feel my gloom lifting this evening, though I believe it has more to do with your presence than the weather." As the horse trotted along, Dave put his arm around Penny's shoulders, wondering if she'd resist this sign of affection. But she didn't, and snuggled up closer to him. The wind, now blowing through the tops of the huge pine trees, was making a sound like waterfalls.

With about a half mile to go, Penny suddenly sat up straight and said, "Dave what's that noise? Oh, my God, look!" When he looked up, he gasped. A huge dead pine tree was falling over right across their road. Dave pulled sharply on the reins to halt the frightened horse, but at the loud crashing sound of the pine hitting the ground, Penny's horse reared up and cried out in terror.

When the horse finally calmed down and the dust and debris had settled, Dave said, "Looks like we can't get by. We'll have to leave your wagon here and walk to your home."

"But it's still muddy out, and I have my best gown on."

"What we can do," Dave said, "is unhitch the horse, leave the wagon, and go on by foot." It was light enough by the moon to see the road.

"How can I get over the tree, Dave? I don't want to tear my gown."

"All right, Penny, come over here." With that Dave lifted her up in his arms and stepped up to the dead tree trunk, which was about three feet off the ground due to the branches holding it up.

"Don't get me dirty, Dave!"

He lowered her carefully on the other side. Then, he unhitched the horse and managed to lead the animal through the woods and around the bottom of the tree, the roots of which were now sticking up in the air about fifteen feet.

"Why do you suppose this happened now, Dave? We could have been killed."

"Yes, but the good Lord spared us. Perhaps that's a sign."

Dave boosted Penny up onto the horse's bare back, noticing how feminine her delicate figure was.

"A sign of what, Dave?"

"Don't know. Mayhaps it pleases the Lord that our time to go and meet our departed spouses has not arrived."

"Your children still miss their mother a great deal. I can hear it in their evening prayers. Last night Lavinia said in her prayer, 'Momma, come back to me. I want you to hug me. Please get a horse and wagon and drive back from Heaven.'"

They soon arrived at Penny's, and the girl from a nearby farm, who had been watching all their children, went home.

After several glasses of the hard cider while they talked about their friends and acquaintances at the frolic, Dave said, "I must go now, Penny. I certainly enjoyed the evening."

"Why don't you stay here tonight? It's so late, and you'll have to get over that tree again. Only problem is, with all the children here tonight, there's no bedding for you."

"Well," Dave said, "I suppose we could bundle."

"Bundle?" Penny said, and her face reddened. "I, ah, I don't know if there's any board here to separate us."

"Give me a lantern, and I'll look in the barn." Dave soon came back with a board, washed it off, dried it, and put it down the center of Penny's bed.

"Have you ever bundled before?" Dave asked.

"No, I – I – my family wouldn't have approved."

"Well, I have. It's interesting, but unless you're exhausted, it's difficult to get much sleep."

"Will you stay on your side, Dave?"

"Yes, of course."

"Do I have your word?"

"Yes, yes, Penny," and he walked up to her and kissed her.

"And you must leave your britches on."

Dave laughed and said, "Yes, I will," and he kissed her again, and they embraced. Her closeness was making him physically excited. Her mouth was sweet, and he could feel her firm breasts against him.

"I must put on my night clothes. Dave, you wait out here in the sitting room till I call you."

A few minutes later she said, "I'm in bed now."

Dave found the bedroom now lit by just one candle. Penny was sitting up in bed and smiling, with her long, golden hair curling down beyond the top edge of her nightgown, which still revealed an ample part of her bosom.

"I think I might get lonely over here," Dave said, as he crawled in under the covers on his side of the bed.

"You might be lonelier should I send you home," Penny said, smiling, and she slid down under the covers. They both turned on their sides, facing each other and put pillows under their heads so they could look over the board.

"Your eyes are very beautiful tonight, Mrs. Todd," Dave said, and he leaned over and kissed the lips of her small mouth.

"Ah, Mr. Hotchkiss, and you are looking very handsome yourself."

"I'm considering climbing over the board, Mrs. Todd."

"But David, you promised," and she kissed him and ran her hand through his hair. "If you crawl over, you'll get splinters in you," and she giggled like a school girl.

They kissed again, but after a few minutes she suddenly pulled away. "You're a very passionate man, I can see. Do you think this bundling is wise?"

"It does seem to be more difficult to keep myself from desiring you, unlike when I was young and bundled; then, we mostly talked and laughed."

"Perhaps you should go, David, though I fear I desire you as much as you do me. Yet until such time as we're married, it's a sin to lust after each other."

"I believe you're right. My carnal needs should not push you into sinning. You are too dignified and beautiful for that," and he sat up on the side of the bed and put on his shirt and shoes.

Penny reached over the board and ran her hand over his shoulders and said, "We need to talk some more soon about what lies ahead for the two of us."

"Yes, you're right." He turned around and kissed her again, thinking, *I sure wish there were no restrictions.*

As he stood up to leave, the door opened, and Sarah stood there. "Hello, Papa. I can't sleep. It's too crowded in there. Lavinia keeps hitting me in the face."

"Yes my Sarie, I'm certain she means no harm," Dave said, and he picked her up. "You can come home with me, and we'll come back in the morning. Say good-night to Mrs. Todd."

They said their good-byes. Dave wrapped Sarah in a blanket, put her on Mrs. Todd's horse in front of him, and they headed for home. It was much darker now with black clouds covering the moon.

Chapter 14

The Strawberry Patch

On the morning of June 15th, as Submit prepared for her wedding, all the Hotchkisses, including their children and spouses, were invited for a breakfast at Gideon's. Among the men at the table was Jesse's oldest son, Asahel, a large, intelligent lad who looked several years beyond fifteen. The ladies bustled around the kitchen and helped Submit to dress.

After the usual greetings, as they began eating, Pa said, "I thought now would be a good time to discuss how you all feel about our situation with the British. First, I should tell you, we just got a letter from Titus. So far he seems to enjoy the army."

"He likes the army," Dave said. "I'm not too surprised, though it's not to my taste."

They discussed the British for a while and what they thought might come of all that was going on.

"Pa, what about the two different Waterbury militias?" Dave asked. "You've got one company whose members support our country, but then there's the other militia under Captain Brown which is almost all Tories."

"Yeah," Gideon said, "and should hostilities occur in this vicinity, mayhaps we'll be fighting them. I believe a formal complaint will be drawn up against Captain Brown for the General Assembly soon."

Just then Anna came into the room and smiling said, "Hey, enough of the serious talk. We have a wedding to celebrate."

"Ah, the wedding," Gideon replied, "we certainly have enough of them. Joe Payne just married Hester, and now we have Submit's. Who will be next?"

"Maybe Dave," Anna said with a mischievous grin.

"Now, now, Anna," Dave said good naturedly, "this is Submit's day. Leave me in the background."

They then all went to the wedding and had a frolic afterward. Penny and Dave were sitting and watching the people dancing to the music, just as they had done at Anna's wedding.

"Joe seems happy now that he's married to Hester," Penny said.

"Yes, he does," Dave responded. "Shall we dance?"

They stood up and joined the others and danced to the "Sir Charles Sedley's Minuet."

After a time, while still dancing, Penny said, "By your countenance, Mr. Hotchkiss, I'd say you're happy tonight."

"And you'd be correct, Mrs. Todd; perhaps it's the rum, perhaps it's the music, or perhaps it's that perfume you're wearing. I feel, for the first time since Abby's departure, contented."

"I'm pleased to hear this, Dave," Penny said.

"Even though you and I have not reached an understanding about our future, over the last few weeks your good nature, natural joy and concern have made my children happy again. Even Sarah seems recovered. I never thought I'd feel this way again." With that, Dave embraced her to the joyful stares of all the Hotchkisses, Paynes, and their friends.

"Oh, David," Penny said, as she blushed, realizing everyone is looking at them, "you are a valuable friend."

"And I love your blue gown, too," Dave said and swung the beautiful widow around to the tune, "Miss Hedge's Minuet."

When the festivities ended, Dave drove the wagon from Salem back to his house with Penny beside him. Dave was still in high spirits and sang:

"Are you joyful, Penny Todd, Penny Todd?
    May I ask you, Penny Todd?
Are you happy, Penny Todd, Penny Todd?
    I can make you happy, Penny Todd,
    Yes I can, yes I can.
    I can make you happy, Penny Todd."

"I'm flattered Mr. H. Yes, I am happy."

"Tomorrow, we shall talk of serious things," Dave said, "but tonight I just feel joy. Look, Penny, at the big oaks!

"Are you joyful, Penny Todd, Penny Todd?
    May I ask you, Penny Todd?"

Just then there was a crack of lightning, which scared Old Buck, and the horse began galloping ahead as the rain started to pour down.

"Whoa, whoa!" Dave hollered, as he pulled in the reins.

After slowing the frightened horse, they continued home while Dave kept singing his Penny Todd song.

"You didn't know I was so musically inclined, did you Penny?"

"No, no, but I'm soaked wet, Dave."

"Here, get under this coat," and he put his coat over her shoulders. Then he continued singing gleefully, as the rain poured down on his face.

When they arrived home, Penny said, "You are joyful all right, Dave, but I think it's the rum. We'll see how you feel in the morning."

Penny went into a bedroom. As Dave took off his wet clothes in the kitchen, he continued, "Are you joyful Penny Todd..."

"Quiet, Dave," Penny said from her room, "you'll wake the children."

The next morning, after the children had eaten their breakfast, as Penny was cleaning the dishes and Dave was still eating some bread, she said, "I notice you have your best shirt on today, David. Is there a special occasion? I would think you would have worn it to the wedding."

"Ah, well, I just felt like wearing it today," Dave replied.

"You said last night you had something serious to discuss with me."

"I did? No, you must be mistaken. What I want to do today is go with you and pick strawberries. I know a good spot not too far away."

Surprised, Penny wiped her hands off and said, "That sounds like fun. I'll get the children."

"No, no," Dave said. "Just you and me. We need to get away from the little ones once in a while."

"But who will mind the children?"

"Ah, hah, here she comes now," and, as they looked out the window, Anna ran up to the house.

"Are you berry pickers ready?" Anna said, with a happy expression on her pretty face. She glanced mischievously back and forth between Dave and Penny and then wiped the sweat from her forehead.

Dave said, "I have a basket all packed, see?" He held up a basket he'd hidden, containing some fruit and a jug of cider.

"Now, now, what's going on?" Penny said. "You arranged for Anna to come over here and mind the children just so you and I could pick berries?"

"Yes, when I saw Anna at the wedding yesterday, I told her of my craving for strawberries, and she agreed to come. Anna, you are precious to come here."

"She certainly is," Penny said. "Watching nine children can be a burden."

Anna laughed and said, "Now that I'm married I sometimes miss being around all of my younger brothers and sisters. This will be fun for me."

"Come Penny, I'll hitch up Old Buck," Dave said, and he got up and went outside, but stopped just outside the door.

He heard Anna say in a low voice to Penny, "Has Dave said anything yet?"

"Hmm, last night he said he had something serious to discuss this morning, but now he doesn't remember even saying that. Too much rum."

Dave walked to the barn and soon drove the wagon up to the back door. Penny came out looking radiant. She had combed her long blond hair down her back and wore a blue shawl around her shoulders to protect her from the cool of the early June morning.

They drove off east on the road to Columbia. "There's this place near my pa's where we used to pick strawberries," Dave said. The sun came out and warmed them as Old Buck plodded along. At Columbia they turned south, and after a short distance, Dave stopped and tethered his horse off to the side.

"Come up here, Penny." After walking several hundred yards through some woods, they came to an open clearing next to a sparkling brook. Colorful green moss covered most of the ground mixed in with the strawberries. Nearby, white birch tree leaves waved in the breeze.

Penny immediately got down on her knees and joyfully began picking the small, tasty berries. "They're so sweet, Dave. Have you tried them?" She removed the stem from another one and popped it into her mouth.

"Yes, they are," Dave said. He hadn't expected there to be so many berries nor that Penny would be so enthusiastic about picking them.

"Look, Dave, over here." She ran to another spot to gather some more. "Dave, be sure to brush the leaves aside with your hand so you can get at the big ones underneath."

After a time Dave took out a blanket he'd brought along and laid it out on the moss. Then he went over to Penny and took her by the hand and said, "Let's stop a while. I've got a blanket we can sit on so you won't stain your dress." He led her by the hand. They sat down facing the stream, the sun heating their backs.

"I'd wager there are fish in the brook, Dave. Did you bring fishing gear?"

"No, no," and he kissed her hand. "I think you surmise why I brought you to this place."

"It's not to pick berries?" Penny asked. She smiled and lowered her eyelashes as Dave turned and kissed her. He then reached out to her, and she moved in close and buried her face in his shoulder. She said, "Oh, Dave, what are we going to do?"

"We'll get married, if you'll have me," Dave replied. He pushed back from their embrace and smiled at her, waiting for her answer.

"Oh, I do want that, if you love me," and tears came to her eyes.

"I find I'm drawn closer to you every day, Penny. I never thought I'd find someone I could love as I did Abby, but I swear I do. Your joy, your beauty, and the kind of person you are have made me get over my grief, and I find I love you very much."

"But, it's so soon. Are you ready Dave?"

"Yes, we're not in our twenties. We don't know when the good Lord will take us. I'd like to marry you soon."

"How soon? Do you think our friends will say we are rushing into this without thinking, without you having a proper time to grieve over your first wife?"

"Our friends and relatives may say such things, but I believe they expect it anyway. Do you want me to take time to investigate all the available young ladies of Waterbury Township to see if one suits me more than you?"

"No, no, David," Penny replied, and she kissed him warmly, clinging to him. "I would rather you took me right now in this strawberry patch in broad daylight than have you go chasing after other young ladies."

Dave pushed her slightly back away from him again, and looking into her blue eyes, said, "I take it that's a yes to my proposal." He kissed the tears on her flushed cheeks.

"Yes, of course" Penny replied. "I do love you."

"How about three weeks from now?"

"All right, Dave, but we should keep the wedding small and without a frolic. We'll just have the children and your immediate family ... What will our life be like?"

"Well, for one thing, I won't sleep in the kitchen. I think we should add on to my house and live there. We'll keep your farm and work it as much as we can. With all the children, the two places will keep them busy with chores."

"Do you wish to have more children, Dave?"

"Whatever the Lord wants will be our blessing."

"I don't wish to die having a twelfth child like your mother did."

"Of course, I understand."

"One promise I wish you would make to me, Dave. Don't go in the army. Let the young single men fight the British."

"I can assure you of that, though I may have to be called away for a few days in Pa's light horse to defend nearby towns. Your answer to my proposal makes me very happy, Penny. Now, if you no longer want to pick strawberries, we can go, or we can just relax here and enjoy the flowing water."

"This is a beautiful spot. I may pick a few more strawberries, but I'd rather just sit here next to you. You're making me feel very safe and secure about my future." She put her arm around his wide shoulders and moved closer to him on the blanket.

"Do you think we shall always live in Judd's Meadow, Dave?"

"Mayhap. But I would like someday to move further west, perhaps after this war. The land hereabouts is not the best, and I hear land in New York is low in price."

"Are you not concerned about Indians in New York?" Penny asked.

"Not too concerned. I don't plan to take the Indians' land from them. I'll buy it."

Penny looked around and said, "Now, we have to bring some berries back, or Anna and the children will think there's something amiss."

"Not yet," Dave said, and he turned and pulled her down on the blanket on top of him and kissed her passionately. When she lifted her head up to look down on his smiling face, her ample breasts now seemed to Dave more luscious than ever; they almost escaped her dress. He could feel his loins stirring as her long blond hair fell down on both sides of his head.

"Oh, Dave, Dave, I'll make you happy. I do love you," and she kissed him again. He had his hands on her back, but gradually moved them down to her buttocks and gently squeezes.

"You have such lovely hair," Dave said, and he ran his right hand through her yellow locks. Then he rolled her over on her back, making her laugh at his weight on her.

"Hey, Mr. H., you're getting rather heavy. Someone's feeding you well." Dave moved to the side of Penny and continued to look down on her, stroke her hair, and kiss her on her lips, her nose and her eyelids.

Penny suddenly sat up straight, a look of fright on her face. "What's that noise, Dave?"

"Don't know," and he stood up and reached for his whip.

"Who's there?" he yelled.

The noise grew louder, however. "Come out here, whoever you are!" Dave shouted even louder. As they stared in the direction of the rustling, Dave began to laugh. "It's just Old Buck." The old horse ambled slowly up to Dave to have his head scratched.

Chapter 15

All One Family

On July 5th, two days after Mabel had delivered to Gideon the nineteenth offspring from his loins, a healthy boy they name Amzi, the Hotchkiss clan gathered at the meeting house to witness the wedding of David and Penny. In spite of the efforts of the bride and groom to keep this a without-a-frolic affair, the rest of the family was so pleased at the news of this union that they all came, except the new mother Mabel. Even Gideon's brothers Stephen and Joshua attended along with some of Dave's cousins, as well as Penny's parents, Mr. and Mrs. Peck.

The nine children of David and Penny sat in the front row with Reuben and Anna. Asey held baby Cyrus on her lap.

Gideon insisted on having music, rum, and cider, and again, after the ceremony, everyone joined in the festivities.

Dave said to his father, "Pa, you shouldn't have done this. I already had a big wedding the first time."

"I know, Dave. But one of the pleasures of having a big family is that there are so many weddings. I love weddings. You've got a beautiful lady, Dave. But, don't forget we're soldiering tomorrow night."

"Yes, Captain, I will be there tomorrow for training."

Little Lavinia came up to Dave and said, "Does this mean Mrs. Todd is our new ma, like Sarah says?"

"Yes," David said, as he picked up the five-year old; "she's now Mrs. Hotchkiss. You know that her children, Amos, Daniel, and Rhoda didn't have a father, and you didn't have a mother. Now you all have both a mother and a father."

"I see, Papa. Then we're all one family, right?"

"That's right, Lavinia," Dave answered.

When Dave and Penny were having supper with Penny's parents, Mr. Peck, a huge, muscular man about 55 years old, wanting to get to know his new son-in-law, began asking questions. "Are you descended from one of the original settlers of New Haven?"

"Yes," Dave replied, "my great-great grandfather, Samuel, came here from England in 1639."

"Was he a prominent citizen in the town?"

"Hah, ha," Dave said, "quite the opposite I believe. He was very young, about eighteen and probably an indentured servant. A few years ago I had a chance to look at the New Haven Plantation records for the time when he was alive.

"One entry said, 'Samuel Hotchkiss and Elizabeth Cleverly for filthy dalliance together, which was confessed by them both, they were both severely whipped.'"

"Really? They put that in the records?" Mr. Peck asked. "They were probably just holding hands," and he smiled for the first time.

"Yes, and that's not the worst of it," Dave said. "A few months later the records said something like, 'Samuel Hotchkiss and Elizabeth Cleverly being desirous to join in marriage and not being able to prove their parents consent, but both affirming they have the consent of their parents, and having sinfully and wickedly defiled each other, making them unfit for any other, we hereby give them permission to marry.'"

"Hah, ha, that they put that in the record is difficult to believe," Mr Peck laughed.

"How is it you never told me that, Dave?" Penny asked.

"Oh, I was saving that for our old age. Think about it. If they weren't unfit for any other, I wouldn't be here."

After a time Mr. Peck asked Dave how he felt about our relations with England. Dave said, "Well, I happened to observe the British being routed by the militiamen at Lexington and Concord. I and my whole family believe we must defend ourselves against the tyrants, especially now that we've shown we can best their army as we did at Bunker Hill two weeks ago."

"Yes, I agree," Mr. Peck said. "Now that Congress has elected George Washington, a man I once met, to be commander-in-chief of all the armies, we should be able to drive the British in Boston right back into the ocean."

"By the way," Mr. Peck continued, "to change the subject, Penny said you might move some day. You wouldn't be crazy enough to move into Indian country in New York State, would you?"

"Mr. Peck, as I told Penny, I'm not going to try and take Indian land. I'll pay for it, though I think it might be some time before I can accumulate enough funds."

"I still say, Dave; it's too dangerous. Don't do it!"

That night, after the children were asleep, Dave said to his bride, "Mrs. Hotchkiss, I think I'd like to retire now."

"Oh, David, stop being so formal. You sound like an old man." Penny came over to him, sat on his lap, and kissed him passionately.

David smiled, lifted her up, and while carrying her to the bed said, "I take it you are ready to go to bed too, Mrs Hotchkiss." He kissed her and put her down gently on the bed.

Chapter 16

The Letter

Almost seven months later, on Sunday, January 29th, 1776, David and Penny piled their children into a big, old, four-runner sleigh, which at one time had belonged to Penny's former husband. "Come, children," Dave said, "I know it's terribly cold, but you can all bundle up under the blankets. I'll carry Cyrus and ride on Old Buck."

"Do I have to hold Raiphe on my lap, Papa?" Asey asked.

"Yes, you do. Are you ready, Penny?"

"All right, Dave, the children are all seated."

Then Dave drove off to the meeting house for the Sunday church service. It was very cold, with about a foot of fresh snow on the ground. Some of the congregation did not have sleighs and walked to the unheated meeting house.

After Reverend Leavenworth preached a long sermon and they spent some time with their friends and relatives chatting, Gideon said, "We've just received an interesting letter from Titus, Dave. I'd like you all to come to supper tonight, and we'll read his letter."

Later, when they were all gathered at Gideon's house and finished the evening meal, the children were sent to play in the large sitting room. The adults were all in the dining room before a roaring fire.

"All right," Gideon said, "here's Titus' letter."

Eben interrupted, saying, "Before you start, Pa, I heard something last night at the tavern I thought you should know. Clyde showed his ugly head, and when he was under the effects of much rum, he said old man Everett was selling whips to the British."

"He did?" Gideon said, raising his eyebrows in surprise. "I'll tell the committee. If we can get evidence of this, we can arrest him and put him out of business. Keep your eyes and ears tuned for any information on this. I'd love to catch that pompous Tory. "Now, here's Titus' letter."

Gideon read the letter, dated, 1/15/1776, in which Titus told about the attempt of the patriots to capture Montreal and how the American general, Montgomery, whom Titus was accompanying, was killed by a cannon blast. The attempt failed.

"My God!" Dave said when Gideon finished. "Titus must have been close to getting killed. I had heard General Montgomery was killed and that we had lost a battle over Quebec, but this is the first I've heard any of the details."

"It would appear that if Montgomery hadn't been killed and Arnold hadn't been wounded, we would have captured Quebec," Jesse said.

Eben spoke up and said, "Pa, I heard that General Lee needs troops for New York City; so tomorrow I'm going to ride to New Haven and enlist."

"Are you old enough?" Gideon asked.

"Just turned eighteen, remember, Pa," Eben replied.

They discussed some of the ideas in the pamphlet, "Common Sense," which though anonymous, was thought to have been written by a man named Thomas Paine.

When the discussion ended, just as the family had done with Titus, the older men began giving Eben advice from their own experience in the army such as, "Keep your powder dry," and "Watch out for diseased whores!"

Gradually, the large family broke up and went their separate ways, some of them on foot, some on horseback, and some by sleigh.

Chapter 17

An Assistant Surgeon

About four months later, Titus arrived home, having been discharged at Montreal on May 1st. He seemed to Dave no worse for the experience and, though tired and thinner than usual, appeared to be in excellent health.

Several weeks later, on a warm spring day, Jesse ran over to Dave's house at noontime and burst in, just as the family was about to sit down for their noon meal.

"Dave, just got a letter from Asa in New York City," Jesse said, as he wiped the sweat off his forehead. "Look what he says. Let's see, here it is.

"'Pa, I'm writing you now especially about Uncle Eben. He's taken ill and is in the army hospital next to the Grand Battery. When I saw him yesterday, he looked very bad. He's got lung fever and bad rheumatism. Unless we can somehow get him out of the hospital, I fear he'll die there.'"

"That's terrible! Dave said. "How's Asa's health?"

"Fine, he says."

"Oh, poor Eben!" Penny said. "Did you show the letter to your pa?"

"Yeah, I did," Jesse replied. "He agrees with Asa. Dave, weren't you about to take a load of whips to New York City, anyway?"

"Yes, I was. I could go see him and figure out what I can do."

"Tell you what," Jesse said. "I'll go with you, and we could take Titus, too."

Two days later the three brothers headed for New Haven with a load of whips. At the harbor of New Haven they hired a boat and sailed to New York City. Upon arriving at Beekman Slip, they hired a wagon and team and delivered their whips late in the afternoon to a large saddle shop on Queen Street.

Then they located Asa in his quarters in a house on Stone Street. Though it was after dark, Asa took them to see Eben at the hospital.

As they entered the building with a lantern, Dave said to Jesse under his breath, "My God, the stench in here!"

It was very crowded with soldiers but few doctors or nurses and apparently little medicine. Many of the men were coughing or retching. Other than their own lantern there were only a few candles lit, giving the hospital a ghostly feeling.

When they found young Eben, who was normally in such good spirits, he was lying in filth on some dirty straw. He hadn't shaved in some time, his clothes were filthy, and he appeared to be very weak.

As soon as Eben saw his brothers and Asa, though, he smiled weakly, turned on his side, and said, "Titus, Dave, Jesse!" As he said this, though, he began coughing terribly, his face turning red.

"We're delivering some whips," Jesse said. "Asa told us you were sick."

Eben spoke in a soft voice, trying not to cough, "This is a death house. Just look at these men."

In truth, Dave thought as he looked around, *the putrefaction appears to be running amuck in their weakened bodies.*

"Can you get me out of here and take me home?" Eben asked. "I'm no use to the army in here. Now, you better leave before you catch this sickness too."

Dave said, "I understand from Asa that General Putnam is here. Since I met him back in '58, perhaps he'll give me a hearing. First, we'll talk to the doctor."

"Thank you," Eben said, and he started coughing again, holding his hand in front of his mouth. He stopped and said "Oh, Dave, this seems unbelievable, but Ezra's here."

"What, Ezra Hopkins?" Dave asked in amazement. "Where is he, the bastard?"

"He's one of the surgeon assistants and works the night duty," Eben replied. "I don't think he's recognized me in the dark, and I didn't want to say anything to him for fear he'd kill me. He's going under a new name, Martin Bradford. Two days ago, though, when I saw the surgeon, Captain Blake, I told him that Ezra was wanted for two murders. I haven't seen either of them since."

"My God! that murderer taking care of sick men?" Dave said. "We'll go see Captain Blake now."

At that moment, however, as Ezra was about to enter the room, the hair on the back of his neck rose as he stopped in his tracks and stared at the men in the lamplight. He said to himself, *The Hotchkisses. Got to get out of here fast!*

When they found Captain Blake in a small separate room he used as an office, the fat, bald, bespectacled doctor was writing at his desk.

After introducing themselves, the Captain said, "Now, who is it you're asking about? Hotchkiss, right?"

"Yes," Jesse said, "Eben Hotchkiss. I think for him to regain his health we should take him home since he's of no use to the army now."

"I believe you're right," the Captain said. "Came in here with the camp fever, but he's gotten worse. I don't have the authority, though, to let a soldier out of the army. But I can write a recommendation that he be discharged. I'm sorry men, but I just don't have the medicine I need to take care of all the illness here."

"Please write your note," Dave said. "Now, could you tell us where this assistant surgeon, Martin Bradford, is? Eben said Martin's the same man who murdered our sister and my wife. His real name is Ezra Hopkins."

The Captain surprised, said, "A few days ago, when your brother told me this, I was skeptical, as Martin worked hard and seemed to be good in caring for the men. Today I told him what your brother said, and he replied, 'This is a big misunderstanding. I don't know anybody named Hotchkiss.'"

"Where is he?" Dave asked again.

"He should be here now," the Captain replied. "I saw him when he came in about two hours ago. Here, ask my other assistant over there."

When Dave asked the man about Martin, he said, "About the time you came in here he told me he was sick and was going back to his quarters."

"His quarters? Where's that?" Dave asked.

"Over on Pearl Street."

"Asa, show us where that is!" Dave said.

The four Hotchkisses ran out the door, and Asa led the way to the nearby Pearl Street. They had left the lantern behind and were running by the light of the faint moonlight.

"Here it is," Asa said. Dave knocked on the door, and a sergeant answered it.

The sergeant explained that Martin had left, carrying a rifle and a bag of clothes. Standing in the doorway munching on his chicken, he said, "Chances are he's either going to try and cross over to Long Island or New Jersey."

"We need to split up," Dave said. "Sergeant, could you show me where the ferry to Long Island is? Then Titus could go with me, and Asa can take you, Jesse, up along Hudson's River."

"I don't need to go with you; the ferry landing is simple to find. Just go east on Pearl Street here."

"All right," Dave said, "let's split up and see if we can find him." Dave and Titus began running over toward Dock Street and soon come to the ferry landing. Even in the evening, the ferry was still running. Soon they could see the ferry approaching from the other side. They looked over the passengers waiting on benches, but Ezra was not there.

"Let's hide in the shadows over there and see if he boards the ferry," Dave said, and they went and kneeled down in some bushes.

The ferry soon landed, and the passengers disembarked. The people in the tavern nearby and those on the benches now boarded the ferry. "I guess he's not coming," Titus said. "Damn it, we missed him!"

Just as the boat was about to leave, from out of the shadows on the other side of the dock area, Dave saw a figure run toward the boat. "There he is," Dave said.

"Let's get him," and they stood up and sprinted toward the ferry. Ezra leaped on board.

"Hold the ferry!" Dave yelled. But already the boat was starting to pull out. "Jump on board with me, Titus!"

But just as they get to the end of the dock, a voice rang out, "Halt, or I'll blow you to hell!"

Dave saw Ezra kneeling on the boat, aiming his rifle over the rail at them. "Damn, you, Ezra! You can't run forever. I'll get you some day!" Dave yelled, raising his fist in the air in frustration.

"Just stay away from me," Ezra yelled back, "Remember, I got my Kentucky rifle."

Dave's face turned red, "He's slipping through our fingers again; damn, damn!" Dave and Titus watched the ferry till they could no longer see the sought-for passenger.

"What'll we do now?" Titus asked. "Shall we take the next ferry?".

"No, I would like that, but we have no weapons except our whips, and we probably couldn't find him anyway. Long Island is huge. He'll probably go up a way and take a boat over to Connecticut. We need to get Eben out of the hospital. Let's go back to the sergeant. Then we'll meet up with Jesse and Asa and find some lodgings."

It took them a while, but they finally met up with Jesse and his son, who were naturally disappointed about Ezra's escape.

"I should report back for duty," Asa said. "Let's walk over to Broad Street together."

They soon found a few rooms available in a small gabled stone Dutch house on Broad Street. It was a one-story house with a low roof and a huge chimney. Asa said, "Pa, make certain you just drink the water from the water carts."

The next morning they all went back to see Captain Blake, who said, "Now, here's your note concerning your brother."

When they went back outside the hospital, Jesse said, "That place is a real charnel house. We've got to get Eben out of there. Who do you think we should see?"

"Let's try Old Put," Dave said. "Hope he remembers me."

"General Putnam's headquarters are right over here at number one Broadway," Asa said. "It's called the Warren House." Leaving Asa outside, the three brothers went in and found a young officer in the front office.

Dave walked up to him and said, "Sir, my name is Dave Hotchkiss. I was a messenger at the battle of Fort Ti in the old war with the General. I'd like to see him for a few minutes. If he doesn't remember me, tell him I'm the son of Captain Gideon Hotchkiss."

The officer went into an inner office, and soon the General himself came out, "Ah, Dave, Dave, it's been a long while," said the portly old general who was now in charge of all of the New York City forces.

"Thought you might not remember me, sir," Dave said, and then introduced the General to his brothers.

Putnam said, "I remember when we were down in that gulch with Rogers, and you had one of the biggest whips I'd ever seen a man carry who wasn't on a wagon. Come on into my office."

The office was large, and a young, serious officer with dark bangs who was writing furiously at a desk nearby. "Men," the General said, "this is Major Aaron Burr." Dave noticed how small Burr was. He looked like a boy.

Burr stood up, smiled, shook hands, and said, "You know, General, I remember Titus from Quebec. One of the fastest runners I've ever seen."

The General suddenly became serious. "We are very busy, men, as you can imagine, preparing for a British attack on this fair city here. So what can we do for you?"

The Hotchkisses sat down. Unlike Burr, who wore a fancy uniform, Dave noted that the General had only a sword belt over his waistcoat; so he looked unlike an officer. Dave said, "General, there are two things. First, our youngest brother, Eben, is in the hospital here and very sick. We have a note here from his surgeon, Captain Blake, recommending he be discharged. We'd like to take him home to Connecticut and nurse him back to health. I fear otherwise he'll die."

Putnam rubbed his double chin and said, "Our policy is to not discharge soldiers who are sick. There are exceptions made, though. Major, would you address this request?"

"Yes," Burr said. "The easiest way to do this is if some family member will enlist in his place. Is there another brother or cousin who might be willing to take his place?"

Titus ran a hand through his hair and said, "Major, I just now returned from Montreal since I wasn't discharged until May 1st. I have many brothers, but I'm the only adult besides Eben in the family not married. Eben and I have always been close, since he's only two years younger than me, and he's a runner too. I'll enlist in his place. My only request is that I enlist in New Haven to be with my Connecticut friends."

"All right," Burr said, "I'll have the discharge papers drawn up, if I have your word that you'll enlist promptly in New Haven. By the by, Titus, last year I went in the Voluntown ten mile race. It was mentioned that a Hotchkiss won the race in '72; was that you?"

"Yeah, it was Titus," Dave said. "He beat Torch Morley in a close finish."

"Torch Morley?" Burr shouted, and his face became flush as he stood up. "Do you know what kind of trick Morley played on us in the race?"

"I can imagine," Titus said.

"What he did," Burr said, "was he…"

"Ahem," Putnam interrupted, "I have much to do here. What was the other matter you men wished to bring up?"

Dave said, "General, a man from our town killed our sister and my wife. When we saw Eben just now in the hospital, we discovered this same man was now an assistant surgeon at the hospital," and he explained who Ezra was.

Burr, raising his voice, said, "You're saying a murdering blacksmith is an assistant surgeon in our hospital?"

"Well, he was," David said, "but he saw us last night and deserted. We split up and tried to head him off. However, he had a rifle and managed to get away on the ferry to Long Island."

"I doubt we can find him," Burr said. "We'll put the murderer on our deserters list. Now, what's his real name?" Dave gave him the information on Ezra.

The three Hotchkisses went outside and, joining Asa, sat on the steps. Jesse said, "We'll have to take Eben to our quarters. I'll stay with him till he's fit to travel."

Jesse, Dave, Titus and Asa returned to the hospital.

"We're taking you out, Eben," Jesse said. "Here's your discharge papers."

"You did it?" Eben asked, unbelieving. "Holy Hallelujah! Lift me up, will you?"

Titus and Dave helped their weak brother stand up. "Can you walk?" Dave asked.

"I think so," Eben responded smiling, but then he coughed. "Come, help me out of here!"

With Titus and Dave on either side, they walked Eben out into the bright sunlight and up into the wagon.

After putting Eben to bed, it was decided Dave and Titus would return to New Haven while Jesse would stay with Eben.

As Dave and Titus were preparing for the return trip, Jesse said, "Be sure to see Charity and tell her it may be several weeks before I return."

Dave and Titus sailed back to New Haven, where Titus enlisted for a year as a sergeant in Captain Parmalee's Company, in Colonel Elmore's regiment. Dave drove the wagon on home.

A very pregnant Penny rushed to embrace her husband. "How's Eben? Did you get him out of the army? Where are Jesse and Titus?"

Dave kissed her and said, "Let's go into the house. I'll tell you everything."

Chapter 18

Two and Two

Two weeks later Jesse brought Eben home, though in order to allow him adequate rest, they took ten days to make the trip.

On June 24th, as Dave was planting flax seed, eleven-year old Asey came running toward him as fast as she could. "Papa, Papa," she yelled as she stopped and tried to catch her breath. "It's Momma Penny. It's her time!"

"All right, Asey," Dave said, "I'll get Mrs. Mollyhouse. You get your Aunt Charity."

Though Charity was pregnant with her eleventh, she came over to help out with the birth.

Penny had a fairly easy delivery, and Dave was pleased to see his new son, Charles Todd Hotchkiss. All of the children made a big fuss over their new half-brother.

One Sunday in mid-July, immediately after the church service, Jesse stood up in the meeting house and said, "I have just received a letter from my son Asa, who's in the army in New York City. I think you'll be interested to hear what he says."

The people nodded to let Jesse know that they'd like to hear news from New York.

"He said,

"'Dear Ma and Pa,

"'Yesterday, July ninth, our regiment was marched out early in the evening up to the Commons. It looked like the whole army was there, but it wasn't.

"'An officer read us the new Declaration of Independence. All the generals were there on their horses, including General Washington.

"'We all gave huzzahs. All the officers shook hands with General Washington. Then they rode on to read the document before other ranks."

"'There is a huge British fleet nearby, and they are landing their troops on Staten Island. I fear a battle soon. I have heard no news of Ezra.

"'Hope this finds you all in good health.

"'Your Loving Son,

"'Asa'

"Let us all say a silent prayer for Asa, General Washington, and all of our men fighting for our freedom."

Upon leaving the meeting house, the people talked excitedly about the meaning of the Declaration of Independence.

"What it means to me," Dave said to Penny, "is that all the colonies are now behind the notion of complete independence from England. There's no turning back now."

By this time, Eben had recovered and was now living at Jesse's house, doing work for Jesse on his farm.

On a hot day in August, the third, when Charity cried out with labor pains early in the morning, Jesse sent Eben off to fetch Mrs. Mollyhouse, but when Eben returned he went to Dave's house instead and yelled from the yard at the house, "Dave, Dave, come to the door!"

"Yeah, what's happened?" Dave said from the doorway where he stood with a glass of cider in his hand from his noon dinner.

"It's Charity. She's having her baby, but when I went to Mrs. Mollyhouse's home, I went in. She and her husband got the small pox. I've been exposed, damn it! Can I stay at Penny's empty house, in case I get it, till I know?"

"Yeah, that's all right with us. You certainly don't want to expose Jesse's children or mine either. I'll send Penny over to Jesse's to deliver the baby."

"Who'll take care of me should I get the small pox?" Eben yelled.

"I think Jesse may have had it. He could do it. Go over to Penny's house and put a pox sign on the door."

Penny, taking her new baby with her, went to Jesse's house and delivered Charity's baby, a boy whom they named Jesse.

Unfortunately, twelve days later Eben did come down with the small pox. Jesse went to take care of him at Penny's house and confined himself right there with him.

A short time later, as Eben was recovering, Jesse also came down with the small pox, and the two men continued to stay together. One day Dave approached the back door to Penny's house, but stayed back a ways. "Eben," Dave shouted, "come on out!" Eben stepped out on to the porch.

"Hello, Dave; good to see you. We're getting a little lonely here, just the two of us."

"How you feeling now?" Dave asked.

"Much better, though I'm very weak. Jesse's having a difficult time, though. He shouldn't have come to take care of me, though I don't know if I would have recovered without his care. I got pox marks all over me."

"How are you getting meals?" Dave asked.

"Beulah brings them over and leaves them on the porch." Beulah was Jesse's fourteen-year old daughter.

"I wish I could see Jesse," Dave said, "but I never had the small pox. I can't take the risk."

As the days wore on, Jesse's and Dave's families increasingly worried about Jesse, as well as the possibility that others would come down with the dreaded disease.

On September 25th Dave came again to Penny's farm. "How's the patient today, Eben?" Dave asked from outside.

"We've got two patients now," Eben said. "Beulah's in here, too." Then lowering his voice, he said, "I fear Jesse won't survive, Dave."

"Oh, no," Dave said with a quivering voice. He'd always been so close to Jesse. "Eben, open the window next to his bed, and I'll talk to him from outside."

Dave went around to the side of the house where Eben indicated Jesse was confined. "Jesse, can you hear me?"

"Yes," a weak voice responded. "That you, Dave?"

"Yeah, how you doing?" Dave asked.

"I confess I don't know as I'll make it. I've no strength at all. The pustules are as big as great green peas. Dave, will you promise me something?"

"Yes, of course, anything."

"If I don't survive, I'd like you to somehow help in the upbringing of my children until such time as Charity remarries."

"I promise, but you'll survive, Jesse. We're all praying to God for your recovery. You'll recover just like Eben did. Promise me you won't give up, Jesse."

"Not much I can do now, Dave. I've given myself up to the Lord."

Tears came to his eyes as Dave said good-bye to Jesse. Dave thought, *Oh, my God! He's got to recover!*

But Jesse did not survive. He died two days later on September 27th, 1776. The large extended family of Captain Gideon all gathered at the meeting house for the funeral. Before the service, Gideon said to David, "I never expected to survive any of my children that didn't die in childhood. Can't understand why the Lord took a man like Jesse with ten children before an old man like me."

"Yes, it's hard to comprehend," Dave said, wiping tears from his eyes. "Jesse thought he'd gotten the small pox in the last war, but it probably was just the chicken pox."

Eben stood up and, after telling of how Jesse saved his life not once but twice, said, "Charity, if you'll allow me, I wish to live at your house and work your farm until such time as your children can manage it. I'll also help in any way I can with the whip business."

Then Dave stood up and came forward. He wondered what he could say that Eben hadn't already said. Dave looked out over the sad faces and said, "I always loved Jesse. From the time we were just children I always admired him and looked up to him more than any person I know, even my pa. Though Charity and Jesse's children will sorely miss him, I find it extremely difficult to think about going on without his presence in my life. Those runs we used to go on I'll particularly remember. We joked and talked about everything. He was always so cheerful." At this point Dave choked up, and he had to wipe his eyes on his sleeve.

"Charity," he continued, "I promised Jesse on his death bed I'd help you. If you ever have need of anything, just let me know. I will also continue to help with the whip business. Now, I think it only proper we bow our heads and say a silent prayer to the Lord for Beulah's recovery."

After the ceremony and the burial, the grieving widow thanked Dave for his kind words, and said she'd be glad to have Eben live with them, as soon as Beulah recovered.

However, Beulah did not survive either and died on October 24th. After her funeral, Captain Gideon talking with Dave said, "How is your new baby?"

"Little Charles is fine, Pa. Looks like you. Penny's holding him right over there. Come look!"

Gideon walked with Dave over to Penny, and, looking at the smiling baby, said, "Two births and two deaths within five months. The good Lord is mysterious."

Chapter 19

Valley Forge

The war continued on. The British drove the Americans out of Long Island and New York City in the fall of 1776.

Though there had been no fighting in the Waterbury vicinity, in April of 1777 the enemy made a raid on the patriots' supply depot at nearby Danbury. Captain Gideon and his whole company rode to Danbury, but they arrived too late to be involved in fending off the attack. The patriots had eighty casualties while the British lost 154. The Danbury patriots' supplies, however, were destroyed.

About the first of January, 1778, Charity received a letter from Asa, and after reading it to her children, brought it over to Dave's. It was dated December 25th, 1777. Asa wrote of the terrible difficulties of the army at a place called Valley Forge.

After reading the letter to Penny and the children, Dave said, "'Tis a great letter, Charity. You can be proud of Asa's serving in the Continental Army under such difficult conditions."

Charity wiped a tear away and said, "Yes, I am proud of him, though I wish he hadn't joined. Losing a husband and a daughter is enough. And, he's so young, only seventeen."

Dave said, "Asa is very strong with a good head for the army. He should survive the experience. Thank the Lord he was inoculated against the pox."

"Have you heard from Titus?" Charity asked.

"No," Dave replied. "All I know is that after his discharge from the army at Fort Schuyler on the Mohawk River last May, he went to Boston and enlisted as a lieutenant of Marines and master-at-arms on board the United States ship Oxford. I believe they've been on a cruise ever since."

One day about the middle of March, Eben appeared at Dave's doorstep, as he often did to go on a run with him. Eben bent forward against the wall to stretch his calves while Dave was in the bedroom putting on his moccasins. "Penny, you look very heavy with child," Eben said. "How are you feeling?"

"Just fine, Eben, except my back occasionally, and I have to be careful carrying Charles around."

Dave came out of the bedroom and went up to Penny, kissed her, and said, "Isn't she beautiful in her condition, Eben?"

"Yes, you are fortunate, Dave," Eben said.

"Hah, I feel like a fat hog," Penny replied. "How is Charity now and all her children?"

"Charity is in good health and pleased by a recent letter from Asa," Eben responded.

"I saw some of the linen she and the family are making," Penny said. "It's very good quality."

It had been a mild winter, and as Dave and Eben stepped outside to start their run, Dave noticed the roads were dry. As they ran along, Dave looked up into the tall pine trees through some heavy fog and said to Eben, "Look at the way the sun is hitting these trees." The needles on the pine trees were covered with heavy dew. As they trotted east, the sun filtered through the fog and the glistening wet pine boughs, giving the scene an eerie, ghostly appearance.

"Yes," Eben said, "it doesn't seem real. Truly, it's like a beautiful dream."

At Columbia they turned south. When they arrived at Gideon's, they stopped in at the leather shop and greeted Abe and Amos.

When the two runners went into the house, Dave said, "Hello, Pa, how are you?"

"Fair to middling, considering I'm an old man of 61 and still got six children living at home. So, what's new with you fellows?"

Eben said, "Charity just got another letter from Asa."

"Thank God he's still alive there," Pa said. "Tell Charity I'll be over soon to read it."

On the way back the runners stopped in at Charity's farm so Dave could read the letter. When Dave continued his run, the fog had lifted and the dew dried up, leaving the pines in their normal, green-needled state.

About a month later, on April 25, 1778, Penny had her baby, a girl this time. They named her Abigail. "Now we've done honor to both our former spouses," Dave said smiling at Penny.

Chapter 20

Captain Ebenezer Dayton

Six months later in September 1778, Dave drove his wagon up to Gideon's, loaded with whips. It was early evening, and Amos and Abe had already gone home, but Gideon was still up, reading his Bible.

"Do you know Ebenezer Dayton, Pa?"

"Yeah, I heard of him. He's an odor on both sides. Robs everyone." Gideon put a bookmark in his Bible, closed it, and carefully laid it on the small table next to him.

"Well, he claims to be a patriot. Anyway Pa, come see what he took off a vessel going to New York City. I ran in to him at Whittemore's Tavern, and I bought a pile of whips from him."

Captain Gideon followed Dave outside with a lantern. Gideon stared at the load. Amazed, he picked up a whip and rolled it in his hand as he studied it carefully under the light.

"It's Everett's all right. Hah, ha, Dave, we got him, the bastard!" and he slapped Dave on the back with glee. "Wait till I show the committee! I've suspected for sometime he's been selling to the British. We have a meeting tomorrow night. Go with me, Dave; I'll drive your wagon with these whips. I can't wait."

I've never seen him this joyful, Dave thought.

The next night at the meeting house the Committee of Safety for Waterbury met. David listened to their discussion.

When the Reverend Leavenworth asked if there is anything which incriminated any Tories, Gideon said, "Yes, I have something. Come see this."

When he showed them the wagon, Leavenworth said, "A load of whips. What about it?"

Gideon and David explained how the whips came into their possession.

The Reverend scratched his wig for a moment and said, "But how do you know Squire Everett made these whips, Gideon?"

"I can tell by the way the core is wound here as well as the lasher. See this, we use five strands on the outside layer. He uses seven, and his are always black with one white strand. See this."

"Nobody else uses that combination?" the Reverend asked.

"No," Gideon said, "it's his method of identifying his product. Now, it'll hang him."

"All right, Gideon," the Reverend said. "Tomorrow get Radcliff and go and arrest him."

The next morning, in a pouring rain, Dave, Gideon, and Constable Radcliff rode up to the barn where Squire Everett made his whips.

"Come out, Squire," Radcliff said in a loud voice in front of the barn.

The Squire opened the door, and seeing his competitor, yelled, "I'm not coming out in the rain. What do you bastard Hotchkisses want? Clyde ain't coming back to you!"

Radcliff got off his horse and, holding his pistol, advanced to the door. "I've got a warrant for your arrest, Squire."

"Arrest, hah! What have these damn rebel Hotchkisses accused me of anyway, making better whips than they do?"

"You're being arrested for selling whips to the enemy," Radcliff replied.

"What? That's ridiculous!" The Squire yelled out, and his face reddened. "For one thing, where is it written I can't sell whips to anyone I want? These are not military goods."

"You know you can't trade with the British," Radcliff responded. "It's the boycott act we've had for four years. We're taking you in."

"Clyde, take over," the Squire replied. "I'll get this matter cleared up. Hell, what kind of proof can they have, anyway?"

"You may be surprised, my friend," Gideon said. The four men rode off in the rain to the meeting house. When they arrived there, four committeemen were seated, including Reverend Leavenworth and Captain James Bronson. Captain Dayton was also seated over in a corner.

"James, what the hell you got Radcliff arresting me for?" the Squire ranted. "So why's it a crime to ship goods to New York city? Everybody's doing it."

James Bronson, a huge, gruff man with a black patch over one eye, said, "As you know, Squire, our committee was formed to enforce the boycott act. These whips were found in a vessel headed for New York City," and he held up one of the whips.

The Squire picked up one of the whips and, after glancing at it, said angrily, "How the hell do you know this is my whip? Anyone could have made it."

"Not so," Gideon said. "You know as well as I do that the pattern on the lasher is yours, and the core is your winding too."

"I suppose it could be mine," the Squire said, rolling the whip between his fingers, "but who's accusing me of selling to the British? Is it just my competitor here? The Captain would do anything to put me out of business."

With that Captain Dayton stood up and rubbing his chin said, "I accuse you, Squire. I took twelve dozen of them off a vessel headed for the enemy in New York."

"And who are you, may I ask?" the indignant Squire asked, his face getting even redder.

"I'm Captain Ebenezer Dayton."

"Dayton? You're Dayton? I heard of you. Damn it, James, Dayton here is nothing but a bloody pirate!"

"I resent that," Dayton said. "I'm a commissioned privateer. Congress has authorized me to disrupt the supplying of the British. I have only taken from those patriots who owed me money."

James Bronson stood up and said, "I think we've heard enough. The committee members will go over in the corner here and make our decision." Gideon went with the rest of the committee, and after a short discussion, they returned.

Bronson said in a loud voice, pointing his finger at Everett, "Squire, I have to tell you; we find you guilty of trading with the enemy. You'll be confined to the Waterbury jail for a year. Also, we are fining you in the amount of 200 of your best whips, which we'll confiscate. Take him away!"

Radcliff approached the Squire with his pistol. Everett started moving, but turned and yelled, "It's all your doing, Gideon! When I get out, I'll get you, I swear!"

"Hah, I should worry about you?" Gideon said smiling.

"I've never seen the Squire that angry," Dave said.

"Serves him proper," Gideon replied. "Wait till I tell Abe and Amos."

Titus Hotchkiss came home from the Navy in November. He served nine days in Waterbury assisting Agur Mallory, a crippled veteran, at nine dollars a day. Then he returned to the Navy.

The following year, on July 25th, 1779, the British attacked New Haven. Captain Gideon and the light horse under his command galloped off to New Haven to do battle. None of Gideon's sons were wounded, but a young apprentice of his was killed by a cannonball. The British, after staying just one night, evacuated without burning the town.

Chapter 21

The Duel

Several months later toward the end of September, late in the afternoon, Captain Gideon was walking toward his house from the barn, going in to supper, when he heard a horse rapidly approaching. The horseman galloped his steed right up to the fence next to Gideon and yelled, "You bastard, Gideon! It's all your fault!"

"Nice to see you too, Squire," Gideon said to Squire Everett. "I see you've served your time." Gideon noticed that the Squire had lost weight in prison and could no longer be considered even portly.

"Of course, you idiot! Now that I'm out, though, what have I got to come back to? My business is almost gone, and it's your fault, Hotchkiss. I ought to shoot you dead right now."

"Oh, I'm to be killed because you chose to sell goods to the enemy, is that it?" Gideon replied.

"Yeah, and I suppose you never did anything wrong," Everett shouted, his face getting rosier, as his horse pranced nervously in circles. "Just 'cause you're a damn light horse captain doesn't make you immune from me demanding satisfaction."

"Satisfaction? You're challenging me to a duel?"

"Damn right! You've injured me grievously. I've a right to demand satisfaction."

By this time Amos and Abram had come out of the shop. "What's the ruckus with the Squire, Pa?" Amos asked.

"He's demanding a personal armed encounter." Gideon said.

"A duel?" Abram said. "He wants to duel you? Hah, ha."

"The varmint is blaming me for his troubles," Gideon said.

"Squire," Amos said, smiling, "are you crazy? Pa's the best pistol shot in Waterbury Township."

"Hey, shootin' at targets is one thing," the Squire shouted, "but facing down another man's gun is something else again. I'll send Clyde over to make the arrangements."

"I ain't accepted your challenge yet." Gideon answered.

"Oh, so the great captain's afraid, huh?" the Squire taunted.

Gideon was thinking, *I should kill the bastard, but dueling is against my religious principles,* but said, "I believe I have the choice of weapons."

"Ah ha, and the great pistol shot is gonna pick something else?" the Squire said, sarcastically. "I s'pose you want broad swords."

"But, Pa," Abram said, with a worried look on his face, "you ain't good with a sword at your age. You'd be out of your mind to pick swords."

"Well," Gideon said, as he rubbed his chin. "Tell you what. We're both in the whip business. The weapons will be whips."

"Whips? Whips ain't no dueling weapon, Gideon," the Squire yelled, and he dismounted and approached Gideon. "I can't get satisfaction from a buggy whip, and you know it."

"I didn't say buggy whips," Gideon said. "You want satisfaction. We'll make it knout whips, and we'll strip to the waist."

"Knout whips?" Amos said. "Pa, I only heard of them from Titus. He saw them in Europe some place."

"I been making whips all my life," the Squire said loudly, "and I never heard of them. What are they like?"

"They got hooks braided into the lasher," Gideon said.

"All right," the angry Squire said, "I'll do it. I'll tear the flesh right off your hide! Clyde will be over tomorrow to establish the details."

Amos and Abram stood there stunned while the Squire mounted his horse and galloped off.

When Dave heard the news of the coming duel, he rushed over to his father's house. "Pa, you're not a young man. I can't understand why Amos and Abram let you accept the challenge." Dave was pacing up and down in front of his father while Gideon just sat in the chair in his living room smiling. "You didn't injure the Squire. He has no right to call you out."

Mabel came into the room and said, "You're right, Dave. Nobody'd ever think your pa a coward should he refuse the duel. Look at all he's done in both wars."

"Hey, all right, I heard you," Gideon said. "I just couldn't do it with pistols. I'd kill him for sure. Also, dueling is against my principles. Now, Dave, when you see Clyde, you have to agree on terms. I suggest we have a circle twenty feet across, and we have to stay in the circle. As to the knout whip, we each make our own, but with no more than ten hooks in the lasher."

Mabel sat down and said, "Why? Why have you got to do this? It's stupid. We've got six children still under our roof who rely on you."

"Now, now, Mabel," Gideon said. "If I refuse his challenge, I'd be worried the rest of my life the varmint might wait in ambush for me and kill me."

"Pa," Dave said, "walk me out to my horse. I want to make sure about the arrangements you want." The two men walked outside, and when they were out of hearing of Mabel and the children, Dave said, "Pa, you heard Titus tell how deadly that knout whip is. He said they use it in Russia to punish prisoners. Some don't survive. A man can get killed by it."

"The Squire knows that, too," Gideon said; "that's why he accepted. But he ain't gonna kill me. After you see Clyde, though, and we make a knout, I'll practice with it. I'd like you to advise me."

Early the next morning, the parties met in a small secluded field next to the foggy Naugatuck River. It was dark from black clouds, and a light breeze was blowing off the water. Dave and Clyde met to examine the hooks on the other party's whip while Amos and Abram drew a circle on the ground twenty feet in diameter.

As the two men took the other's whip Clyde said, "I figured you'd use the Long Distance Reaper. Got a pretty heavy lasher, huh. Well, we did much the same thing."

Dave looked over the Squire's whip and said, "These hooks are sure sharp. This is stupid, this duel. These two old men may both suffer and for what?"

"Yeah," Clyde said, "it's all a matter of pride."

"The Squire looks nervous," Dave said, "and he should be."

The duelists, standing about 50 feet apart, were taking their coats and shirts off. Gideon was wearing heavy leather breeches.

"Are you ready, Everett?" Gideon called out.

"Yeah, I'm ready," Everett growled, and turning his back to Gideon, drew his whip back and took a big practice swing, making a loud crack.

"Do you wish to withdraw your challenge at this time?" Gideon asked.

"Ah, no. Just want a drink of rum, though. Clyde, where's the crock?" Clyde brought the rum over. Everett cradled the crock in his left arm while he held the butt of the whip handle in his right hand and took a big swig.

Dave went to the center of the circle and announced, "Pa, Squire, here are the rules you agreed to. You'll stand back to back. Upon the signal you'll walk three paces forward, then turn and lash."

Dave was thinking about his practices with Gideon. They had fastened straws to a log, and his father had tried hitting them with the knout whip. It took him a while, but with Dave's help he had begun to get the feel of the knout with it's heavy lasher and just how much wrist action to use.

Amos said, "Pa, you sure you don't want to back out of this?"

"No, I'll proceed," Gideon said. "Just be sure Everett obeys our rules."

"All right, Pa, Squire, come here and stand back to back," Dave said.

As the two men approached each other in the center of the circle, with their whip handles held straight up and the whip itself hanging down behind their backs, Dave thought, *Pa sure is short compared to the Squire.*

"When I signal," Dave said, "I'll count off your steps."

"Ready now; go; one, two, three." Both men walked off three steps, then turned and faced each other. As Gideon brought his whip behind him, the Squire rapidly pulled his whip back over his shoulder and then brought it quickly straight over his head forward and down, aiming for Gideon's head.

Oh, God, here it comes, Dave winced as he saw the wave of motion of the rapidly thrown whip come down, but Gideon leaped a yard to his right. The hook-laden lasher made a loud but harmless crack.

At the same time, Gideon brought his whip around in a tremendous circular side motion. The Squire could see it coming but couldn't dodge. The deadly lasher wrapped around his buttocks, the hooks digging through his breeches into his skin.

"Ah - ah - a - ah!" the Squire hollered in pain. Gideon pulled the whip back, and because of the hooks, it spun the Squire around and ripped huge holes in the back of his breeches.

Dave yelled, "Squire, that's it; the duel's over!"

"Damn, damn, Hotchkiss. I ain't through," and he pulled his whip back for another lash, this time ready to make it a sideways lash, but before he could bring the whip back around forward, Amos moved quickly up behind the Squire, grabbed his wrist, and said sternly, "No more, Squire, you had your chance."

Dave said, "Squire, you've defended your honor. This ends it. You need to cover your backside," and he put his hand over his mouth to stifle a laugh. Abram and Amos, however, did laugh out loud at the Squire's appearance.

"God damn!" Everett shouted, "these were my new britches."

"Yeah," Dave said, "well, you're fortunate my pa chose to hit you low rather than rip the flesh off your back and chest."

Clyde came up with a cloth to wipe the blood off the Squire's rear. "Don't think I can stay in a saddle, Clyde," the Squire groused. "Guess I'll have to walk home."

Just then a wagon came into view. Mabel jumped down, her red hair all tousled, and ran up to the Captain. "Are you injured, Gideon?"

"No, I'm fine, Mabel," the Captain said as he put his shirt back on.

"Thank God!" and she hugged him.

Dave came up to his father and said, "Our plan worked, though I was scared you leaped away too soon and that he might be able to adjust his whip throw."

"I was scared too, but I watched the direction of his arm before I even saw the whip. Don't think I ever want to do this again."

"If you attempt this again, I'll lock you in the outhouse," Mabel said, and she laughed, mostly from relief that her husband wasn't injured.

Chapter 22

The Expedition

About six months later, one day in March, 1780, Dave had just returned from a trip to Hartford to deliver whips. There had been a tremendous snow storm which had held him up for a whole day at a small tavern.

He had only been home an hour and was standing by the fire to take the chill from his bones telling Penny the rigors of the journey, when Eben burst through the door. Stomping the snow off his feet, he said, "Dave, you got to get your horse and come with us."

"Wait. What's it all about?" Dave replied, and he looked out the window to see his brothers, Gideon, Amos, and Abram mounted on their horses in the road.

"You ain't heard? Captain Dayton's wife got robbed by a band of villains when Dayton was out of town a few days ago. They got some of Dayton's captured goods. We're all gonna try and catch them."

"Do you know where they are?"

"We tracked them to Gunntown and then south to Captain John Wooster's, and we want to continue following them now that the storm's let up."

"But why us? We're not deputies." Dave said.

"But one of the robbers, Mrs. Dayton said, they called Martin, and he had weird eyes. It's got to be Ezra Hopkins. Also, there's a man named Graham in the band and two of the Wooster boys. Oh, by the way, they stole Chauncey Judd."

"They did? Why would they capture Chauncey?" Dave asked. "He can't be more than fifteen."

"Don't know. The guess is that Chauncey saw them with their loot late at night so they took him with them rather than allow Chauncey to identify them. Could be dead by now, I suppose."

"All right Eben," Dave replied, "give me a minute to saddle up Old Buck."

"But Dave," Penny said, "you just got here."

"Penny, we can't pass up the chance to get that murderer, Ezra Hopkins."

After saddling up his horse, Dave joined his brothers, and they picked up two of Chauncey's older brothers and proceeded toward Captain Wooster's, whom Dave was told had harbored the robbers. On the way, Dave's brothers told him more of the details, including the fact that a Captain Steele was now leading the band of men intent on capturing the robbers, partly because Captain Dayton had offered a reward for their capture.

By the time they arrived at Captain Wooster's it was dark. Dave noticed there were quite a few men there already. Dave went up to talk to Captain Steele.

"The robbers must be going to Derby to pick up a boat at the landing there, since they have no horses," Captain Steele said.

"How far is it from here?" Isaac Hotchkiss asked, a cousin of Dave and his brothers.

"About six miles, I reckon," Steele said.

Though it was dark now, they set out on their horses slowly through the dark and snow, looking all the time for any sign of the robbers.

"We should inquire at Daniel Wooster's house," Dave said; they did, but there was no sign of them there.

The pursuers pressed on, and as daybreak came and they approached Derby, they saw some tracks in the snow. Steele said, "It looks like our quarry is just ahead. Hurry, men!" and they galloped rapidly forward and crossed the bridge over the Naugatuck River.

As they came down to the landing, Dave yelled out, "Jumping Jackfish, look! There they are in a whaleboat!" When they looked down the 150-yard-wide Housatonic River, which the Naugatuck flowed into, they could see the boat rounding a rocky point called the "Devil's Jump," which projected from the eastern shore.

"Where's the ferryman?" Steele yelled. "We've got to cross the Housatonic and ride to Stratford to intercept them."

During this delay, while they aroused the sleepy ferryman, the local people, hearing about what was going on, joined the pursuit. Finally, after crossing the river, the pursuing horsemen rode off at a gallop for Stratford, fourteen miles away.

At the "half-way house" they stopped, and since most of them had had no refreshments since the preceding evening, they decided to halt here for breakfast. But first, a few men were stationed by the river-side to give notice if the boat was sighted. However, the sentinels were not very observant, and the whaleboat floated silently and swiftly down the river in the shade of the opposite bank. Before the alarm was given the thieves had left their enemies behind.

Dave and the party of pursuers immediately began their chase again along the Housatonic. When they arrived at a spot opposite the boat, it was at a point where the river was about 200 yards wide; the boat clung to the eastern bank. A few shots were fired, but the distance made them ineffective. The only answer was a loud, "Huzzah" from the boat as they came to the water of Long Island Sound.

"Damn, damn!" Dave shouted in frustration. "What'll we do now?"

The men gathered together and looked to Captain Steele for advice. Steele said, "If we are to make a successful expedition across the sound, we must first return to Derby. Then we must gather a few good boats and a force of men that can overcome an enemy force we might encounter. Also, we need to talk with Captain Clarke."

"Why Clarke?" Dave asked.

"Because," Steele said, "like Dayton, he used to live in Brookhaven over on Long Island. He even went on privateering expeditions. Maybe he'll agree to lead our forces into the enemy's territory."

A few persons were assigned to watch the course of the robber's boat from up in the Stratford meeting house belfry with a spyglass and to note where the boat might land on the Long Island shore. Dave and the other men then returned to Derby.

After talking to Steele and Dave, Captain Clarke, a salty man with the longest queue of grey hair Dave had ever seen on a man, agreed to not only help the pursuers, but to lead the expedition to try and capture the robbers and rescue Chauncey.

Clarke looked over the large group of men in the town square and began giving orders. "Ay, there men! First, I want just 30 men, fifteen in each boat. Every man must have a pistol or a musket. We'll leave at three this afternoon. Now, we need to gather up some victuals for the voyage. Oh, and Joe, get Captain Harvey. I want him to lead the second boat. Remember men, we're going into enemy territory. If we're discovered by the British, we'll have to fight our way out."

Eben said to Dave, "I hope Clarke knows what he's doing. The Wooster boys shouldn't be a problem, but Ezra and this Graham fellow, from what Mrs. Dayton told us, could be real dangerous."

At three o'clock the two craft, with their sails unfurled and manned with well-armed rowers, started down the river. When they stopped again at Stratford, the observers in the belfry reported the point of landing of the robbers.

"Ah, hah! Come on, men," shouted Captain Clarke, eagerly. "We can not go amiss." He stared across the sound, smiling. "They've gone to Brookhaven, and I know the very house where they'll be found. We'll trap them all before morning. Pull away, men!"

Long Island Sound was about twenty miles wide at this point, and the passage, even with a favorable wind, often required three to four hours. Eben said to Dave, as they rowed side by side, "Do you think the robbers will expect us to come after them and maybe ambush us?"

"Perhaps," Dave replied, "but I'm hoping they'll feel safe on Long Island and not foresee us following them."

"Hope you're right, Dave," Eben said. "I keep having this picture in my mind of Ezra pointing his damn rifle at us as we come through a tavern door."

Dave was exhausted when late in the evening the boats reached their destination. He hadn't slept the night before, and his hands were blistered from rowing, but in spite of it all, he felt excited and lighthearted, thinking, *At last I'll bring Ezra to justice.*

They pulled up into a small cove at Crane's Neck, about three miles west of Brookhaven. Two men were left to guard the boats, and the rest began walking quietly in the dark toward Brookhaven.

At one point, when walking next to Clarke, Dave said "Captain, where do you think they are?"

Clarke threw his long grey queue over his shoulder and said, "There is a tavern kept by a man named John Bailey. He's a Tory, and his house is a favorite den for persons in that party as well as British officers stationed in the vicinity. After all that the robbers have been through, they'll need food and rest." Just outside the town they stopped. Clarke told them his plan for the capture. They waited some time to be sure their quarry would be settled down for the night.

When they arrived at the town, all was quiet. Dave saw no lights, except one at Bailey's tavern. Clarke stationed most of the men around the outside of the tavern out of sight from the door.

Then, he and Captain Harvey, along with Chauncey Judd's brother, Walter, and Dave, approached the front door, and Clarke knocked.

After an interval of a few minutes, as if there was a consultation with another person, the door was unlatched, and an attractive, blonde young lady appeared.

When Clarke asked for lodging, Miss Bailey replied, "I am very sorry, but we cannot accommodate you. Another party of travelers arrived here today, whom we have been obliged to entertain, and our beds are all full."

Captain Clarke again turned to Harvey, and in a low voice said, "This is all we need to know." He came out of the night shadows and dexterously slipped by the young lady, at the same time saying, "Give no alarm, miss, on peril of your life!"

Miss Bailey backed up and silently sat down, her face turning white from fright. Dave looked around and, seeing the door of a downstairs room, opened it, only to find a man in bed with a young lady. When he quietly asked the embarrassed man his identity, he revealed he was a British officer. Clarke assured him, if he remained silent, no harm would come to him.

In the meantime, Miss Bailey told the men that the travelers were in the upstairs bedrooms.

While most of the men waited below, Dave, Eben, Captain Harvey, Captain Clarke, and Walter Judd silently ascended the stairs. Dave noticed that there was a room on the right at the top of the stairs. He took out his whip and had his pistol in his left hand.

Dave's heart beat fast at the anticipation of seeing his old enemy.

Clarke quietly opened the door.

Is Chauncey still alive? Dave wondered.

Clarke held up the lantern, and Dave could see that the travelers were all sleeping, with Chauncey next to a man in uniform. Walter Judd reached out and, putting his hand over Chauncey's mouth, carefully lifted the exhausted boy up in his arms and carried him out while the robbers still slept.

Most of the robbers had their faces turned away so Dave couldn't see which one was Ezra. Clarke, holding the lantern just below his face, shook one of the thieves. What the robber first saw on awakening was Clarke's stern face, and he yelled, "God almighty!" waking the rest of the burglars.

For a moment all was confusion, but the robbers, seeing that they were facing pistols, didn't resist; the rescuers jumped on them, pinning them down in order to tie their arms behind them.

Dave looked frantically for Ezra, but didn't see him. "Where's Martin?" Dave yelled. Just then Dave heard a noise in a nearby room. He ran out into the hall and opened a door on the opposite side of the hall, and there he was. Ezra, his dark hair hanging in his eyes, was sitting on the sill of the window, with one leg outside, about to jump out.

Hearing the door open, Ezra looked back, and seeing Dave, yelled, "Oh, no, Hotchkiss!"

"Halt, Ezra!" Dave shouted, but Ezra pivoted around, quickly putting his other foot out the window. Dave cut lose with the big whip, lashing Ezra across the back.

"Ah h h h," he screamed as he dropped to the ground outside. He began running up a road in the dark, limping some from the fall.

Dave turned, dropped his whip, leaped down the stairs, and ran outside the house and up the road he had seen Ezra take. There was a half moon, giving some light. He could just barely see Ezra up ahead when the road was straight. The muddy-rutted road ran through bushes and woods and made many twists and turns. On and on the two men sprinted.

I'm closing in on him, Dave thought.

"Stop, Ezra, or I'll fire this pistol!" Dave yelled, but Ezra, having recovered from the drop out the window, kept running.

Dave was thinking, *When I get up close enough, I'll have to jump on him. Don't want to kill him. I want the bastard to be hanged for his crimes.*

After about a half a mile, Ezra was still about 50 yards ahead. But when Ezra rounded a sharp bend, Dave lost sight of him. When Dave sprinted around this turn in the road, though, he could now see several hundred yards ahead, and Ezra was not in sight. Dave stopped. *Maybe I can hear where he is in the bushes,* he thought. But, at that moment he saw a flash of light on his left and heard a loud report.

Oh my God, I'm shot! Dave said to himself. The pain that went through his upper left arm made him wince and cry out, "I'm hit!" and he dropped to the ground for a second. Then, realizing that Ezra would not have time yet to reload, he got to his feet and rushed into the bushes and trees toward the spot where he'd seen the flash, but Ezra had already moved on.

Now he could see the blood spurting from his arm, and he felt faint. "Damn you, Ezra!" he screamed. "I ain't dead! I'll get you yet, you bastard!" Tears of frustration and pain came to his eyes.

Now, the exhaustion from the accumulation of no sleep, little food, all the rowing, the running, and the loss of blood took its toll, and as Dave stumbled back out toward the road he felt faint and collapsed just off the road and fell. Just before becoming unconscious he thought, I'll never get him now, Abby.

When he awoke, he heard a voice yell, "Dave, Dave, where are you?"

"I think he's over here, Gideon," Eben said, and the two brothers soon found him.

"Dave, are you all right?" Eben asked.

"He shot me, the slippery varmint!" Dave said. "Got me in the arm here. He's long gone now. Damn, damn! I was so sure we'd capture him this time. Must be he was the only one who wasn't asleep."

Gideon bent down and said, "Dave, we've got to get you some medical help. Come, Dr. Carrington can bandage that up."

Eben and Gideon helped Dave to his feet, and they supported him as they walked back toward Bailey's. Amos and Abram now approached. Eben said, "Amos, Abram, help Dave here. I'll get Dr. Carrington. Dave's shot and bleeding bad."

Gideon said, "Eben, ask Clarke if we can form a party to go after Ezra." Eben ran back to get Carrington.

"Dave," Abram said, leaning on his cane, "sit down here on this stump and rest."

Dave sat down and said, "How is it no one shot Ezra when he jumped out the window?"

"One of the men we left outside did fire his pistol," Amos said, "but it mis-fired."

Carrington soon appeared with his bag. "Here, bite down on this musketball, David."

Dave took the bullet in his hand and said, "Eben, what did Clarke say about pursuing Ezra?"

Eben wiped the sweat off his forehead and said, "Clarke said it's too danger-ous. Ezra could be three or four miles away by now, and where we don't know. Also, there's British Regulars stationed not far from here. Ezra may tell them of our raid."

As Dave put the musketball in his teeth and bit down hard, the doctor used his instruments to remove the ball in Dave's arm and then bandaged the wound. After this, Dave stood up, and they all slowly walked the rest of the way back to the tavern.

Clarke talked to Dave about what has happened to him, after which he said, "Come men, bring our captives and their loot, too. We've got to get back to our boats before word is spread we're here, especially since one of the bastards got away."

"Captain, what about our British friend here, his wench, and Miss Bailey?" Gideon asked. "They may try to talk to the enemy before we reach our boats."

"Yes," Clarke replied, "we should take them with us. We'll take them at least part way and then let them go.

"Tell you what," Clarke said, "let's take the British officer's horse for Dave."

As Dave mounted the horse with some difficulty, he said, "How's Chauncey?"

"He's weak and tired, but otherwise seems all right," Walt Judd said.

"Just put him up here with me," Dave said.

The men then lined up their captives in a single line.

As Dave and Chauncey rode together, Chauncey said, "Mr. Hotchkiss, do you believe in prayer?"

"Yes, Chauncey, I often pray; makes me feel better."

"I prayed not to be killed," Chauncey said. "Then I prayed that I'd somehow get away from those robbers. My prayers were answered. The Lord must truly want me to live."

"I wish I'd prayed more to capture Ezra Hopkins - Martin to you. Tell me all that happened, Chauncey."

As they rode along behind those on foot, Chauncey told Dave the whole story of how he was captured and forced to go with the robbers.

After several miles, Captain Clarke let the young ladies go, but the party of raiders kept the British officer, knowing he could later be exchanged for an American officer.

At the boats, the prisoners were split up between the two boats. Dave and Chauncey were covered by a sail, putting them as much as possible out of the reach of the wind. Clarke shouted, "Ay, my fellows, set a straight course for the mouth of the Housatonic."

Chapter 23

A Sailor's Return

It was past sunrise on Saturday morning when the boats were spotted from Sentinel Hill as the rescuers rounded the point in the river and headed toward the landing in Derby.

The patriots in the boats shouted their success to those on shore, though Dave still felt despondent about Ezra's escape. The people all gathered to hear the news, and even before the landing, the joyful peals from the meeting house bell sent the glad news throughout the town. In a short time, hundreds assembled to express their pleasure at the results and to be of help, if needed, in bringing the criminals to justice. They all made a fuss over Chauncey, who was smiling and chatting joyfully with all those who spoke to him.

The prisoners were tied up and placed under guard until after the Sabbath.

Dave and his brothers, along with the Judds and Reuben, mounted up and headed back to Judd's Meadow. Dave was feeling sick and a little weak.

As they rode along, Dave said to Eben, who was riding next to him, "Isn't it odd that of the seven robbers the only one to escape is the murderer, Ezra."

"Odd isn't the word for it," Eben said. "It's really eerie. He's escaped our grasp three times."

Upon arriving at Dave's home, Dave and Eben dismounted. Dave led Old Buck to the barn. "Pa," Raiphe, who was feeding the piglets, said, "what happened to you?"

"The man we were chasing shot me," Dave responded.

Raiphe turned and ran ahead of his father to the house yelling, "Ma Penny, ma Penny! Papa's been shot in the arm!"

Penny, aroused by Raiphe's cry, ran out the door, almost running into Dave.

"Oh, sorry, Dave. You're shot in the arm? Has it been attended to?"

"Yes, yes," Dave replied. "Doc Carrington got the ball out and bandaged me up."

"Hello, Eben," Penny said, and she kissed Dave and embraced him, being careful not to touch his arm. "Come in and sit down. Let me look at your wound; I'll change the bandage."

"Ezra shot me, Penny" Dave said. "I was chasing him. He must have stopped, hid in the bushes, and then fired his pistol when I got close, the dirty scoundrel. It was at night and fairly dark; I couldn't see him."

"Tell me the whole story. Did the others get away too?"

Eben interrupted, saying, "Penny, who's the pretty young lady with Asey?"

"Mary Sanford," Penny replied. "Asey, introduce Mary to your Uncle Eben."

Dave then covered all the details of the expedition and capture while Penny attended to his wound.

"My God, Dave!" Penny said. "Forget about Ezra! I already lost one husband. Thank the Lord, Ezra didn't kill you. We've got eleven children between us and another on the way."

"I don't think you need be concerned about that anymore," Dave replied. "The way the war has been going it may be years before I'll have any reasonable chance of capturing Ezra. Damn! we were so close! Right now, though, I just want to sleep."

A month later, on a sunny spring morning, Dave felt well enough to go out and run. He ran to his father's house.

Dave went into the house to discover Titus was there. They hadn't seen each other since May of the previous year when Titus had signed onto the *Dean Frigate* for a one year's cruise with the Continental Navy. Titus was in bed. Dave was surprised how pale and emaciated he looked.

"You just need some good country fresh air and Mabel's cooking," Dave said. "It isn't simple to stay healthy on the food the army gets, and I suppose the navy is the same."

"Mayhaps you're right, Dave. We certainly didn't get the best, and I was an officer. I'm as weak as a newborn colt now. Tell me, Dave, how's Rachel?"

"You mean Rachel Garnsey? She's still unmarried last I knew. In fact, when I last saw her she asked about you."

"She did? That's encouraging. I hear you got yourself shot trying to catch Ezra."

"Yes, I don't see how we can capture him now till the war's over," Dave replied, and then he told Titus the whole story of the robbers and Chauncey Judd. Though Titus was weak, he described for Dave his long voyage aboard the *Dean Frigate.*

A few months later, when Dave returned from the long journey to deliver whips to a man named Cooper in New Jersey, he said to Penny, "This fellow Will Cooper said he had his eye on some land in northern New York. He thought that when the war's over he could sell it in small parcels to the soldiers after they leave the army."

"Mayhaps we could buy a parcel," Penny said.

About a month after Dave returned home, on October seventh, Dave and Penny, who was extremely pregnant, were pleased to attend the wedding of Titus and Rachel Garnsey. Five days later Penny had her baby, a blue-eyed boy, whom they named Gilead.

Chapter 24

Porter's Tavern

Winter came for the large Hotchkiss family, and early the following year, on February 15th, they were all pleased to see Eben marry Mary Sanford. Not to be outdone by his uncle, the 21-year-old veteran of Valley Forge, Asa Hotchkiss married Sarah Williams on March 23rd. Since all the siblings of Asa were girls except the baby, the two men, Asa and Eben, continued to live with their brides in what had been Jesse's home in order to run Charity's farm.

On June twenty-first Dave accompanied his father on horseback to the Waterbury town meeting. While trotting north, side by side, Dave said, "What business do we have to take up at the meeting, Pa?"

"We have to contrive ways and means for processing the town's quota of soldiers for Horse Neck and the Continental army."

"But haven't we tried everything we can think of to get the seven men?" Dave asked.

"I believe if we put up enough hard coin and even neat cattle we'll get the seven men."

As they near Waterbury, they noticed a number of people on foot or on horseback going toward the center of town. "What's going on?" Dave asked of a young man.

"It's the French; they're marching through," was the happy reply.

"Hey, I want to see this, Pa," Dave said.

When the two arrived, Gideon said, "Alleluia, Dave! I'm pleased for sure that they're fighting on our side."

"Yeah, look at them, Pa. Does the column have an end?"

Gideon said, "Jumping Jupiter! The head of the column is out of sight on West Side Hill, and the other end hasn't even come into sight at the hill where George Nichols lives." People lined the road all through the town and cheered the French. Several French bands played exciting songs as they marched by, increasing the enjoyment of the Waterbury citizens.

At the meeting Dave found out that the French were to meet Washington's army near King's Bridge over in New York State.

On the way home Dave said, "Pa, I've been thinking. Some day I may move west, clear some land, and start all over. What do you think of this concept?"

"I would hate to see you leave, but Dave, don't go into Indian country. You heard what happened at Cherry Valley just three years ago. The Loyalists and Indians captured many people and burned their homes."

"I know, Pa, but that was due to the war. I'll wait till the war's over."

One morning, a few months later, in late October, 1781, as Dave was about to go for a run with his son Fred, who at age twelve had recently begun running with him, Eben and Titus appeared at the door out of breath. "Dave, Dave," Eben yelled, "the war's over! Cornwallis surrendered at Yorktown, Huzzah!"

"Are you joking?" Dave said and then shouted, "Hey Penny, the war's over!"

As Eben and Titus stretched their legs and Penny came out to greet them, Titus said, joyfully. "The mail rider just arrived. Gave us the good news."

"Just where is this Yorktown, Titus?" Dave asked.

"As I understand, it's on the coast of Virginia, near Williamsburg," Titus replied.

As the four runners began running toward Gunntown, Dave noted the fall maple leaves looked a shiny bright red, with the early sun beaming through the dew on the foliage. He also noticed how healthy and fit Titus was now, compared to when he was discharged from the Navy the year before. Fred said, "Pa, what about the British forces in New York City? Is the war actually over or not?"

"You're right of course," Dave said. "But this is such a terrible loss for the British. I can't imagine they'll continue trying to take back our country. Of course, they still have major forces controlling Charleston, and Savannah, Georgia."

Titus said, "I understand the British and Hessian forces that surrendered amounted to 10,000 men. Now, if the British would just abandon New York and Long Island, we could capture Ezra."

"Do you think Washington will attack the British in New York City?" Eben asked.

"I don't believe so," Titus replied, "from what I've heard and seen, the British Navy is just too powerful."

For late October, the day was warm, and the rutted road was dry, making it still comfortable to run. The fall leaves were now rustling in a slight breeze.

"Dave," Eben said, "will you want to move west now?"

"I'll be investigating the possibles of purchasing some land," Dave said. "But I'm sure it'll be some time before I can move. Also, of course, like you said, Titus, if it's possible, we want to bring Ezra to justice before I leave here."

"Do you think we could just organize a trip to Long Island and capture him?" Eben asked.

"I suppose that's possible, if we just knew where he was on Long Island," Dave said, "but we don't even know if he's still on the Island. For now, let's get together tonight at Porter's Tavern for a few rums to celebrate the victory."

When Dave and his brothers arrived at the tavern that evening, what Dave saw surprised him. Instead of men joyfully drinking toasts to the victory, all the rooms were filled with exhausted and sick soldiers.

Eben talked to Mr. Porter, and when he rejoined his brothers, said, "These soldiers are all ones that got sick on the long march to Virginia; they were sent home, and this is as far as they got." Some men were lying on the floor while others sat on the floor with their backs against the wall.

"Have they got the small pox?" Amos asked.

"I don't think so," Eben said. "Most of them are just exhausted from the march and their sickness, which is mostly the rheumatism and ague."

Dave went over to the bar and, turning around to face those in the main room of the tavern, said loudly, "Gentlemen, my brothers here and I are very grateful for the sacrifices you have made in order to serve our country. With the surrender of Cornwallis it is time for a little celebration. I am asking Mr. Porter to pour each of you a mug of his good rum, with the cost to be borne by me."

The soldiers immediately perked up. Some yelled out, "Huzzah," and even the sickest managed a smile at the thought of the refreshment.

"That was very generous of you, Dave," Abram said.

"Well, I was hoping you fellows could support my offer with some coin," Dave replied. "There's many a parched throat among these good men."

When the rum was distributed a number of hearty toasts were made to General Washington and the victors at Yorktown. Dave thought, *The soldiers who survive their illnesses should remember this night at Porter's tavern for many years.*

Chapter 25

West Point

In February 1782, the first smallpox inoculation in Waterbury Township was performed by Charles Upson.

In May, after Dave recovered from his own smallpox inoculation, he felt well enough to make a journey to Burlington, New Jersey again, going by way of Fishkill and West Point to deliver a wagon load of whips to the Quaker, William Cooper.

When Dave, Titus, and Eben arrived at West Point, they were amazed to see a peculiar sight. In a large field about a thousand men were working on a curious edifice about six hundred feet long which was supported by over one hundred large pillars made from tree trunks. It was covered by both American and French military colors.

As the three Hotchkisses stood outside the tent they'd set up, observing this unusual sight, as well as all the extensive fortifications on the cliff overlooking the Hudson, they saw two runners in the distance coming toward them from the south along the top of the high riverbank.

One was a short man with a mustache and the other a tall blond young fellow. Their path led them right by the Hotchkisses, and they both stopped a moment.

"Sir, what is this colorful display?" Dave asked, addressing the tall blue-eyed runner.

"Well, it's in honor of the birth of a baby in France they call the Dauphin," the tall soldier runner said. "Mr. Hotchkiss, it's a pleasure to see you and your brothers again."

"You know my name?" Dave asked. "Have we met somewhere?"

"Yes, I'm Pres Redway; it was at a footrace years ago in Hartford when I was just nine years old. I was with my two older brothers and my cousin Polly Hall. She was the one who was shot during the race."

"Oh, my God! Yes, I remember. Titus, Eben, remember this fellow? Waugh, you've certainly grown tall since then."

They shook hands, and Pres said, "This is my friend Torch Morley."

Torch, who had rather scraggly dark hair and a wide smile, with his short stature looked odd beside his tall young friend. He said, "I see you're here for the big race tomorrow."

"Race, what race?" Dave said. "We're just passing through on our way to New Jersey."

"Torch, you should have kept your mouth closed. Now we'll have to race these Hotchkisses."

A few days later, when Dave arrived in Burlington with Titus and Eben, they found that William Cooper had moved from his previous store into a shop in the center of Burlington. As the Hotchkiss brothers entered the shop, Dave noticed a man talking with Cooper in a serious manner. He said, "George Croghan just isn't paying us, Will. Thought you might want to take over my shares in this property."

"Where is this land, again?" Cooper asked. He was a rugged-looking large man, dressed like a Quaker in black and grey.

"It's on a lake west of Albany, Otsego Lake."

"If Croghan can't pay thee, what makes thee think I could do better?" Cooper said.

"Croghan doesn't live there, plus he's got so much other land he bought on credit. There's thousands of acres."

"Hmm, I've heard there's enemy Indians up there, but I'll think on it," Cooper replied. "Hello there Dave Hotchkiss. Got my whips, I imagine. This is Abel James." Dave shook hands with Cooper and Mr. James and introduced them to his brothers.

"Do you have other land for sale in that vicinity, Mr. James?" Dave asked.

"No, what we have is a company, the Burlington Company, which owns the mortgage on a large patent of land." Mr. James said. "I'd like Will here to buy my shares."

"Well, maybe when the war is really all over," Cooper said.

NEW YORK
STATE
FRONTIER

MASS.

C.T.

CANAJOHARIE

MOHAWK RIVER

ALBANY

HUDSON'S RIVER

HUDSON

CLAVERACK

SHEFFIELD

CANAAN

GOSHEN

LITCHFIELD

WATERTOWN

WATERBURY

JUDD'S MEADOW

KATS KILL

ACRA

PATEROH

KATS KILL (?) MOUNTAINS

HARPERSFIELD

CHERRY VALLEY

OTSEGO LAKE

COOPERSTOWN

FRANKLIN

UNADILLA RIVER

WEST BRANCH DELAWARE RIVER

NOHAQUA

FR BRANCH DELAWARE RIVER

KOOK HOUSE

SUSQEHANNA RIVER

UNADILLA RIVER

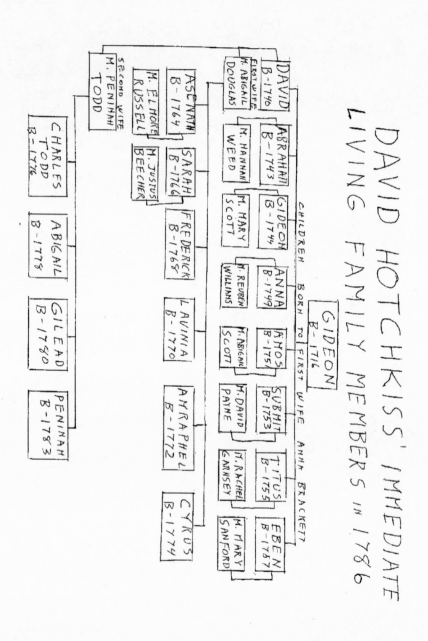

DAVID HOTCHKISS' IMMEDIATE LIVING FAMILY MEMBERS in 1786

Chapter 26

A Frontier Auction

In the years after the war ended, Dave, his father, and all of Dave's siblings gradually recovered financially from the deprivations they suffered from during the war, which were primarily due to the deflation of the currency.

The war officially ended in 1783. It was in that year that Penny had another baby, a girl they named Peninah, the thirteenth child under their roof. Dave, Penny, and their children continued to farm the two properties. Late in the same year on December fifteenth, Dave's oldest child Asey married the veteran Elmore Russell of New Haven.

Chauncey Judd courted Dave's half-sister, Mabel, and two years later, on September tenth 1785, they married.

All during this time Dave kept on delivering loads of whips for large orders.

One day, a few weeks after Mabel's wedding, in late September, when Dave arrived at the leather shop, Abram said, "We have a big order from your Quaker friend, Cooper. There's a note with it."

"Let's see it," Dave said.

The note read, "David Hotchkiss, please, would thee deliver the enclosed order to me in Albany on or about October fifteenth."

"Albany? Now that's surprising," Dave said. "Must be he's got customers there like he does in Philadelphia."

"Well, Albany is still the largest county in New York State, with about 50,000 people," Abram replied.

When Dave arrived in Albany he accompanied Cooper in delivering the various quantities of whips to Cooper's customers so that he could collect the money owed and in turn pay Dave. As they drove back to a tavern after the last delivery, Dave said, "Whatever happened to that land west of here that Abel James wanted you to invest in the mortgage that was held on it?"

Cooper thought for a moment and said in a low voice, "That's odd that thee should ask. Croghan owned a good share of the land, but he died a few years ago. Because payments were not made to the note holders, we, that is my partner Craig and myself, finally arranged through our attorney, Alexander Hamilton, to have the property auctioned. We intend to buy it. We're advertising this in the Albany Gazette."

"When and where is the auction?"

"It's in Canajoharie on January thirteenth," Cooper answered.

"Where's that?"

"It's about 50 miles west of here in the Mohawk Valley. It'll be in a tavern owned by Albert Mabie. Why don't thee come to the auction? I'm anxious to break up this Otsego patent and sell off the land. We'll finance most of the purchases."

"Hmm," Dave said, "sounds interesting. I'll have to think on it."

Dave discussed the purchase of the land with Penny. "But Dave," Penny said, "both my pa and your pa think it's foolish and dangerous to move into New York."

"Don't worry, Penny, the Indians won't bother us."

Dave also talked to Titus and Eben. After much soul-searching, they said they'd like to buy some. Although somewhat reluctant to leave their friends and grown children behind, Penny agreed with Dave that if the price was right that now might be a good time to make the move west. "Why is land suddenly becoming available in New York State?" Penny asked.

"As I understand it," Dave replied, "all during the long war those holding mortgages often weren't able to collect payments from those they had sold land to, especially where Indians had attacked the settlers. Then too, because the Iroquois supported the British, much of their land is being taken from them and sold in large patents to wealthy men or men with important political friends. The same is true of land that was confiscated from certain Tories. Now, this land in turn is being broken up and sold in small parcels to the soldiers coming out of the army as well as to others who can't find land they can afford in New England."

On January twelfth, Dave rode into the small town of Canajoharie along with Raiphe and Dave's older son, seventeen-year-old Frederick. It had been a long trip in the January weather, and they were anxious to get in out of the cold. As they rode their horses down the main street, with the wind howling, Frederick said, "Pa, why do you suppose they're having the auction in this little frontier town instead of Albany, New York City, or Philadelphia?"

"I imagine Cooper had Hamilton arrange this here to try and keep others from bidding on or even knowing about the auction."

When they arrived at Mabie's tavern, they found Will Cooper in the nearly empty barroom stirring a fire in the large fireplace with a long sharpened stick. After being welcomed by Cooper, Dave and his sons had supper with Will and his partner, Andrew Craig, whom Dave quickly deduced by his dress was also a Quaker.

During the meal, Cooper brought out a rough map of the Otsego patent. It clearly showed how the lots which were to be sold were placed around the lake. Frederick was particularly interested and asked a number of questions about the terrain and the prices of the different lots. As they were finishing their victuals, a thin, small man entered the tavern, stomped the snow off his boots, and came over to the table all excited. Cooper introduced the man as his lawyer, Christopher Yates.

"Will, we've got a problem," Yates said. "A Dr. John Morgan and a man named Ireson have gotten an injunction to stop the auction."

"What?" Cooper asked in a loud voice. "After all we've gone through to get this auction arranged. How did this happen?"

"This man Morgan represented Croghan's heirs and creditors," Yates replied. "They used a young attorney, Aaron Burr, who married one of the creditors, and he petitioned the New York Chancery Court. They claimed that under a shadow conspiracy and using the cover of William Franklin's name that we had secretly and clandestinely revived Croghan's judgement without giving notice to George Croghan's heirs, executor, and creditors."

"But, that's ridiculous! It's still an auction," Will Cooper said, his voice raised in anger.

"I know, but they claim we're trying to get the Otsego patent at a price far below its fair value, thereby defrauding the rival claimants."

"Does Sheriff Sam Clyde know about this?" Cooper asked as he took a swig of his cider and ginger.

"Yes, he's the one who told me about it. They went to his home in Cherry Valley yesterday and delivered the injunction. The injunction says he'll be fined 10,000 pounds if he proceeds with the auction."

"10,000 pounds!" Cooper exclaimed. "By all that's holy, the Sheriff will never go ahead with it, Chris!"

Yates rubbed his chin and said, "Well, you could threaten to sue the sheriff."

"Yeah, Chris. Good notion," Cooper replied, and he banged his fist on the table. "Tell the bastard we'll sue him if he doesn't go ahead with the sale. Also, thee can assure him I'll assume the responsibility for any legal penalty he should receive for conducting the auction."

"But 10,000 pounds," Craig said. "I can't participate in that!"

"We won't have to pay it, I'm sure," Cooper said. "But don't put anything about this in writing, Chris."

At this point Dave spoke up, "I met Aaron Burr several times. I don't think he'll give up too easily, and if he doesn't, how good will your claim be to the patent?"

"Don't be concerned, Dave," Cooper said. "Burr's not here. By the time they figure out what to do we'll have resold most of the lots with new deeds. Chris, have the sheriff meet us here for breakfast."

The next morning at breakfast, when Dave and his sons sat down at the same table as Cooper, they found him vigorously arguing with the sheriff, who was a fat, red-faced man in a bearskin coat. Cooper loudly proclaimed that the auction should proceed, explaining that he'd have to sue him if he didn't carry off the auction today.

"Sue me?" Sheriff Clyde said, "I think I'd rather be sued than pay a 10,000 pound fine. Hell, I could never raise that kind of money in a lifetime."

"Tell thee what," Cooper said. "On my word as a good Quaker, if thee has to pay any fine, I'll pay it."

"You will?" the Sheriff said, raising his dark heavy eyebrows. "Well, now, Mr. Yates, you're the lawyer and know the law. What am I required to do?"

Yates took a big bite of his eggs and said, "Sheriff, Mr. Cooper is an honest Quaker man. If he says he'll cover any fine, he will. Further, don't forget you'll earn your fee of 35 pounds for conducting the auction."

Pausing for a moment, the sheriff said, "All right. We'll proceed," and he smiled for the first time. "I wonder if Morgan will bid against you."

When the auction was about to start, Dave and his sons sat at a table close to the roaring fire while Sheriff Clyde took off his coat and stood behind the bar. The two Quakers took a table close to the bar. "No opposition," Cooper said to his partner with a grin. "This is to my liking."

But a few minutes before noon two men arrived, the cold wind blowing some snow through the doorway as they entered. They announced themselves as Dr. Morgan and Mr. Ireson. Morgan and his friend took off their coats and hats and sat down at a table away from Cooper. Morgan was a thin grey-haired man with a pinched face.

Sam Clyde said, "All right, gentlemen, the auction will now commence on the Otsego patent."

Morgan stood up and yelled, "Wait, Sheriff! What about the injunction? You can't start the auction! It's not legal!"

"I've consulted the only lawyer here, and he says I can proceed with it; so you either have to bid on the property or be quiet. Now, do I hear a bid?"

Cooper spoke up, "I will bid 1,000 pounds."

Morgan said, "You won't steal the land with that bid. I'll bid 1,500 pounds."

"1,600," Cooper responded.

The bids continued going back and forth, the tension growing with each bid. "What do you think, Pa?" Frederick asked. "Will Cooper win out?"

"I don't know," Dave replied.

After a number of bids back and forth, Morgan said with authority, "3,500 pounds."

Dave could just barely hear Craig whisper to Cooper, "3,600 is all we got. Shouldn't we quit now?"

"3,600," Cooper called out.

Sensing Cooper might have reached his limit, Morgan said, "3,625."

"That's it," Cooper said, and he and Craig sat down at Dave's table. Cooper's round face was red with rage. "After all we've been through, damn it!"

By this time it was 2 o'clock. Dave and his sons, along with Cooper and his partner, went ahead and ordered some dinner while the sheriff went into another room with Yates to write up the deed for Morgan.

After a time Sheriff Clyde returned and said, "Where's Dr. Morgan?"

Cooper yelled out, "Gone to hell! The varmint has fled town as hard as he could drive and will never return."

"Hmm," The sheriff said and then in a loud voice, "I hereby make a public cry for Doctor John Morgan to appear and pay for the patent he's purchased. Is Doctor Morgan about?"

"No!" Cooper yelled. "I already told you. He's gone!"

"Ah, Mr. Yates, what'll we do now?" the sheriff asked.

"You must start the auction all over again," Yates said emphatically.

"All right, I'll open the auction again," the sheriff proclaimed, and he went behind the bar again. "Do I hear a bid?"

"Yes," Cooper said, after consulting with Craig, "I'll bid 2,700 pounds."

"Are there any other bids? No? Then the Otsego patent is hereby cried off to Mr. Cooper."

"Huzzah!" yelled Cooper. The sheriff went into the other room to draw up the new deed while Cooper and Craig toasted each other with a mug of rum.

But after only a few minutes Dave saw Dr. Morgan reappear in the doorway, the winter wind blowing cold on Dave's feet. "Where were you?" the sheriff demanded when he came into the tavern room. "I made a public cry for you."

"I didn't want to be around this scoundrel, Cooper," Morgan said. "So I walked to the blockhouse down the road. I never heard a public cry. You just made a cry within doors. You're only paying obedience to Will Cooper. Sheriff, you must do your duty!"

"All right, all right, you may be correct, Dr. Morgan," Sheriff Clyde said. "I'll award you the property at the price you bid, 3,625 pounds. Now, I need your money. Here's the deed."

Once again Cooper's face turned red, and he put his head down on his hands on the table.

Morgan looked at the deed and with indignation said, "Hmm, this is no legal deed, Sheriff; I can't accept it. It's a botched and defective performance replete with misnomers and other errors. I want you to come with me to Albany to have my lawyer prepare a proper conveyance."

"Go all the way to Albany you say?" Sam Clyde replied. "I must consult the lawyer." He went over to the table where Dave and his sons, along with the two

Quakers, were now sitting with the thin lawyer and said, "Mr. Yates, what'll I do now?"

"It's obvious to me that he's stalling," Yates said. "He doesn't have the money, and the auction requires the money be put up on the day of the auction. He's refused the deed. Therefore, you must give the deed to Mr. Cooper, who does have the money."

When the Sheriff announced he was giving the deed to Cooper, Dr. Morgan shouted out, "This is all a fraud, Cooper! You scoundrel! You haven't heard the last of me yet," and he shook his fist at Cooper.

Cooper said sternly, "I resent thy remarks, sir. If I was not a Quaker, I'd challenge thee to a duel."

Morgan, swearing under his breath, put on his coat and hat and, along with Ireson, walked out of the cozy tavern into a roaring blizzard.

After a few minutes, in which Cooper and Craig enthusiastically congratulated each other on their good fortune, Cooper turned to Dave and said, "Now, Dave, thee know we hold title to this land. Would thee prefer a 250-acre farm property or a small lot to put up a house and a store or a shop on in the town that I'm starting here at the foot of the lake?"

"Is that where it says Croghan's Forest?" Frederick asked.

"Yes, that's where my town will be."

"What will you call the town, Mr. Cooper?" Raiphe asked.

"I plan to call it Cooperstown for lack of a better name," Cooper replied.

"Why not Craigtown?" Frederick asked, grinning.

"Because I plan to live there," Cooper said, "I'm putting up a large house right here, and he points to a spot on the map at the foot of the lake.

"How about Craigcoop Village?" Raiphe asked, smiling.

"No, no, that sounds too much like a chicken coop," Craig said. "Cooperstown is fine with me."

"Now, how about it Dave?" Cooper asked. "Which property would thee like to buy?"

"I appreciate your giving me first choice, and the prices seem reasonable," Dave replied. "But, I'm concerned how valid your deed is. Also I'd like to see the properties before buying."

"Hmm," Cooper said, thoughtfully stroking his chin. "Tell thee what. I'll lower the price to eight shillings New York currency per acre, and if thee buy a tract of at least 250 acres, I'll give thee a village lot, 35 feet by 150 feet, free."

"This is very generous of you," Dave said, "but I still want to see the land first. When can we view the property?"

"We plan to advertise the sale of the tracts, and I will be at the location at the foot of Otsego Lake in early May. By then the surveyors will have laid out all the tracts. At these prices, which are about half of what others are selling tracts for, we should sell it all off by the end of May. So why don't thee pick out a tract now, and I'll save it for thee till the fifteenth of May? Then thee can come and see the tract before buying it."

"This seems like an excellent notion, Pa," Frederick said. Dave then selected a tract, as well as one for Eben and Titus and three different free lots in Cooper's village.

The next morning, excited by the prospect of a future home in the wilderness, Dave and his sons rode off slowly in the snow along the frozen roads toward home. "Pa," Frederick asked, "Are you going to go through with the purchase of the tract?"

"I'm not certain, Fred. I want to see the property, as I told Cooper."

"How much land do they have in the patent?" Fred asked.

"It must be at least 40,000 acres. There should be enough land for everyone."

Chapter 27

Azubah Jones

A few months later, about a hundred miles east of Judd's Meadow on a farm near Killingly, Connecticut, a raucous voice, bursting with song, woke Pres Redway up on this early 1786 spring morning. "Oh, my heart's a twitter in the spring, by jove. My heart's a twitter over you," the voice boomed out.

Oh, no, Pres said to himself as he put his pillow over his head to try and drown out the dreaded sound. *Aunt Burt! I forgot she's visiting.* He remembered the many times this great-aunt, Beatrice Redway, had sung a loud song early in the morning, and though it disturbed his sleep, he couldn't help but grin at the terrible sound.

Today he planned to do some planting on this farm where he lived with his mother. Pres' three older brothers and two sisters had all married and left home, but lived nearby. Pres' father had died when Pres was just twelve. Being the youngest and only offspring still living at home, the full burden of running the farm fell to Pres, though his brothers who lived closest occasionally helped out. At 21 he was a three-year veteran of the Revolution.

When Pres arrived at the table, Aunt Burt, a fat and rather ugly lady, almost eighty years old, was already seated and eating. The family all loved her, since she always made them laugh with her boisterous laughter and bawdy stories. She was telling Pres's mother all the latest gossip around Killingly and Pomfret.

"And, Mehtie, when the Reverend bent over, his pants split," Aunt Burt said, and she began laughing so hard her fat belly shook the table.

"Ah, Pres, my boy," she continued. "When you gonna pick yourself a wife? Surely, there's some young lady out there that would fancy a tall, yellow-haired, blue-eyed lad like you."

"Now, now, Beatrice," Pres' mother, Mehitabel, said, "don't bother the boy! He's got his hands full right here."

"I tell you Aunt Burt," Pres said, "when the right young lady appears, I'll know, but I don't have much to offer her. I'm just a young farmer with no place of my own."

Just then there was a knock at the door. When Pres opened it, a young teenage girl, dressed in a white hunting shirt and leather breeches, stood there. Her long, straight brown hair with streaks of yellow was in a long braid. She was about five-foot-nine inches tall and had high cheekbones and hazel eyes. In spite of her youth, she appeared to be fully developed.

"Pres, can you come and take me to the fair?" Azubah Jones said in a hoarse voice.

Pres looked down from the doorway at his step-niece. He had been her step-uncle now for about five years, after his sister, Mehtie, married Aza's widower father, Daniel Jones. "Aza, I'd love to take you, but I've got planting to do. Come on in, though; I'm eating breakfast. Aunt Burt's here."

"Hello, Aunt Burt," Aza said, as she came through the door, her big smile lighting up the room. "Pres, you need to get out once in a while. Can't you plant after?"

"Not today, Aza," Pres said. He wondered why Aza's voice was always hoarse. He also noticed, though muscular, how graceful she was, with a very thin waist.

"Pres, call me Jonesey," Aza said. "I don't like to be called Aza any more."

"And why not?" Aunt Burt asked.

"Because boys make sport of my name, calling me Assa," Aza replied.

Aunt Burt took a bite of the eggs on her plate and said, "Pres, I heard that you and your big brothers, Comfort and James, are going to New York State to buy some land that's for sale. Is that true?"

"We're going to just look, for now," Pres said.

"When are you going?" Aza asked, excitement in her voice. "I want to go with you," and she stood up and walked back and forth, her brown braid swinging side to side. "A journey to New York State. I love the notion. I could do all the cooking. Then when I get back I could tell Pa all about the land. Pres, you got to take me!"

"But you're just a girl, Jonesy," Pres said. "It's about two hundred miles. It's no place for a proper young lady, and also there's the physical demands."

Aza Jones hugged Pres from behind and said, "Aunt Burt, you know some day I'm gonna marry this rascal," and she smiled mischievously.

"You are?" Aunt Burt said. "Hah, hah," and she almost spat out the cider she was drinking. "What are you, Aza, fifteen? Your pa ain't gonna let you get married for a long time. Also, your pa wouldn't let you go on this long journey with three men."

"I agree with Aunt Burt, Aza," Pres said. "Your pa won't let you go."

Jonesey put her hands on her hips and glared at Pres and shouted, "And don't call me Aza anymore, Pres Redway," and she quickly went out the door and ran off down the road, her braid bouncing back and forth with each step.

Chapter 28

Shipman

At a family breakfast meeting a month later at Captain Gideon's in April, 1786, after all his brothers had exchanged the latest news on their various farms and businesses, Dave said, "Penny and I have talked it over, and I'm going to Otsego Lake to look over Will Cooper's tracts. Now, Eben and Titus, are you going to go with me?"

"Can you tell us what this place is like, Dave?" Eben asked. "I want to be able to tell Mary."

"Yes," Dave said. "Cooper printed a broadside that he'll be sending out called, 'Guide to the Wilderness.' Here's what he says; 'I was alone three hundred miles from home, without bread, meat, or food of any kind; fire and fishing tackle were my only means of subsistence. I caught trout in the brook and roasted them on ashes. My horse fed on the grass that grew at the edge of the water.'

"'I laid me down to sleep in my watchcoat, nothing but the melancholy wilderness around me. In this way I explored the country, formed my plans of future settlement, and meditated upon the spot where a place of trade or village should afterwards be established.'"

"Dave, suppose we find the land unsuitable," Titus said. "Will we have made the long journey for naught?"

"Well," Dave answered, rubbing his chin in thought, "I came across Will Macclure the other day."

"The fellow who used to be our school teacher?" Titus asked.

"Yes, he's a surveyor now. When I told him where I was going, he said I ought to look into some land south of there along the Susquehanna River near the Pennsylvania border. He'd done some surveying there and said it was good land; so we could go there also."

"All right then, I'll go," Titus said, "I've found a group of clockmakers who want to buy my farm, which will give me the money to buy a tract."

"I'll go too," Eben said. "Pa, will you loan me the money to put down the initial payment?"

"Yes, this appears to be an excellent investment, if the title is clear." Gideon replied. "But make sure there's no problem with hostile Indians."

"Then it's set," Dave said. "We'll set off on the twenty-eighth. I'm taking Fred with me. We'll take a boat from Fishkill to Albany."

Just then Reuben Williams came bursting into the room all out of breath. "Is Anna here?" Reuben shouted, and he looked around the room anxiously for his wife.

"Not that I know of," the Captain said. "Why, what's happened?"

"I don't know," Reuben replied, and he flopped down in a chair. "We had a little disagreement at supper. We went to bed, and when I woke up in the morning, she was gone."

"Gone?" Dave said. "Could she be at your parents' house?"

"I've already looked there," Reuben replied. "She's just disappeared. Do you suppose someone took her in the middle of the night when she went downstairs for something?

"She's not at any of your houses, is she?" Reuben looked around the room intently at each of Anna's family members. Getting no reply, he sunk his head in his hands and cried out, "It's all my doing. She must have left me."

Dave said, "She may have been perturbed with you, Reuben, but would she leave your two young children? We must spread the word of her disappearance. We can have a broadside printed up describing her. But first we must mount up and ride to all the towns around."

Dave, his brothers, and Reuben immediately left and rode separately to all the towns in the area as far away as New Haven, Danbury, Stratford, and even Hartford and Torrington. But no one had seen her. Constable Radcliff and all the family members searched around Reuben's house for clues that might tell them something about Anna's whereabouts, but there was nothing. The broadsides were printed and mailed to constables in all the towns around. Then they waited, but they heard nothing.

A few days before Dave and the others were to leave for Otsego Lake, Reuben came to see Dave and said, "I'd like to go along with you, Dave. I can search for Anna on the way, covering Fishkill and Albany. My only problem is the children. Would Penny mind having two more in your house?"

"I suppose not," Dave replied. "Yes, if you should decide to buy land, I'd enjoy continuing to have you as my neighbor."

Several weeks later on a rainy, early May day, late in the afternoon, Dave, Titus, Eben, Fred, and Reuben led their horses up a long narrow mountain trail. At the top they saw some smoke rising from a campfire.

The five travelers proceeded single file through the thick, budding bushes and trees in the direction of the camp fire.

As they approached, Dave saw a strange sight by the light of a campfire. Sitting on a log under a lean-to, which extended out from a twenty-foot-high cliff, were two men.

One of the men, dressed in leather, looked up from the fire. He was sitting next to an Indian, and said loudly, "Gentlemen, I suppose you're coming to buy some of that patent that Will Cooper claims he owns. I should drive you off to Cherry Valley, but some others would just replace you. So, here, sit down and have some venison."

"What'll we do, Pa?" Frederick asked.

"Follow me," Dave replied, and he walked up to the leather-clad stranger and said, "You're right. We've come to examine the land Cooper's selling. My name is David Hotchkiss, and these are my brothers Titus and Eben, my son Fred, and this is my brother-in-law, Reuben Williams."

"My name is David Shipman," the stranger said. "They call me Ship. Come on in under here out of the rain."

"And who's your friend?" Dave asked, as they all gathered under the shelter and sat down on another log.

"My name Captain John," the Indian said. "Many have come for land; land that is my father's."

Captain John, Dave noted, was a fierce-looking Indian who appeared to be in his mid-50s. He had long, grey-streaked black hair that was parted in the center and pulled back, exposing his high forehead and dark eyes. He had large holes in his earlobes, in which were twisted ornaments of silver, beads, and even porcupine quills, all mixed together. Similar items were suspended from his nose and fell below his lips, resting on his chin. He had red paint streaking across his forehead, and his arms were colored in the same way. Several hound dogs, tied to a small tree, were yapping at the visitors.

Shipman stood up and, taking out his big hunting knife, cut some pieces of meat from the deer carcass which hung from the lower branch of a nearby pine tree. "Here, put these on those sticks there," Shipman said. The travelers, breathing in the mouth-watering aroma of the roasting pieces of deer meat, quickly began cooking their own venison steaks.

"Mr. Shipman," Dave said, "do you intend to buy some land, or do you already own some?"

"Hah," Ship replied. "How do I know Cooper's claim is a good one? But, even if it is, does he own the deer, the foxes, the bears and rabbits? I'm not a farmer. I do have a cabin over on Oaks Creek. If Cooper tries to force me to leave, he'll find me unwilling."

"Where does Captain John live?" Dave asked.

"Captain John lives wherever he finds shelter," the Indian said.

"Captain John, how did you happen on your name?" Dave asked.

"John went to Christian Seminary south of here by Mr. Hartwick," Captain John responded, continuing to use the third person in his speech.

Dave then turned to the hunter and said, "Is Cooper at the foot of the lake now, Ship, as he said he'd be?"

"Yes," Shipman replied.

"Did you meet any of the men?" Titus asked. "What are they like?"

"I met some, but I didn't stay too long. Cooper has a man he calls his sheriff, a fellow named Sam Clyde. Then, as I was leaving, I saw a fellow running on the path around the lake. He appeared to have been running some distance."

Curious, Dave asked, "Hmm, what'd he look like?"

"He was young, light-haired and tall," Shipman answered. "Also, he had a girl running with him."

The men settled down for the night under the shelter. As Dave was close to dozing off, he noticed Captain John was still sitting by the fire. He seemed to be staring down his nose at the decoration resting on his chin.

In the morning, when the travelers awoke, they found that Shipman and Captain John had gone. The sun soon came out, and as Dave and his party descended the hill on the east side of the lake, they came to a spot at the top of a cliff which dropped off at least 100 feet to the water, giving them an excellent view of the beautiful lake below. "My God!" Eben said, "it's like Cooper said, as transparent as crystal and as smooth as a sea of glass."

When they arrived at a clearing cut out of the forest at the south end of the lake, they saw Cooper, dressed in his usual black clothes, seated on a stump with a large map of his patent on his lap. Cooper greeted the Hotchkisses warmly, but he seemed very serious and nervous, rather than his usual exuberant, joyous appearance. Dave introduced Reuben to him.

"Is everything ready for our inspection of the properties you reserved for us?" Dave asked.

"Yes, Dave; here, I'll show thy brothers and Mr. Williams the properties on this map," Cooper said. He pointed to the lots he'd set aside that adjoin the one Dave had reserved, all on the west side of Otsego Lake. "The properties are all surveyed. Thee will see the markings."

"I see you have a building here already," Dave said.

"Yes, I put up this log meeting house. Thee are welcome to share it with the other settlers who've come to buy land. Have some rum, too."

"Now, how and where could we ship out our timber, wheat, and other crops?" Titus asked.

"Thee have two possible routes," Cooper said, as he laid down his map and stood up in order to better express himself to the men around him. "Our lake here is the start of the Susquehanna River," and he pointed east to the outlet of the lake just a short distance away. "Runs all the way down through Pennsylvania, including Harrisburg, and ends up in the Chesapeake Bay. Or, when we build a road over to Cherry Valley, thee can go north from there and connect with the Mohawk River leading to Hudson's River."

Dave went over and looked in at the door of the crude meeting house. About thirty men were sitting at tables, some playing cards and some just drinking rum and talking about the land they were contemplating buying and settling on.

Dave and his party then mounted their horses; they rode west and then north around a narrow trail along the west side of the lake. They began riding and walking around the borders of the lots reserved for them, observing the area which could be farmed and what timber there was. Then they camped for the night in a spot near the lake.

"The land appears to be suitable for growing crops or raising cattle," Dave said, "but it is very hilly, not the flat land that would be more suitable for wheat."

Anna Hotchkiss Williams was sitting alone on the dirt floor in a small darkened room. *How long has it been?* she wondered. *Will I ever get out of here and get back to my children? I wonder where I am?... . I hate these Indian clothes.*

What was it Dave told me about Chauncey Judd when he was held captive? The Bible passage about Joseph in a well? ... I wonder if he has a Bible.

Anna got up on her knees, and, putting her hands together, said, "Lord, please give me the strength to endure. Watch over my children, Hulley and little Lewis, and my dear husband, Reuben. And Lord, please deliver me from this prison as you did Joseph and Chauncey Judd."

A crack of light appeared at the door. *Oh, no, he's coming again. O, how I hate him. Will I ever see Reuben again?... . But I must survive!*

Chapter 29

A Runners' Reunion

The next morning, Dave and his family members rode back to see Cooper. As they approached the stump Cooper was seated on, using it as an outside chair and desk, they heard someone shouting. "Damn you, Cooper! You can't sell these lots. We're suing you for violating that injunction!" Dave realized it was Dr. Morgan standing in front of Cooper, angrily waving his finger in Will's face.

"Look!" Cooper replied, still sitting on his stump, "that auction was legal, and thee refused the deed."

"No, it wasn't legal," Morgan yelled, and the men in the meeting house came out to hear what the commotion was all about. "All you men, this man Cooper has no right to sell this patent!"

Cooper now stood up, but keeping his voice low, said, "Now Morgan let's be reasonable. If we pay thee 800 pounds, will thee drop thy claim to the patent?"

Morgan scratched his chin and lowered his voice a notch, "800 pounds, huh? Well, I'll have to take it up with my associates. In the meantime, stop selling lots!"

"I'll do as I please, Morgan!" Cooper said loudly, as he rose from the stump. "The patent is mine and my partner's. Now, I want thee to leave here, or I'll have my sheriff lock thee up."

"On what grounds, damn it?" Morgan said, his face flushing.

"Just leave, will thee? It's been a sad time," Cooper said.

"Oh, yeah, I heard about the shooting. All right, I'm leaving. I'll write you concerning the 800 pounds."

"What's this about a shooting?" Dave asked. "Did one of your settlers get drunk and shoot a neighbor?"

"No, no, it happened several days ago, before thee arrived," Cooper said, as he sat back down on his stump. "Somebody murdered my servant, Orange Ballard. He had been a trapper, and I was very fond of him, a good earthy man."

"How did it happen?" Eben asked.

"Orange was escorting my daughter, whom I brought with me on this trip, from the meeting house back to our little cabin over there, when a shot cracked out. It hit Orange square in the chest, and he fell dead at her feet. Scared poor Hannah half to death, too. She hasn't come out of our cabin since."

"Who did it?" Eben asked.

"I have no notion," Cooper replied. "Mayhaps it was that hunter, Shipman, though I doubt it, or some damn Indian. The shot must have come from the forest."

Dave scratched his forehead and said, "Was there anyone here at the time who's not here now?"

"Ah, let's see, there were a couple of settlers who bought lots and left for home to get their families," Cooper said.

"Anyone else?" Dave asked.

"The only other one is a man I hired to go down to Ononaquaga to look over some land I'm interested in. Said he'd been there before and knew the area. He had an Indian with him. Maybe he's some relative of thine, Dave. Said his name was Ezra Hotchkiss."

Dave looked at Eben. "Ezra," Dave said, his face suddenly losing color. "What'd he look like?"

When Cooper mentioned the unusual eyes, Dave flopped down on a log near Cooper. "Will, he's your killer. His real name is Ezra Hopkins. He kills for no apparent reason, though it has something to do with girls or ladies he admires. He killed my wife and sister. We've been trying to find him for years. I'd like your permission to go after him. Have your sheriff make us deputies. Where is this Ononaquaga?"

"It's about 80 miles southwest of here on the Susquehanna. At one time it was an Indian community. Joseph Brandt was the chief. When the war went against the Indians, those that survived, including Brandt, went to Canada."

"Let me talk this over with my friends and family here," Dave said.

"I'd certainly appreciate it if thee would catch the scoundrel," Cooper said. "If thee bring him back here, I'll have a speedy trial and hang him. As soon as thee decide who's going, we can make thee deputies."

Dave and his group went inside the meeting house for dinner. "My God!" Titus said, "Look at the crowd here. There's more and more coming here every day."

They had just squeezed in on benches at a table, when a familiar voice spoke up, "Hey, fellows, are they gonna have a footrace here?"

"Pres," Eben said, shaking hands with the tall, young Pres Redway, "Jumping jackfish! what are you doing here?"

"I've come with my two brothers looking for land." Pres shook hands with all of his running friends. "After being at West Point for three years, I wanted to see what the land was like that I heard other soldiers tell of."

"Who's the girl with your brothers?" Dave asked.

"Oh, she's my step niece, Azubah Jones," Pres said.

"You brought a young girl way out here in this wilderness?" Titus said. "That's crazy!"

"Bring your brothers and your niece over," Dave said. "We've got some business to discuss over dinner." Pres went and brought Comfort and James, as well as Jonesey, and introduced them to those of his friends whom they had not already met.

Comfort said, "Yes, I remember you fellows from that race we were in at Hartford. I was just thirteen. James and I are both married now."

Dave noticed that Comfort was even taller than Pres and that James looked as handsome as he did when he was at Hartford years ago.

James ran his hand through his dark curls and said, "How's your sister Anna, Dave? I remember well dancing with her at Hartford."

Dave said, "'Tis a mystery I wish we could solve. She's married to Reuben here, but she disappeared a while back, and we have no notion where she is."

As the men at Dave's table started their meal and shared Cooper's rum, they talked about the lots they'd inspected.

Dave was quiet and appeared to be lost in thought. Noticing this, Titus said, "Dave, what do you think of Cooper's lots?"

Dave looked up from his plate, cleared his throat, and said, "The discovery of the location of my wife's murderer has taken hold of my thoughts, if not my soul, making it difficult for me to think of land, but here's my belief. While Cooper's price on his land is very reasonable, with the low interest rate of seven percent and the throwing in of a free lot in town, still the loan has to be paid off completely in ten years. But what bothers me is his unclear title. I was at the auction in January, and the whole transaction seemed somewhat questionable. I'm not certain Cooper's heard the last of Dr. Morgan, especially with Aaron Burr representing some of the claimants."

"Aaron Burr?" Pres said. "I've met Burr. That alone would scare me off."

"However," Dave said, "that colonel you introduced me to at West Point, Alexander Hamilton, represents Cooper and is the one who set up the auction."

"Interesting," Pres said, "Burr against Hamilton, the two young officers I admired the most during the war."

"Remember, men, I like Cooper," Dave said, "but his land isn't the only land available. There's land in Hoosick, New York. Also, there's the Oquago Valley, which my map shows as just below Ononaquaga on the Susquehanna River.

"What I'd like to propose to you all is that we get some canoes and paddle down the river. We'll try to find and capture Ezra, and then while we're in the area we can explore land in the Oquago Valley near the Allison patent."

"I'm inclined to go with you," Comfort said, "but tell me more about this fellow Ezra."

Dave explained in detail how, after Ezra's first escape, he had managed to elude his captors two other times.

"Though I pray it's not true," Reuben said, "I've often wondered, Dave, if Ezra could have captured my Anna and killed her and buried her somewhere."

"You may be right, God forbid," Dave said. "We'll find out, if we capture him."

Dave continued, "Now, while I'm sure that Eben, Titus, Fred, and Reuben will join me, I'd like to have the rest of you men go with me as well. In fact, I'll pay for your time to go with me as deputies. I should warn you, though, Ezra is clever and dangerous. In addition to killing three people that we know of, he shot me and Polly Hall. Well, how about it? Will you men go?"

"How long will it take us?" Pres asked.

"If it's 80 miles, probably only about two days to get there, since it's downstream," Dave replied.

Pres talked to his brothers and Aza a moment. Then James said, "We'll go with you. Having gone this far, we'd just as soon go the extra miles to see some property, and we don't mind earning a few dollars for our efforts in capturing the murderer. My niece, Jonesy, though, she insists on going with us."

"You want to bring a girl on this trip?" Dave said. "I see she's pretty, but we're going after a murderer. I say no."

Aza blushed and spoke up with her hoarse voice, "Mr. Hotchkiss, I'm pleased you think I'm pretty, but I'm not here to be admired for my appearance. My father may want to buy some land; so I wish to go. But also, I can help you. I can shoot a musket and paddle a canoe, and you won't have to pay me."

"I'll keep an eye on her," Pres said. "She's as fast a runner as your sister Anna was."

Dave said, "I may need all the help I can get; all right, you can come."

Young Frederick smiled at the outcome of the discussion and, looking at Aza, said, "I'm glad you're coming with us, Jonesey."

"One item," Pres said, "none of us are familiar with the area. How will we even know when we reach Ononaquaga? Mayhap we need a guide." After talking it over with the others, Dave decided to hire Shipman for their guide.

When Frederick was alone with his father he said, "I'm pleased, Pa, you're letting Aza come with us. She's pretty and the most intriguing girl I've ever met."

After supper, as Dave and the others were sitting around the table in the meeting house, Aza turned to Pres and said impishly, "Mr. Redway, can I take a walk with Fred? He wants to show me a lookout spot with a great view of the lake up on the eastern side."

Pres consulted with Comfort and then reluctantly said to Aza with a frown, "All right, but for only one hour, and, Fred, you better guard her well."

Fred and Aza stood up and walked off hand-in-hand.

About sundown Titus and Eben returned with Shipman and Captain John.

Dave observed Ship's appearance, something he hadn't really noticed in the dark at their previous meeting. He was about as tall as Pres, but very thin, almost emaciated looking. On his head, which was covered with wispy, grayish sandy hair, he wore a cap of fox-skin. His face and neck were red from constant exposure to the elements, and his grey eyes looked out from under shaggy grey eyebrows. He wore a dressed deerskin coat with the hair on, and on his feet he had deerskin moccasins decorated with porcupine quills. He also wore tarnished buckskin breeches and leggings. Over his left shoulder was slung a belt of deerskin from which hung an enormous ox-horn. It was plugged at both ends to hold his powder. But what Dave noticed particularly was the length of his rifle. When he rested the butt on the ground, the barrel extended to the top of his cap.

Dave said, "I'm pleased you agreed to guide us, Ship, but is Captain John going to go with us?"

"Yeah," Ship said. "He's an excellent tracker; also, he's a Mohican, a tribe that's lived at one time in the area we're going to. Do you know what the word Mohican means? It means, 'the good canoe man.'"

Three hours later Fred and Aza returned, still all smiles, but Pres was furious and scolded Aza.

Jonesey said. "You sound like my father." She flung her hair over her shoulder. "Don't be such a grouchy!"

"A grouchy, huh?" Pres shouted. "Damn it, Jonesey, they had a killing here, and we don't even know for sure where the killer is. I should make you stay here with Cooper and his daughter."

"No, no, don't do that!" Aza said, in a pleading voice. She came around in back of Pres and hugged him from behind. "I think you just don't want me to be alone with Fred. He's a handsome lad, I believe, don't you?" and she looked across the table at Comfort and James with a sly, devilish smile.

Pres, appearing to Dave to be rather dumbfounded, said, "Ah, what can I say when his father's right here? I suppose he is, though I'm still angry with him as well for not getting you back sooner. Look, it's almost dark out."

Chapter 30

The Susquehanna

The following morning, near noon, Dave's party launched three light-colored bark canoes from Otsego Lake's shores, and they paddled to the nearby outlet, the start of the Susquehanna River. In the first canoe, Dave was seated in the front, Ship in the rear, and Captain John sat cross-legged in the bottom in the center. Reuben, Eben, Titus, and Fred were in the second canoe while Pres, Jonesy, Comfort, and James occupied the third one.

The stream initially was very narrow, about fifteen feet wide, but the spring-melted snow and the recent heavy rains made it deep enough for them in most places. Ship skillfully steered the lead canoe to avoid hitting the shore, sunken logs, or islands covered with brush and trees. "Do as I do," Ship yelled to the other canoes behind him. "Watch out for that sweeper, Dave." A low hanging large tree branch was sticking out from the shore.

"Sweeper?" Dave said, as he used his paddle to push off from the obstruction.

"Yeah," Ship replied. "Those branches can sweep a man right out of a canoe. Now the ones that are really low-hanging we call strainers. They can hold a man under water. In fact I saw a canoer almost drown once from a strainer."

The thin river twisted and turned sharply, making the skill of the rear paddler important. After they passed the point where Oaks Creek flowed into the river, the Susquehanna widened.

After a few miles, when the Cherry Valley River joined the Susquehanna, the river again widened, making the maneuvering easier. Dave noticed that the brownish-red sumac fruit, still hanging on its branches from the previous year, along with the red buds on the maple trees, gave a pink glow to the banks and the hills beyond, much like autumn colors. It was a warm day, with only a slight breeze blowing from the west. On the nearby riverbanks a few bushes already had their leaves, though on some of the trees just light yellow-green, miniature leaves were visible.

Dave said, "I'm glad to see you have a rifle, Ship."

"You need it in this country, Dave. As you know, muskets just don't have the accuracy you need for hunting."

"I should warn you," Dave said. "Ezra owns a rifle too. Tell me would you, what do you know of this Ononaquaga territory we're going to?"

Ship thought a moment, paused while he steered the canoe around a large rock, and said, "At one time it was the largest Indian town on the Susquehanna with about forty houses. It was a group of villages on both sides of the river. Years ago a Reverend Jonathan Edwards established a mission there to convert the Indians to Christianity.

"Now, some of the Indians kept their long houses with many families in one house, while some lived like white people in log cabins and stone houses. They even had a large building that was both a fort and a meeting house for those Indians who were Christians."

"What happened to all this?" Dave asked.

"Well, when the war started, Joseph Brandt, the Indian Chief, used Ononaquaga as a base and led parties in attacks on settlements in Springfield and the Mohawk Valley. People who were around Otsego Lake couldn't be neutral; so the patriots went to Cherry Valley, and the Loyalists, mostly Indians, went south to Ononaquaga. Then in October of '78 the patriots from Cherry Valley attacked Ononaquaga and burned the villages and destroyed their crops. Many Indians were killed, including children."

Dave said, "Really, they murdered children?"

"Yes, they were brutal! Then, wanting to avenge their loss, a month later a force of about 500 men, mostly Iroquois, but some white men, marched and surprised the sleepy garrison at Cherry Valley."

"I did hear about this," Dave said, "but not much detail."

"The fort there managed to hold out," Shipman continued, "but I believe sixteen soldiers were killed, including the commander, and thirty-two citizens were massacred."

"Then I suppose the patriots attacked the Indians again," Dave said.

"You've probably heard of Clinton's Expedition," Ship said.

"Was this the one where they met up with General Sullivan?" Dave asked.

"Yes, it was eight years ago in August. Clinton was at Otsego Lake and dammed up the outlet raising the level of the lake three feet. Then with 120 boats and 2,000 men he broke the dam, and the boats were poled and paddled down the flooded Susquehanna. They burned every Indian village they saw."

"After meeting up with Sullivan's army at Tioga Point, they had a big battle with the Indians, led by Joseph Brandt, forcing the Indians to flee."

Dave said, "The one thing people fear back in Connecticut are Indians. It makes me wonder if I should really bring my family here. Tell me, are the Indians here abouts mean or fierce?"

"Well, they can be."

As they paddled on, Dave occasionally saw a cabin alongside the river, looking very new, but most of the land was vacant. "This land is groaning to be farmed," Dave said.

Late in the afternoon, near the confluence of the Unadilla River, they stopped when they saw a cabin, and after climbing a muddy riverbank, Dave asked the young farmer if they could camp there for the night. He and his wife were only too glad to have visitors and asked many questions about Croghan's Forest, as they called Cooper's new settlement, and what was going on with Mr. Cooper.

Dave then said, "Sir, we wonder if you've seen anything of a man using the name Ezra Hotchkiss? He's now supposed to be in Ononaquaga."

The man thought a moment and said, "Ononaquaga is at some distance from here. I do see canoes go by once in a great while, but I know nothing of the man you speak of."

His wife spoke up and said, "George, tell him about the Indians we saw."

George said, "Ah, yes. About two months ago, when we were having a big flood, we saw five Indian canoes go by. They were all painted up like warriors."

"How were they painted?" Ship asked.

When George described their dress and how they were painted, Captain John said, "Those men Delawares. I not see them. Must have come back from Canada. Delawares could be at Ononaquaga."

"Was there a white man with them?" Dave asked.

"I don't know," George replied. "I didn't see one, but they went by so fast, and I wasn't close to the river. They were busy trying to stay free of the large blocks of ice."

"It might just be a hunting party," Ship said, "but from where?"

After the evening meal, at which Aza and Fred had spent considerable time talking with each other, Pres went down to the riverbank and sat on a log, looking out over the fast-flowing water. He was wondering, *Why did I ever agree to let her come on this expedition. If I don't lose her to Ezra's murderous ways, I could lose her to Frederick.*

Just then Aza appeared and after walking around in front of Pres, said, "Fred and I want to go for a little walk, Pres. We promise we'll be back in an hour. Can I go?"

Pres stood up, his six-foot-three inch frame towering over the young beauty. "Look, young lady!" he said, frowning down at her, "you're my responsibility. If you want to go for a walk, you'll go with me, not Fred."

Do I sound possessive? he wondered.

Aza paused for a moment, as if undecided whether to go back and appeal to Comfort and James. Instead she looked up at the young man and said, "All right, let's go." She smiled and took hold of his hand.

Pres remembered back to a time when Aza was just nine years old and he had first met her. Now, as he looked down at her, he noticed how her breasts filled out her hunting shirt, leaving no doubt that she was flourishing in her womanhood, even at fifteen.

"Where do you want to go?" Pres asked.

"Oh, let's go back to that grove over there," Aza said, pointing west.

They wandered slowly west and entered the apple orchard, which Pres thought was probably planted by Indians since the trees were not in neat rows as the white settlers usually planted them.

"The trees are in full bloom, Pres." Aza said. "Aren't they beautiful, all covered with white blossoms?

"Come and sit beside me, Pres. I was wondering. You didn't know any of the people Ezra killed or wounded; so why did you agree to go on this mission?"

Pres sat down next to Jonesey, "Well, actually I do know Polly Hall since she's a distant cousin of ours. Then, as we said to the Hotchkisses, we could use some of the dollars Dave's willing to pay. Also, we want to see the land. The final thing that convinced me was you wanting to go so bad."

"I see," Aza said, as she turned and smiled up at Pres. "Now that we're so close to our destination I'm pleased you're here. I'm a little scared, especially if we should find Indians."

"Don't be scared, Jonesey. I'll be with you all the way. Wish you'd let me call you Aza, though. I like it better."

At this point Aza got up on her knees, and, turning around, she straddled Pres' outstretched legs and facing him, gave him a hug. "When are we going to get married anyway, Pres?" and she kissed him on his neck.

Oh, she smells so fresh, Pres mused. Then he pushed her back, saying, "What are you doing? You're not a little girl anymore playing around with your uncle. You're teasing me now. And you're such a beautiful young lady."

"I'm beautiful am I, and with just these hunting clothes?" she replied, as she turned sideways to Pres and arched her back. "I never heard you say that before." She threw her braid over her shoulder, looked into his eyes, and ran her hand through his thick blond hair. "Your eyes, Pres, are so blue, and I love your hair, too."

"But what about Fred Hotchkiss? I thought you fancied him."

"Oh, he's just a little older than me. I always fancied you, Pres, from the first time I met you, when I visited your house with my father and you took me out to the barnyard to see the animals."

With that she kissed Pres on the lips, "Oh, Pres, I do love you. Why else would I come on this crazy expedition all the way from Killingly?"

"But what did you do with Fred yesterday for three hours?"

"Ah, you are jealous, aren't you?" Aza said, her voice seeming more hoarse than usual.

"Of course not, but you didn't answer my question."

"Fred took me on a long hike up through the forest, and we had a beautiful view of the lake and saw the sun go down."

"But it still shouldn't have taken you three hours," Pres said.

"Now, you're sounding like an old grouchy again," and once more she kissed him. With that, Pres put his right arm around Aza, squeezing her to him. Then he laid her down on her back and turned over on his stomach beside her, looking down at her.

"You don't act like an old grouchy, though." She smiled and with her right hand pulled his head down so she could kiss him again. To Pres the smell of her hair mixed with the fragrance of the apple blossoms seemed overpowering.

"What am I going to do with you?" Pres said. "You're only fifteen. We can't get married now. But you've gotten so pretty," and he kissed her soft lips again. Aza turned on her side and gracefully wrapped one leg over his back.

Pres looked down at her beautiful bosom, his maleness expanding. He was about to caress one of her breasts when he remembered the stern words of her father. "Pres, I'm relying on you and your brothers to be perfect gentlemen with my daughter at all times! Is that understood?"

Suddenly he stopped and pushed himself away from Aza, "Oh, I love you so, my Aza, but I promised your father. No, this is not right. While we're here on this expedition I'm your guardian, not your lover."

"But Pres," Aza said, "I want you to love me."

Pres stood up, tucked his shirt in and said, "No Jonesey, Aza, Aza Jones, Azubah Jones, daughter of my sister's husband Daniel Jones. No, I can not do this! I must put the devil behind me."

"All right, Pres," Aza said, as she took her hand and brushed some loose hair away from her face and looked off into the distance, "but will you still love me?"

"Sure will, Jonesey," and he reached down and picked her up in his arms and kissed her forehead. "How about a ride around the orchard?"

"Yeah, yeah," and she smiled and lifted her head up and kissed his cheek. "I guess Pa couldn't complain about that."

Pres put Aza up on his shoulders and ran around the orchard crookedly, yelling like a crazy man and dodging around the apple- blossomed branches while Aza giggled, trying not to fall off. Finally, he ran under a low-hanging branch which caught Aza about shoulder high, and they both fell backward on their backs into the soft grass, laughing uncontrollably at the ridiculous accident. "Was that a sweeper or a strainer?" Aza said, and they laughed even more.

"Well, if we can't make love," Pres said, "at least we can have fun." He picked up a piece of grass and chewed on it.

Aza stopped laughing and, turning around so that she faced Pres, said, "But I don't want to be treated like a child, Pres. I want you to respect me and treat me like a lady you're courting."

"All right," he said, "if you'll stay away from Frederick."

Aza agreed, and the two young lovers hand-in-hand returned to their camp and settled down for the night.

In the morning Dave decided to change his position in the canoes and took Pres' place in the rear canoe with Comfort and James while Pres moved along with his niece to the lead canoe.

The river was now about 50 feet wide. As the morning wore on, the clouds became dark, and the wind increased, rippling the surface of the water. The riverbanks, which seemed so bright and pink the day before, now looked to Dave just a dark brown. Muddy, twisted, brown vines clung to the mostly leafless trees. Every so often some evergreens were seen, but the banks and even the hills seemed very dark. Dave wondered, *Those Indians George saw. Will they be at Ononaquaga?*

At noon they had a meal on an island in the river. Debris left by the earlier flood was hanging from the trees

Shortly after they launched the canoes again, Dave looked over his shoulder and noticed a storm was brewing. He saw it roll in from the east with the wind blowing wildly. The skies became almost black, the rain whipped at his face, and waves rocked his canoe. Dave yelled out, "Comfort, I can't even see the canoe ahead of us." Thunder was crashing all around.

"Yeah," James said, "we'd better pull over to the shore before we hit something and capsize." They paddled to the western shore and pulled the canoe up on the bank. "Get the oilcloth, Comfort!"

After they got the oilcloth out, the three of them huddled under it on the edge of the riverbank.

After an hour, the storm subsided, but it was still dark and cloudy. Just as Dave and his crew were about to push their canoe back into the Susquehanna, Dave saw a canoe upstream approaching. "Hah, it's Titus, Eben, Reuben and Fred," Dave said. "They must have stopped before we did."

Dave, James, and Comfort yelled to their friends and pushed out into the swollen river. When they came close to the other canoe, they agreed that Titus' canoe should follow the east bank looking for the missing canoe while Dave and his crew would watch the other shore. Both canoes moved slowly along close to the riverbanks, where the water flowed slower.

Aza was soaking wet and shivering high up in a tall pine tree, high enough so that she couldn't be seen from the ground. She was thinking, *My head hurts so. That Indian must have hit me with something when I was trying to help Pres after he was shot in the leg. Oh, my love! God, please protect my Pres.*

She thought back to how their canoe, as soon as it had approached the shore so that they could seek shelter from the storm, had been shot at by some Indians with muskets. Since she had been facing the front, she had not seen what had happened to Captain John and Shipman. *I hope they're not injured. Perhaps they can help Pres with his wound, if the Indians didn't kill them all. The only thing I remember, after I was hit, was falling into the water.*

When she had awakened she found herself snagged on a tree branch that was jutting out from the shore. She had looked up the stream, but couldn't see anything or hear any voices.

I've got to get back to where the canoe is so the others can find me, she had thought. She had slowly emerged from the water by clutching to the branches and, hand-over-hand, pulling herself toward shore. Then she had climbed up the slippery, muddy bank.

Aza then had walked north along the shore, the water dripping off her breeches.

Finally, she had come to a little clearing and saw their wrecked canoe, which was partially sunk beside the shore. Looking around quickly she had spotted the large pine tree nearby and climbed it.

She mused, *I hope those in the other two canoes weren't captured too.*

Comfort, who was paddling in the front of his canoe, yelled, "Look! That must be it!"

Dave looked to where Comfort pointed and saw one end of a half-sunken canoe sticking out of the water right at the western shore. Dave shouted out, "Pres, Pres, Ship! Where are you?" but there was no answer.

"Is that their canoe, Dave?" Comfort asked. When the other canoe arrived, the six men studied the wrecked canoe.

"Looks like the same one all right," Titus said. "Look at the footprints. They're all over the ground."

All of a sudden Dave caught sight of Jonesey running toward them from the woods as fast as she could go. She stopped when she came near, and somewhat out of breath, in her hoarse voice gasped, "Indians attacked us. Pres was shot in the leg. Thank God, you're all right!"

"What happened?" Dave asked.

Aza, still shivering, sat down and said, "Have you got a blanket?" While Fred went and took a blanket from his pack and brought it over to her, Aza quickly told them what she knew.

"You've got blood on the side of your head there, Jonesey," Dave said. "Titus, get a clean cloth with some water to clean that wound. I'm happy that you're safe. Do you know where they went?"

"Yes, I saw fresh tracks going south," Aza replied. "These Indians are mean; we've got to rescue them. Keep your weapons ready! Poor Pres; he was hurt bad. Have you got any dry clothes?"

Eben said, "I think mine might fit you," and he took out a pair of his breeches and a shirt from his knapsack. Aza went into the woods to change.

The men then all stared at the tracks. Comfort squatted down. "Ah, hah, they're all moccasin tracks, except these big ones here. These are Pres'. I recognize his shoe. And what's this? There's blood next to Pres' tracks. This agrees with what Jonesey said. The damn Indians got our brother all right. We need to get going!"

"Damn, damn!" James shouted. "Why the hell did we come on this stupid journey, anyway?" and he pounded one hand into the other in frustration.

"There's blood all over the center of the canoe, too," Titus said, "just where Captain John and Jonesey were sitting."

"We'll follow the tracks," Dave said, "but we should be careful. We don't want to be ambushed."

After putting some food in their knapsacks, they all began walking rapidly south, taking turns sending one person about one hundred feet ahead in the lead. The tracks continued going south along the bank of the river. They followed the twisting tracks as fast as they could, considering they were carrying backpacks, for another four miles. All the way they had to dodge prickly bushes and low hanging branches, some with dead leaves, mud, and sticks caught up in them from previous flooding.

Aza, over Titus' objections, had taken a turn and ran up ahead of the men. As Dave and the others were about to cross a small stream, they heard a woman's scream south of them. *Either she's dead or she's captured,* Dave thought. *God, be with her!*

Titus turned to the others and put his fingers to his lips in a sign to be quiet. Then, silently following Comfort for another 40 yards, they came to the end of the forest and peeked out at a clearing. Judging by the number of freshly cut stumps, it must have been recently enlarged. There was no sign of Aza, but what Dave and the others were particularly interested in was a rather large log building or house in the clearing. It was set back about 150 yards from the river.

"Look," Titus said, "the tracks lead right to it."

"Yeah," Dave said, "and there's another out-building in back of it."

The clearing appeared to be at least ten acres and was surrounded by trees, mostly pines and spruce trees. They quietly retreated into the shade of the evergreen forest to talk about what to do next. Drops from the previous rain continued to drip from the tree branches on to their heads.

Eben said, "Why don't we just attack now from two different directions?"

"No, no," Titus said emphatically, keeping his voice low. "We have to know what we're facing, how many there are, where they are in the building, and where our friends are who are being held. I sure hope they're all still alive."

"You're right, Titus" Comfort said. "We should wait till after dark and then sneak up and spy on them to see and hear what these savages are up to. Then we can decide just how to attack."

"I agree," Dave said, "but in the meantime I'm going to skirt around the edge of the clearing to see what I can discover while it's still light out."

"All right," James said, "but be sure to stay in the forest."

"Let me come with you, Pa," Fred said.

"No, you stay here. I'll be back within the hour," Dave replied.

He began walking carefully west, stopping frequently and peering ahead before going further. Many of the bushes already had their spring leaves, helping him to remain concealed. He looked out on the field from time to time, but saw no humans. As Dave neared the end of the clearing and was about to turn south he heard a sound to his right that made his heart jump. It was a mournful sound, a low moan.

Approaching carefully, Dave was shocked to see an Indian stripped to the waist, standing with his hands and feet stretched far apart and tied to two trees. His belly had a big red gash, and the blood from this flowed down on to his breeches. His head was slumped forward, his long grey hair hanging down over his face. "Captain John," Dave whispered. "My God, what have they done to you?" He cut the leather straps which bound the Indian, who then slumped down to the ground.

Dave bent down over the Mohican. He could see Captain John was trying to say something; so he got down on his hands and knees, bringing his head down to the Indian's face. "To find Ship, find tunnel," the Indian said.

Dave heard a noise behind him. He looked up quickly, just in time to see a rock held by an Indian crashing down on his head.

Chapter 31

Indian Chief

Dave opened his eyes, and from his prone position on the dirt floor he saw the red-faced Shipman smiling down at him. "Hey, Pres, Dave's waking up. Hello there, fellow."

"Where are we?" Dave asked, as he sat up and looked around in the gloom, noting that he and his two friends, along with Aza, were in a small room with log walls which went all the way up to a slanted roof. "My God, my head hurts." In one corner sat two other men and a woman Dave did not know. Small horizontal slits, about two inches wide, served as windows. Dave could see that it was near twilight. Pres was sitting on the floor against a wall, looking pale and with a blood stained cloth wrapped around one of his knees.

Pres said, "We're in a room of an Indian band led by your old nemesis, Ezra Hopkins."

"Huh, I'm not too surprised he's here," Dave said, "but leading a band of Indians? How extraordinary! Now, how'd you get here?"

Shipman spoke up, "When the storm hit, we kept going for a ways before we beached. But just as we landed, a couple of shots hit us. One got Pres in the leg and the other hit Captain John. Wish I knew where he is."

"I saw him," Dave said. "They tied him up to some trees to let him bleed to death. Waugh, the pain in my head!" and he lay back down again for a moment.

"Did he die?" Ship asked.

"I don't know," Dave replied. "He collapsed when I cut his bindings. Then some Indian hit me with a rock. Pres, how's your leg?"

"Not good, Dave," Pres said as he looked down at his shattered knee cap. "Hurts like the divil. Don't think I'll be running in any races again. How the hell are we gonna get out of here?"

"I think our friends will attack, once they determine just what the amount of this Indian force is," Dave said. "Who are our fellow prisoners here?"

"I'm John Doolittle," one worried-looking, young man answered, who hadn't shaved in several weeks, "and this is my wife."

"I'm Captain Knox," the other man said. "I was living nearby here when they stole me."

"How did they happen to capture you, Mr. Doolittle?" Dave asked.

"I came here with my wife by paddling up the Kats Kill River," Doolittle said. He had a round red face, a jutting chin and black curly hair. "Then we crossed by land through Acra, Windham, and Harpersfield to Unadilla. They caught us paddling down the Susquehanna."

Dave stood up, but his head still ached, and he began to feel dizzy. He sat down next to Pres on the other side from Aza, who was holding Pres's hand. "I see you suffered another head blow, too, Miss Jones," Dave said.

"Tell me, Pres, do you know why they're holding us? They could have killed us."

"We don't know," Shipman replied.

"Who else they got in this fortress?" Dave asked.

Pres said, "I heard Ezra in the next room talking with someone named Anna. Could that be your sister?"

"Anna? Are you certain he said Anna?" Dave asked, and he stood up and began walking back and forth.

"Yes," Doolittle answered, "I'm sure he called her Anna, though I didn't hear much of what they said, since Ezra talked softly."

"Pres, do you think she's still in the next room?" Dave asked.

"I don't know," Pres said, "it's been quiet in there for quite a spell."

"Is there any small opening in the logs between the two rooms?" Dave asked.

Ship pointed at a small crack between the logs.

Dave went over to the crack that Ship had pointed to and putting his mouth up close to it said softly, "Anna, is that you in there? It's Dave."

After a moment a female voice answered, "Dave? my brother Dave? He's captured you, too?"

"Yes, yes, it's me. Take heart, Anna, there are others with me. We'll get you out somehow."

"Oh, Dave, I've been here so long," Anna answered, "I..."

"Quiet, Anna!" Dave said. Someone was opening the barricaded log door.

A thin man came in, holding a pistol. At first Dave thought he was an Indian due to the dim light and the fact he was dressed like an Indian.

"Ezra?" Dave said as he stared at the man. "Is that you, you bastard?" Two Indians entered behind Ezra, holding muskets, and one carried a stool.

"Yeah, it's me Dave Hotchkiss," Ezra said, as he grinned, took the stool, and sat down on it near the door. "You finally caught up to me, though it will do you no good, but just the opposite." Ezra laughed out of the corner of his mouth, his eyes seeming to look in all directions at once. In addition to a red cloak that he wore over his Indian clothes, he wore a chief's headdress of turkey feathers dyed red. The two Indian warriors on either side of Ezra stared blankly ahead, ready to do any duty Ezra should give them. They wore deerskin breechcloth with a flap in front and back. Tattoos decorated their faces, and they had on heavy-beaded colorful vests.

"Now that you've rendered me incapable of doing you harm," Dave said, "tell me, why did you kill Hulley and my Abby?"

Ezra, smiling out of the corner of his mouth, said "I suppose you won't believe me, though at this point I don't care if you do or not, but I didn't kill them."

"You liar!" Dave said. "We found the whip that matched the lasher near where Hulley was killed in your barn. I know it's you! Damn you, you dirty varmint!" and he stood up and approached Ezra, his face flushed crimson. As he did this, though, the two Indians brought their muskets up, aiming at Dave's chest.

Ezra said, "Better back off, Dave; don't want you to get yourself killed."

"Yeah, yeah," Dave said, and he backed up, still seething, and sat down, putting his face in his hands.

"You found a whip, but not my whip," Ezra said, with a smirk on his face.

Dave looked up and shouted out, "Yeah, well if it wasn't your whip, who the hell else would leave the murderer's whip in your barn?"

"Tell him, Squire!" Ezra said to one of the two Indians behind him.

The older of the two Indians, who was rather dignified, looked at Dave and said, "I Squire Antonio. I sorry to say, my son Abraham killed those ladies. He told me about two moons ago."

"He did?" Dave said incredulously. "What does he look like?"

"He bad brave," the Squire said and briefly described Abraham.

"He does sound like an Indian I met in Hartford years ago, but I still find it hard to believe you two. Ezra, if you were innocent, why did you run away rather than just staying and denying the crimes?"

"'Cause you Hotchkisses were determined to hang me, and I had no proof it wasn't me."

"But how did Abraham manage to get in and out of our area with no one seeing him?" Dave asked.

"I guess no one suspected an Indian. He used to come and see me about once a year and trade pelts for iron products. I'd let him sleep out in our barn. He did say once that he met the man who killed his grandfather at Fort Ti and wanted revenge, but he didn't say it was you. I didn't even suspect it was him until the Waterbury race when Macclure matched up the lasher to the whip. Tell him the rest, Squire."

The Squire, his arms folded across his chest, said, "Abraham was drinking too much fire-water one day; he told me he had got revenge on Hotchkiss family for the man who killed my father at Fort Ticonderoga. When I told him he is coward for killing ladies, he get very angry. He pushed me into a burning fireplace. My braves saved me. I not see Abraham again. I think he killed Orange Ballard. Orange good friend of Squire."

"Why would he kill Ballard?" Dave asked.

"Don't know. Maybe so Ezra and Squire get blame."

Dave's mind was swimming at the thoughts of someone else besides Ezra killing his wife and Hulley. It was hard to think with his head still throbbing from the pain of the blow he'd suffered.

Shipman then spoke up. "Ezra, you ain't no Indian; why the chief's head-dress?"

"I am their chief. The Squire and I went to Canada and brought them down here to this land that rightly belongs to them." Ezra put his moccasin-covered feet up on the table. "Then, while they were building our house here, I took a small party back to Judd's Meadow, stole Anna one night, and brought her back here. I wanted her to be safe from that murderer, Abraham. How the hell, Dave, did you ever find us?"

"I was talking with William Cooper and figured out it was you that he had sent down here to scout out the land," Dave replied. "Have you hurt Anna?"

"Hmm, how come you were alone when you were found next to that damn Mohican?" Ezra asked.

"I was riding in their canoe, but I got out just before the storm. Then we got separated," Dave said, hoping Ezra would believe him. "Now, what about Anna?"

"So you found my men's tracks and followed them here," Ezra said. "Well, welcome to my home."

"Some welcome!" Ship said, as he removed his fox cap. "Now what are you to do with us?"

"Well," Ezra said, as he took his feet off the table and crossed his legs, "as you men know, when the peace treaty with England was signed two years ago, the Iroquois, which you know as the Five Nations, had to give up most of their land. When I went to Canada, I convinced these men we should try and get their land back."

"That's crazy," Dave said. "How do you expect to get all the Iroquois land back with just a party of Indians?"

"Hostages," Ezra said. "I've got you, and I'll capture more. Then I'll exchange you all for Iroquois land. Now, let's see that leg, Redway."

"Hah," Dave said. "You think New York State will give the Iroquois land back to the Indians after they fought with the British in exchange for just a few unimportant people?"

"Mayhaps not," Ezra said, as he removed the cloth from Pres' leg, "but I might settle for the Ononaquaga land. Your knee is festering, Redway. I got to cut that leg off."

"What? Cut it off? Hell, no!" Pres yelled.

Aza came to life now, her eyes widening. "Cut off his leg? No, no! What do you know about medicine?"

Ezra shrugged and said, "I was an assistant surgeon at one time in the army." He turned to the older Indian and said, "Squire Antonio, bring me my instruments, my clay pipe, and a crock of rum."

"Instruments?" the gray-haired Indian asked, looking puzzled.

"Yeah, you know," Ezra said, and he made a sawing motion with his hand.

Antonio went out, scratching his head.

"Ezra, you varmint!" Dave said loudly, "Pres needs a doctor, not an amputation."

"Oh," Ezra said, "and you're saying I don't know when a limb has to come off. If Redway does nothing, he'll die. It's got to be cut off."

"Yes, and why should we believe you?" Dave asked.

"I want Redway to live. I can't exchange dead men. Now, I can do it in here, or I can do it in the outer room with all my warriors around holding him down."

"All right, do it here," Pres said. "I don't want to die."

"Oh, my God!" Aza cried out, and she began to cry and cling to Pres' side as she tightened her grip on his hand, making her knuckles turn white.

"I don't see how we can trust this murderer," Dave said.

"You don't have any choice, and I'm not a murderer," Ezra said. "If you resist, it will hurt more."

"And you didn't kill the Indian, Captain John?" Dave asked.

"He's just a victim of war. I had nothing to do with him. The Mohican was still alive the last I knew. Now, Redway climb up on this table." With Aza and Dave's help, Pres struggled to stand up and then climbed up on the table and lay down.

"Shouldn't the young lady here go into the other room during the amputation?" Dave asked.

"No, no," Aza cried. "I'm not a child! I want to stay with Pres." Ezra just shrugged his shoulders.

When Squire Antonio returned, the surgeon took a swig of rum, lit up his clay pipe, and said, "Antonio, keep an eye on these men while I'm working here. Shipman, come here and hold this candle up so I can see better." Ezra removed his pipe and blew a cloud of smoke over his patient. Then he took off his Indian headdress to improve his vision.

Ship held the candle and said, "Here, Pres, put this musketball in your teeth."

Pres complied, and Ezra reached into a leather bag and pulled out a long curved knife.

"Oh my God," Pres said through the musketball, and his eyes widened as he looked at the large knife.

After putting a screw tourniquet around Pres' upper leg and tightening it, Ezra took the long knife and began cutting into the flesh of Pres' muscular right thigh. Pres spat out the musketball and screamed, "Ah h h, Dave, Ship, help me!"

Aza screwed up her courage, and as Pres lay flat, she leaned over him, bringing her upper body down to his chest. Looking into his red, pain-filled eyes, she said, "How many children do you think we should have, Pres?"

Pres, gritting his teeth, said, "Oh, maybe eight or ten, Jonesey. You think you want a one-legged veteran for a husband whose only possession is twenty acres of land back in Killingly?"

"Yes, yes, Pres," Aza replied, as the tears streamed down her cheeks. "I do love you."

Ezra, looking at the bloody leg, just said, "I have to saw through the bone now. Knox, you and Hotchkiss hold his leg steady," and he took another swig of rum, put his clay pipe back in his mouth and took a deep pull. He then removed a saw from his bag and began to cut through the bone. Pres let out a horrible scream and passed out.

"Thank, God!, he's unconscious," Aza said.

Completing the amputation, Ezra threw the leg on the dirt floor, and after cauterizing the stump, he started bandaging it up. Aza stroked Pres' blond hair.

"Ezra," Dave said, "perhaps you followed the righteous course in removing Pres' leg, and if it was the correct thing to do, we appreciate it, but tell me, you still haven't said how Anna is. Did you hurt her?"

"I have a great affection for your sister. She's my queen."

"But you're holding her against her will," Dave said.

"It's for her protection. In time she'll learn to care for me," Ezra replied. "Now we must go and tend to the nets. The shad are running." He then took another drink of rum and left the room with the two Indians.

The slam of the barricaded door aroused the twenty-two year old Pres Redway. "Oh, Aza, the pain!" Pres then noticed his amputated leg on the ground. As he stared at it, his face lost its color. "I may be sick to my stomach. Dave, did he leave any rum for the pain?"

"No, the murdering weasel took it with him," Dave replied.

Chapter 32

An Inspection

Still waiting in the woods, Fred was beginning to worry. "Titus, it's been over two hours, and my pa isn't back yet."

"Yeah," Titus said, "I think I'll go after him."

"I'll go with you," Fred said eagerly.

"No," Titus said, "I'll just search around in the woods around the clearing to see if I can see anything."

"I'm coming with you," Comfort said.

"All right," Titus replied, "but we must be quiet."

The two men had not gone very far when they came upon Captain John, who was still alive despite his wounds and loss of blood. They lifted him up and carried him back to the hiding place where the others were waiting. Captain John, though very weak, when asked about Dave and the others, said, "All captured. They left Captain John to die. Dave cut John down. Then they took him." After this, he became unconscious again.

Titus then bandaged Captain John as best he could.

"Shouldn't we go back and look for my pa now?" Fred asked.

"No," Titus said, "we must wait till it's dark. I fear that either your father is dead, or he's been captured."

Fred sat down dejected; "Damn Indians!" and he wiped tears from his eyes.

About ten at night Titus said, "Here's what we'll do; Eben and I will go out and sneak up on the far side of the building so the Indian sentinel out front won't see us. Jim, I want you, Comfort, Fred, and Reuben to stay here till we get back."

Titus and Eben crawled down to the riverbank and walked along the edge of the river south till they came to the woods on the south edge of the clearing and proceeded west. They noticed an Indian sentinel in front of the building squatting. When they arrived opposite the side of the building, but out of sight of the sentinel, they crept up through the clearing to the south side of the building. Titus peeked through the slot in the wall and saw a large room full of Indians. They were sitting around a fire on the dirt floor, drinking rum, and gnawing on some venison. A hole in the roof let the smoke out. Looking left inside the room, Titus could make out the doors of three separate rooms side by side, taking up the whole back half of the log building. The outside of the three rooms looked identical, all made of pine logs.

Titus ducked down and whispered to Eben, "Let's look through the other opening." They sneaked along left toward the rear of the building. Titus again peered through the slit, but there was no light inside. So he and Eben listened.

A voice said, "Shipman, you have lived around here a long time. What's this about catching shad?"

"These fish swim upstream at this time of year, thousands of them, and they're caught with nets. They go out at night, and.... Sh h, I think I hear someone outside."

Titus said softly, "Dave, are you in there?"

"Is that you Titus?" Dave said in a low voice.

"Of course, you idiot!" Titus said. "Eben is here, too. Remember how Torch Morley got Jack Briggs out of that prison in New York City?"

"No, I don't think so," Dave said.

"I do," Pres said, "Titus, watch out for those that are out there netting shad."

"Is Ezra here?" Titus asked.

"Yeah, he amputated Pres' leg," Dave replied, "and Anna's in the next room."

Titus said, "We'll be back later. Hold on Pres."

After meeting up with Comfort, James, Fred, and Reuben, Titus told them what they had found.

"Are you sure he said Anna was in there?" Reuben asked with excitement. "That's great news. I thought she must be dead by now."

"Yes, I'm certain," Titus said.

"How many Indians are encamped there?" Reuben asked.

"I reckon eighteen, not counting the two females and Ezra," Titus said. "We must wait till they finish bringing in their shad and go to sleep." They whispered to each other about the best way to attack.

Reuben said, "We've got to do this right. Who's going to lead us now that Dave ain't here?"

Eben spoke up, "It's obvious to me. Titus has had years of experience in the military."

"I'm even more anxious to capture that Ezra now," James said. "No thanks to him our young brother will have to go through life with just one leg."

Chapter 33

Attack

Back in the prison room of the fortress, after Titus and Eben had left, Dave said, "Pres, what did Titus mean about getting Jack Briggs out of prison in New York City?"

Pres shifted his bandaged stump slightly, wincing with pain, and said, "It was about five years ago. Jack Briggs - he's from eastern Connecticut like me. He was sent to New York City by General Arnold when it was occupied by the British. He was under a flag of truce and had a pass. It's rather a long story, but Jack got arrested and thrown in King's College, which was being used as a prison. Torch Morley crossed over to New York with a keg of powder and blew a hole in the wall of the prison, and Jack and two other men were able to escape."

"You think Titus is going to blow a hole in this wall?" Doolittle said.

"I don't know," Pres said. "I don't think they have enough powder, but we better stay away from the outer walls anyway."

A while later Fred was sitting in the woods with his face in his hands. "My God, Titus, my pa could be dead by now. Let's attack now!"

"No, Fred," Titus replied, "they just came in with the shad. We need to wait some more."

It was almost dawn, and Dave began to drop off to sleep on the dirt floor, when he heard an explosion toward the front of the house.

A voice yelled, "None of you move! We've got guns on you."

Another voice shouted some Indian words. Then Dave heard a shot and a scream from someone.

"They're attacking," Pres said. "What can we do?"

"Not much," Dave said. Just then, the door banged open.

Titus yelled, "The Indians surrendered with only one shot fired. Where's Ezra? Come on, Dave! You all right?"

"Yeah, I'm coming" Dave said. "Aza, stay with Pres!" Just then James and Comfort came in.

James gasped when he looked at Pres' bandaged stump and said, "Damn that Ezra! He did amputate, the bastard!"

"Well, he had to," Pres said. "He said I'd die if he didn't do it."

Dave got up along with the other prisoners, except Pres and Aza, and went out of the room. He saw the Indians all sitting or lying on the ground, with Titus, Eben, and Fred holding pistols on them. At this moment Reuben opened the middle door, "Anna, Anna, It's me!"

"Reuben?" Anna said, squinting in the darkness. "Is it really you? Oh, Thank God!" She began to cry for joy as Reuben picked her up and carried her out.

Dave hardly recognized her. She was so pale, and she wore Indian clothes, including a fancy beadwork shirt with a red beaded headband with several feathers in it, a skirt, and knee-length leggings. Her hair was twisted in one long braid.

As Dave came up to his sister, she said, "Dave, don't let Reuben go into Ezra's room!

"Reuben, I want to bathe."

I got to find Ezra, now, Dave thought, and he ran to the door of the third room and pulled it open. Titus and Eben were right behind him. No one was inside.

"Oh, my God! Look at this room!" Dave said, and he quickly scanned the four walls. "No wonder Anna doesn't want Reuben in here." On the walls were large drawings of Anna in various poses. In each of these she was wearing just Indian beads around her neck and a beaded headband. Though the drawings were beautifully done, Dave believed, it was obvious in each of these that Anna was not pleased to be posing in frontal nudity. Several of the drawings pictured her being held down by two Indian females.

Dave noticed that Ezra's room, unlike the other rooms, had a wooden floor. "Look, there's a trap door," Dave said. "Give me a pistol and hand me my whip. This must be the tunnel. I'll go down and follow it."

After Dave took the pistol and his Reaper from Titus he pulled up the trap door and could see the tunnel below. "I need a light. Eben, hand me that candle! You two go outside and see where the tunnel leads from the fresh ground. Hurry!" Dave then dropped down and began following the four-foot high tunnel. He could see it had been dug like a ditch and then branches and logs had been put over the top and earth on top of that.

Is Ezra waiting for me in the dark? Dave wondered, as he progressed slowly, walking bent over. After 200 feet he reached the end of the tunnel. There was a trap door over his head. He put the candle out and lifted the trap door slowly just a crack and saw that it opened to the inside of another building. Corn was piled at one end, and Dave could see Ezra and Squire Antonio near the door looking out of the two slit windows.

Suddenly, the door burst open, and Eben came crashing through, immediately followed by Titus. Ezra swung his pistol and hit Eben on the head, knocking him to the floor unconscious. Then the Squire swung his musket, catching Titus in the neck, causing him to fall just in front of Dave. Ezra held his gun on Titus and said, "Don't go for your pistol, Titus, or I'll have to kill you. Now, turn around so I can tie you up."

Dave brought his pistol up. He opened the trap door another two inches and yelled, "Ezra, drop the gun, or I'll put a ball through your head!"

Ezra turned quickly at the sound of Dave's voice and fired without really seeing Dave in the dim light of early dawn. The shot missed Dave, but caused him to lower the trap door. Before Dave could raise the door again and bring his pistol back up to fire, Ezra yelled out, "Let's get out of here!" and with that, he and the Indian rushed out the door.

Dave quickly climbed out of the tunnel, as Titus and Eben, recovering from their painful blows, slowly struggled to their feet.

"Come on!" Dave yelled, "we can't let him get away now!"

The three of them rushed out the door just in time to see Ezra and Squire Antonio shove off in a canoe. "There they are!" Titus shouted, and the three of them ran to the riverbank.

"Here's another canoe," Dave said. "The paddles are still in it. Titus, you get in the stern; Eben, get in front; I'll take the center." They quickly launched the canoe, and as Dave looked up ahead, he could see Antonio paddling in the stern and Ezra in the center with his rifle, about a hundred yards south.

As Dave sat down in the center of the canoe, he said, "Titus, try and steer directly behind them so Ezra won't be able to shoot; the Indian will be in his way."

Titus and Eben paddled as hard as they could and began gaining on the canoe ahead. By skillful steering, Titus was able to keep their canoe in line directly behind Ezra's, but when they closed to within 50 yards Ezra's canoe made a hard left turn following the curved path of the river, thus allowing Ezra a clean shot at his pursuers.

Dave saw Ezra rest the barrel of his rifle on the gunnel of his canoe and point it toward them.

"Drop down, Dave," Titus said. "He'll aim at you for sure."

But just as Dave thought Ezra is about to shoot, Dave fired his pistol. Though the bullet missed Ezra completely, the noise threw him off so that when Ezra fired he only hit the side of the canoe just below the gunnel rim. *That was too close,* Dave said to himself.

Ezra frantically tried to reload his rifle while Dave did the same with his pistol. Now they were again directly behind Ezra and approaching fast as Dave's canoeists dug their paddles in deep and pulled through hard. Eben just kept his head down to increase his power, letting Titus do all the steering. When they were just ten yards away, Ezra yelled something at Antonio, who bent way forward, allowing Ezra to rest his rifle barrel on Antonio's shoulder, pointing it right at Dave's canoe.

"Get down, Eben," Dave yelled, and Eben leaned backward to get himself as low as possible. Ezra's canoe now had no one steering it. Just as Ezra was about to fire, his canoe hit a rock, making it turn sideways, tipping the canoe, and throwing Ezra almost out of it. Fighting for balance, he dropped his rifle to the bottom of the canoe. At the same time, Dave fired his pistol, which hit Ezra's canoe below the water line so that it began filling with water.

"Damn it all!" yelled Ezra, as he tried to recover his balance. He quickly picked up his rifle before it got wet. By now Dave's canoe was along side Ezra's about ten feet away.

Dave picked up the Reaper from the floor of the canoe. While Ezra was again bringing his rifle up to aim, Dave gave a mighty sideways crack of the whip, wrapping it right around Ezra, just as he'd done with Anna at the Hartford fair. He yanked on it hard, pulling Ezra right out of the canoe into the water, his rifle falling as well.

Though Ezra's canoe tipped so that it almost capsized, Squire Antonio managed to stay in it and continued paddling off down the river.

Dave's canoe was almost on top of Ezra now, but Ezra, standing in three feet of rushing water, took his hands and, struggling vigorously, quickly unwrapped the whip. Dave aimed his pistol and yelled, "Ezra, I got my pistol aimed at your damn head. Raise your arms up high!"

Ezra, realizing he would be killed at such a close range, raised his hands and said, "Don't shoot me, Hotchkiss!"

Dave replied, "I should shoot you, you stinkin' bastard, after all you've done. Instead, you're gonna stand trial. Eben, here take this pistol. Titus, hold the canoe steady!"

Titus was back paddling furiously to keep the canoe from going down the river.

"Now, Ezra, turn around and walk slowly toward shore," Dave said. Ezra did as he was told. When he was close to shore in only one foot of water, where the current was much slower, Dave yelled, "Halt now!"

Dave stepped out of the canoe into the cold spring water with the whip in his hands and walked toward Ezra, who still had his back to Dave. When Dave was within a few feet of Ezra so that his body was now blocking Eben's sight of Ezra, Ezra suddenly turned, pulled a large hunting knife out of his belt, and lunged at Dave yelling. "I got you now, Hotchkiss!"

But Dave, being wary of Ezra anyway, stepped back and brought the coiled whip in his left hand up in front of him so that Ezra's knife arm caught in at least three coils. Dave then quickly twisted the coiled whip several times around Ezra's arm, and said, "Who's got who!" At the same time Dave stepped to one side, giving Eben a good view of Ezra.

"Drop the damn knife!" Dave yelled.

Eben took up the cry too, "Ezra, damn you, you slimy weasel! I'll blow your stupid head off! Drop the knife!"

Seeing that he was helpless now, Ezra let the knife go.

"Titus, paddle closer to the shore so we can get the varmint in the canoe," Dave said.

Dave then tied Ezra's hands behind him, using the whip as a rope. He had Ezra climb into the canoe carefully and sit down on the bottom, after which Dave tied his feet together.

"What'll we do about that Indian that got away?" Titus asked.

"Let him go. I don't want to risk losing Ezra. We still got to paddle upstream to Ononaquaga."

"Ezra, you murderer!" Eben yelled, "you're gonna hang now."

"Unfortunately, he's not the murderer," Dave said, and he explained to them what the Squire and Ezra had told him.

Chapter 34

Home

Upon reaching Ononaquaga, they marched Ezra back to the main building with his hands tied behind his back. As they came into the building, Dave looked around and saw that the Indians now were all tied up, their heads hanging down and the two females crying. Anna was sitting on Reuben's lap, her head cradled in his shoulder. Doolittle, his wife, and Captain Knox were sitting on the same large log that Reuben was on, and James, Eben, Shipman, and Fred were sitting on the dirt floor, still holding their weapons on their prisoners. Pres, looking very pale, was lying flat on a blanket which Aza must have taken from the Indians. Captain John lay next to him.

As soon as Anna saw Ezra, she yelled out, "Don't let him near me, Reuben!" and she hugged her husband and buried her head in his chest. The once vibrant, athletic young lady, who had been afraid of no one, appeared to Dave to have been reduced to a frightened child.

Titus, Eben, and Dave went up to Anna to greet her and help comfort her. She was so pleased to see her brothers that she stood up and clasped Dave to her bosom. But, as Anna did this, Reuben glared at Ezra while his face became tense in anger. He leaped up and ran forward, yelling, "Hopkins, you filthy God-damned bastard!" and he rammed his head into Ezra's chest, knocking him to the ground. Then Reuben got on top of him and began choking him with both hands.

"Don't kill him, Reuben!" Titus yelled, as he grabbed Reuben by the shoulders and tried to pull off the determined, vengeful man. Reuben finally stood up and shouted, "Ezra, how could you do this! You've hurt and soiled my Anna. You won't get away with this, I swear!"

"I do love Anna," Ezra said, as he lay on the ground, his face still red from the choking. Once he saw Reuben wasn't going to attack again, he struggled slowly to his feet and sat down on a log.

"Dave," Eben said, as he waved his hand around, "what are we gonna do with all these Indians? It's eighty miles back to Cooper's place. Not counting the Doolittles and Captain Knox, there's just eight of us, and Pres can't help any. There's eighteen Indians here. Should we let them go?"

"I don't know," Dave said. "They did help Ezra, almost killed Captain John, wounded Pres, and held Anna, but it was Ezra's doing, really. Ship, you know more about Indians than any of us. What do you think?"

The old hunter, leaning on his rifle, paused and then said, "Let me talk to their leaders now that Chief Ezra and Squire Antonio are no longer among them." Ship went over and talked to the Indians for a while in their tongue.

When Ship came back to Dave and the others, he said, "The Indians say they no longer believe in Ezra. I got them to promise that, if we let them go, they'll return to Canada."

"How do we know they won't attack us shortly after we let them go while we travel to Otsego Lake?" Eben asked.

"We'll take all their weapons," Titus said. "They won't be much of a threat that way."

"Is Anna fit to travel, Reuben?" Dave asked.

"I can answer for myself," Anna said. "I'm a little weak, but I can make it, I believe," and she smiled at all her rescuers.

"We can lay her and Captain John on the bottom of two of the canoes with the supplies and the Indian weapons," Titus said.

Dave and his party began to discuss going to look over the Allison patent. "It's only a few more miles," Dave said. "I'm sure anxious to see that land, but I'm even more anxious to bring Ezra to the fate that justice will provide him."

"Why can't you do both?" Comfort said. "You and Doolittle and Shipman could go down there and look it over; we'll wait here for your return."

"I think I'll go too," James said.

Dave, along with the three others, took one of the canoes and paddled south. After about four miles, Ship said, "This is the country you wanted to see."

They all disembarked and looked around. Dave said, "This is good farmland and flatter than the parcel Cooper picked for me." It was mostly rich earth, fairly level on both sides of the river with hills rising gradually several hundred yards back from the riverbanks. The flat land closer to the river appeared to be high enough to withstand most flooding.

Doolittle was pleased too and said, "I don't see any Indians around to fight with. If I can get good title to some of this, I'd buy it."

After beaching the canoe, they studied the area on both sides of the river, noting where the surveyors had made blazes on trees, and then camped overnight there. Doolittle and Dave discussed the attributes of the property. In the morning they paddled up the river to meet the others at Ononaquaga.

When they arrived, Dave sat down and described to Frederick, his brothers, and friends the land he had seen.

"Look Pa," Frederick said, "see what I bought off the Indians. He held up some pelts. "I'll see if Ma Penny can sew them into a coat."

"What else you got?" Dave asked, as he checked the quality of the fox and rabbit pelts.

Clarence Hotchkiss

"Well, I got a tomahawk," and he held up proudly the stone-headed toma-hawk. "It didn't cost me a penny either, since I found it."

They soon released the Indians and sent them on their way. Dave and his party proceeded as best they could back up the river in canoes. Captain Knox, however, merely returned to his home nearby.

At Unadilla they all stopped for a meal. Doolittle said he wanted to return the way he'd come with his wife. Reuben said, "I think I should take Anna back with Doolittle. It's too long a journey to Otsego Lake for her in the condition she's in. How about you, Pres? Do you wish to come with us?"

Pres paused for a moment and said, "I appreciate your offer, Reuben, but I'll go with the others to Otsego Lake. My horse is up there too. We'll bring yours back with us."

Anna stood up smiling and formally thanked each of her rescuers. Dave noticed how pretty Anna looked now that she had had a chance to clean herself up after her ordeal.

Early the next morning the group split up. Dave along with his brothers and Fred, plus James, Comfort, Pres, Aza, and Ship, escorting Ezra and Captain John, began the trip back north. The canoes were paddled and poled up the river to Otsego Lake.

Upon arriving at Cooper's encampment, they took Ezra to Will Cooper, who said, "Ah, I see thee caught the murderer. We'll have the trial right after our noon dinner. Even though I'm the magistrate for this patent, I can't take too much time for this. I'm busy."

"One thing, Will," Dave said, "though I've thought for years that Ezra was the killer of my sister and my wife, I believe now that he's not the killer."

"He's not?" Will shouted. "But thee brought him back. What are thee charging him with?"

"Well, he was one of the gang that robbed Captain Dayton and stole Chauncey Judd. Then he shot me when we tried to arrest him. Also, we found that he stole my sister Anna, kept her against her will, despoiled her, and had his way with her. Further his band of Indians shot Pres Redway and Captain John and were holding three other people against their will."

"Hmm," Cooper said, and he scratched his head. "There are two lawyers here looking to locate here. Let me talk to them about representing the two sides in the trial."

After the noon meal, Dave sought out Cooper. "Well, who are the lawyers, Will, and when's the trial?"

Cooper sat down on his stump. "We'll have the trial at the meeting house tomorrow at ten o'clock. The lawyer for the people will be Abraham Ten Broeck. He's well trained; clerked under Alexander Hamilton."

"How about Ezra's lawyer?" Dave asked.

"Don't know much about him. He's an unlicenced pettifogger from Cherry Valley, named John Bull. Thee better talk to Ten Broeck this afternoon." Dave went and found Ten Broeck, a bald young Dutch man from New Jersey.

The next morning in the meeting house a group of back-woodsmen and farmers picked by Cooper agreed to serve as the jury, and Ten Broeck briefly presented the charges against Ezra who sat in a chair with his head down next to John Bull. Ten Broeck then called on Dave to testify. "Now, Mr. Hotchkiss tell us how you know Ezra here was with a gang of robbers back in Connecticut who robbed a certain Captain Dayton and stole a boy named Chauncey Judd."

Dave told the story of what had happened. Several times Ezra whispered something in his lawyer's ear.

John Bull then stood up and said, "Mr. Hotchkiss, I understand that at the time of this robbery you were under the impression that Ezra Hopkins here had shot and killed your sister and your wife. Is that correct?" and he turned and smirked at the jury.

"That's correct," Dave said; "since then I've learned another man killed them."

"Then you were extremely anxious to capture the man you thought was the murderer. Isn't that correct?"

"Yes, I was."

"Now what made you think that one of the robbers was Ezra?" Bull, asked.

"Two things. First, I was told by my brother that Mrs. Dayton said that one of the men who robbed her was called Martin, which was the name he used when he served as an assistant surgeon for the American Army in New York City in '76. The other reason is she described Ezra including his unusual eye condition."

"Didn't you tell us you only saw Martin for a second when it was dark out?" Bull asked, winking at the jury.

"That's right," Dave said.

"And how far away from him were you when this man Martin jumped out the window?" Bull asked.

"About fifteen feet," Dave replied.

"Ah hah," Bull cried out, "and you expect these good men to believe you recognized a man you hadn't seen in five years when you only saw him from the back for just a second when it was very dark?" and he stood before the jury with his eyebrows raised.

"I have a question for Mr. Hotchkiss," Ten Broeck said as he stood up.

"Go ahead," Cooper said, "get to it."

"Tell me, didn't Martin cry out something when he saw you that made you certain the man who called himself Martin was Ezra?"

"Yes, he said, 'Oh, no, Hotchkiss!'"

"So there was no doubt in your mind that Martin was Ezra?" Ten Broeck said.

"Absolutely none," Dave answered.

"But Mr. Hotchkiss," Bull said, as he stood up and began pacing back and forth with his hands behind his back, "wasn't it very noisy with all those men in the adjoining room arresting the others in the gang?"

"Yes, it was noisy," Dave said.

"Then how could you clearly hear the man you thought was Mr. Hopkins," Bull said, and he turned and glared at Dave.

"I heard him all right," Dave said, and he glared right back at Bull.

"I think not," Bull said, and he sat down.

Then Ten Broeck stood up again and said, "Now Mr. Hotchkiss tell us what you know of Ezra Hopkins more recent crimes."

So Dave told how Pres and Captain John were shot and how he had been captured and held prisoner along with Pres, Aza, and Shipman and how he had discovered his sister, Anna, was being held by Ezra in a separate room.

Then Mr. Bull stood and said, "Now, Mr. Hotchkiss, did Ezra actually shoot Pres Redway and the Indian, Captain John?"

"No, but he was the chief of those Indians that did."

"Isn't it true that Mr. Hopkins amputated Redway's leg to save his life," Bull asked.

"Yes, or at least that's what he said," Dave said.

"And did he not do a professional job?" Bull asked.

"It appeared so," Dave replied.

"Then why would such a villain, as you call Mr. Hopkins, do such a good Samaritan deed?" Bull said, and he smirked again.

"Because his intention was to hold us all to exchange to New York State for land. He wanted Pres alive for his own financial gain."

"Hah, gentlemen of the jury, do you believe that someone of normal intelligence would believe that New York State would ever do such a thing?" Bull said, as he looked at the jury. "I think not."

"Now, Mr. Hotchkiss," Bull continued, "about your sister Anna, when you found her did she appear to be injured in any way?"

"No," Dave said, "but she was extremely vexed about being taken from her husband and two small children and held in a windowless room against her will?"

"You said that Mr. Hopkins had his way with her."

"Yes," Dave said.

"Did she say that?" Bull asked.

"No, she said she was despoiled."

"It is my understanding that despoiled means to undress a person. So she did not say that Mr. Hopkins raped her?"

"That's correct, though, I believe he did," Dave replied.

"Ah, what you believe. You once believed Mr. Hopkins had killed your wife and another sister. Is that correct?"

"Yes, but…"

"And is it not true that Ezra Hopkins learned several months ago from the Indian, Squire Antonio, that another Indian, his own son, Abraham Antonio, intended to kill your sister Anna?"

"That's what I was told by the Squire," Dave answered.

"And didn't Mr. Hopkins tell you he captured her so that Abraham Antonio couldn't kill her."

"Again, that's what I was told."

"And they had no reason to lie to you at the time since they had captured you. Isn't that correct?"

"Yes, but…"

"So, since Anna was not injured or violated and was not killed by Abraham, he merely protected from danger a young lady he considered to be an old friend. I have no further questions."

Ten Broeck then stood up, scratched his bald head, came forward, and said, "Mr. Hotchkiss, what did you see on the walls of Ezra's bedroom?"

"He had drawn pictures of Anna with no clothes on. In some of the pictures she's being held by other Indians."

Then Ezra was asked some questions, though nothing new was revealed.

Ten Broeck said, "Now Mr. Hotchkiss, do you have anything else to say about Ezra Hopkins being in the gang that robbed Captain Dayton?"

"Yes," Dave replied. "You remember I said I lashed Ezra across the back with my whip. I'd like to see his back."

"I object to such a request," Bull said.

Cooper stood up and said, "Ezra, stand up and turn around." With that Cooper pulled Ezra's shirt way up. The jury leaned forward to have a look.

"Ah, hah," Cooper said. "That mark across the back looks like a whip scar to me."

Titus spoke up, "I've seen whip scars many times in the military. It looks like one to me too."

Ezra sat down and whispered something to Bull. Bull got up and said, "My client says that mark is from when he was whipped once for sleeping on guard duty in the army; so this is not from Mr. Hotchkiss' whip."

Cooper sat back down and said, "Is there any more evidence against Ezra Hopkins?"

"Yes," Eben said, and he stood up.

"Who is this man?" Bull bellowed.

"I'm Eben Hotchkiss. I was in the hospital in New York City in '76 when Ezra was an assistant surgeon. He used the name Martin. When he saw my brothers come to visit me in the hospital, he immediately left and crossed on the ferry to Long Island."

Seeing that there was to be no more testimony, Cooper, addressing the scruffy-looking men of the jury, said "Now, gentlemen of the jury, thee have heard the evidence against Ezra Hopkins. Thee must decide if he is guilty or not of:

"One - Being part of the band who robbed Captain Dayton and stole a boy named Chauncey Judd six years ago in Connecticut.

"Two - Did he steal and hold the lady Anna Hotchkiss Williams and did he violate her?

"Three - Did he lead a band of Indians who shot two men and held some others against their will to exchange for New York State land."

Cooper then asked everyone to leave the meeting house so that the jury could decide Ezra's guilt.

After several hours, Dave and the other people along with Ezra, his hands still tied behind his back, were called back into the meeting house. Cooper said to the spokesman for the jury, "How do you find the defendant, Ezra Hopkins, on the charge he was one of the robbers of Captain Dayton in 1780?"

The spokesman, an old trapper, said, "We find there is not enough evidence of his guilt to convince us he took part in this robbery and the stealing of the boy, Chauncey Judd."

"And the other charges?" Cooper asked.

The trapper, his chapped red hands grasping the back of the chair in front of him, said, "We believe Ezra Hopkins did capture Anna Williams, holding her against her will, and though he despoiled her, we don't see enough evidence to convince us he violated her."

"And on the third charge?" Cooper asked.

"We find Ezra Hopkins guilty of leading an Indian band who shot two men and of capturing and holding six hostages against their will."

Will Cooper thought for a moment, his chin resting on his fist and said, "Thank thee men for these careful deliberations. Ezra Hopkins, for your crimes you will be taken to Albany and held there in jail for twenty years."

"Twenty years!" Ezra gasped. "Oh, my God!"

Bull stood up and said, "Your honor, I will not argue with your decision on the sentence, but I'm wondering, should the murderer Abraham Antonio be captured and brought to trial, and if Ezra were to testify against him, would you reduce his sentence?"

"I believe that could be arranged," Cooper said.

After they'd all gone outside David Shipman said, "I must return to my cabin."

"By the by, Ship, are you going to buy any of Cooper's land?" Eben asked.

"No, I was in my cabin before he came. He'll not throw me out." Dave, Titus, and Eben, along with the Redway brothers and Aza, went to say good-bye to Will Cooper.

"Well, how about it, Hotchkisses?" Cooper said. "I've some other settlers interested in thy lots. Do thee want them or not?"

"We appreciate all you've done for us, Will, and your offer is very generous," Dave said, "but I'm still concerned about your title; besides I like the Oquago Valley land better. In fact, we're thinking of doing what you're doing with the Oquago Valley land now that the state just bought much of the Indian land west of the Fort Stanwick Line."

"But that's awfully far from civilization," Cooper replied. "It must be 120 miles from there to Albany."

"Yes, I know," Dave said, "but it's only a short distance from there to a branch of the Delaware River, which goes all the way to Philadelphia."

Pres spoke up, saying, "My brothers and I want to thank you for your hospitality, Mr. Cooper, but just knowing you're being opposed by Aaron Burr would scare me off. I've met Mr. Burr. He is a very determined person, and with his wife personally involved, he may just fight your title tooth and nail. So, we'll not be buying, though it is beautiful country."

"Don't worry about me, men," Cooper said. "At the prices I'm offering and the way it's going, I'll have all the lots sold by the end of the month. By the way, Quakers are not supposed to be vengeful, but I would be very pleased if someone should capture Abraham Antonio."

Dave said, "I'm anxious to capture him as well, but even his father doesn't know where he is. I believe the chances of us finding him are remote."

Some days later in Judd's Meadow, Penny was hanging up wash on the line when eight-year-old Abby ran up to her mother and said, "Look, Momma, Pa's back! See him coming down the road?"

Penny looked off toward the road and could see a wagon coming and some riders and said, "It's your Pa? I can't see that well. How can you tell?"

"He's riding Old Buck, see?" Abby said. Sure enough, Dave soon trotted up, followed by Eben, Titus, Frederick, James, and Comfort, with Pres and Aza following behind in a wagon.

Dave yelled from his horse, "Hello, Penny; you may not believe it, but we captured Ezra."

"Yes, I heard that from Anna, Dave," Penny said. "Did he stand trial?"

"He sure did," Dave said, as he dismounted, "and Cooper had him put away for twenty years, thank God!"

As the other riders dismounted, Penny said, "Who are your friends, Dave?" By now the large brood of Hotchkiss children came out and greeted Dave, Fred, and their uncles while Dave introduced his family to the Redway brothers and Aza Jones.

"James, Comfort, Pres, and Jonesy are going to stay a few days to recuperate before heading home," Dave said.

Pres with Jonesey's help descended from the wagon. Then he picked up a couple of crutches. Dave explained to Penny what had happened to Pres. "Watch him get around, though, Penny."

Pres tucked the crutches under his arms and slowly approached Penny and Dave. "I'm getting used to these now, Dave. I think I can even use an ax to chop up wood one of these days."

"Isn't he amazing, getting around so well?" Aza said, as she walked along beside him, smiling.

"By the way, Dave," Penny said. "The five-mile footrace in Waterbury Center is on Saturday. Also, earlier today a man named Torch Morley stopped by. Said he was in town for the race on Saturday. And what about Cooper's land? Did you buy any?"

"No, Penny, I don't think we'll be moving to Otsego Lake. It's a long story that I'll tell you later, but I don't think his title is too strong. I believe we should buy some of the land in or near the Allison patent. We can farm some of it and sell off lots to others."

Saturday morning, when Dave went to Waterbury Center he and his friends entered the footrace.

Near the end of the race a slight fresh breeze was blowing as Dave, along with the rest of the lead pack, crossed the Mill Street Bridge. The people were gathered along the main road, cheering on the runners.

All the thoughts of the horrors of the war, the deaths of Jesse, Hulley, and Abby somehow seemed so long, long ago.

As he prepared for the final sprint, Dave thought, *I'm sure gonna miss my brothers, sisters, and friends and the running ... Ah, but the frontier is luring me, just like it did Will Cooper.*

Chapter 35

Heading West

"Wake up, Gil, wake up!" fifteen-year-old Raiphe yelled at his little seven-year-old half brother. "Today's the day we go west." Dave could hear him from the table as he ate his breakfast. Penny and most of the children were gathered for a farewell meal. It was April 16th, 1788.

Dave had spent a good deal of time in the last two years since returning from Ononaquaga attempting to purchase land in the Oquago Valley. Finally, with some partners: William Moore, John and Jacob Springsteen, Josiah and Daniel Stow, and Joseph Beebe, they were able to buy from New York State a sizable tract of land, which covered both sides of the Susquehanna River near the Allison tract not far from the Pennsylvania border.

Penny poured some more tea for Dave and said, "Dave, do you really think that Gil at seven is old enough to go with you?"

"Yes, I think so," Dave replied. "He's healthy, and we'll need all the help we can get to establish ourselves. Then, as we discussed, I'll come back and get you and the rest of the children, except the grown ones. I'm pleased Fred that you're willing to stay here so you can manage the farm while we're moving."

"I'd like to go, Pa," Fred said, "but you're right; Ma Penny can't manage this place alone with just my sisters. Besides, I want to continue courting Rhoda and studying the law, when I'm able. With Raiphe, Cy, and Charles, you should have enough hands, even if Gil just minds the chickens."

"How many cattle we taking, Pa?" Cy, who had just turned fourteen the day before, asked. He was a strong boy, Dave believed, noticing the muscles in his arms. Now as Raiphe came into the room with Gil for breakfast, Dave realized that Cy was almost as tall as the six-foot Raiphe.

"I think we'll just take fifteen cows and that young bull, Handsome," Dave replied. "That should be enough to start a good herd."

"I've got a present here for you, Raiphe," Penny said, as she brought out something from behind her back.

"Oh, it's a book, thank you," Raiphe said as he looked up from his breakfast.

"Not just a book," Penny said. "It's a journal. You can write down each day what happened on your trip to Oquago Valley."

Raiphe thanked her again and after finishing his meal packed up the journal.

Dave thought back to a few months ago when he had told Penny he wanted to move to Oquago Valley.

"Aren't you apprehensive at all about this move to the wilderness?" Penny had asked. "You've spent your whole life in this civilized community, and now you'll be moving us all to the frontier where there's no doctors, no law, no meeting house, and no other people, and then there's the Indians."

"Yes, I know," Dave had replied, "but we've talked about this. The land here is so stony and almost worn out for raising cattle or growing wheat. It will be a great deal of work, but when the people in our Waterbury Township find out from us how much land they can cultivate and raise cattle on, they'll want to come too, and we can sell them some of our patent. People will come. I saw what happened on Cooper's patent. As to savages, I didn't see any there. As I told you before, they gave up their rights to the land when the peace treaty was signed."

After breakfast Raiphe, Cy and Dave packed supplies on an ox and one of the horses.

"Cy," Dave said, "Did you pack the ax and the auger?"

"Yeah, Pa," Cy replied. "I put in two axes and an adze and several hammers."

"Good," Dave said. "We've got to pack some seed, too."

"Here are the chickens, Pa," Charles said. He handed Dave a small coup of chickens to be strapped to the ox. They soon had the two animals loaded down with the tools, clothing and other necessities. Fred helped saddle up four other horses.

"Wish you were going too, Fred," Gil said, as Fred lifted him into the saddle behind his brother Charles.

Dave's daughters, Asenath and Sarah, both having married a few years before, had moved out, as well as the three Todd children. Dave's other daughters, Lavinia, Abby, and Penny were still at home. Fred and the three girls stood beside Ma Penny, who had tears in her eyes, and waved to Dave and the boys as they began their trip down the road.

Dave and Raiphe led the way, with the ox, cattle, and the four small pigs and six sheep following. Charles, Cy, and Gil followed the animals, with the tethered supply horse bringing up the rear.

Again Dave thought back to just a few months ago, when he and his partners had been able to purchase the patent for $1265. It was agreed that he would go and live there and, like Cooper had done, be the agent to sell off lots to settlers. He thought, *I hope I've made the right decision. Sure going to miss the family and all our friends. I've got to convince some of them to move there.*

After reaching the Naugatuck River and turning north, Raiphe turned to his father and said, "You said, Pa, we wouldn't be taking the route up to Canajoharie, then over to Otsego Lake and down the Susquehanna; so just how are we going?"

"I want to take a shorter though more difficult route. It goes up the Kats Kill Creek, much as Reuben and Anna did when they returned home two years ago."

"So is that why we're not taking a cart or wagon?" Raiphe asked.

"That's right. I understand from Reuben that much of the route is just Indian trails."

At Watertown, Dave stopped at a farmer's place he knew of, and he and the four boys all slept on the floor while the animals grazed in the farmer's field.

The next morning Dave and his sons were up before dawn, and after rounding up the animals, started out again north. After going through Litchfield, they stopped at Goshen at a tavern run by a man named Thompson. The boys took turns watching the animals while the others ate breakfast. They then set out again, going through Canaan and took some refreshments at Sheffield in Massachusetts.

By now it was getting dark. "Good work today boys. We covered close to forty miles."

In the morning it began to rain. Gil said, "Pa, can't we just stay here today out of the rain?"

"No, boys, we need to keep going. We must get to Hudson to take the horse-boat across Hudson's River. Put your oilcloths on." The boys, grumbling some, arose and rounded up the animals again. They proceeded through Egremont and then turned west going into New York State and came to the town of Clavarack. Dave noticed several new handsome houses and a new court house and jail. About an hour and a half later they arrived at the town of Hudson which was right on the river. Dave discovered the town had been almost entirely built up since the war. It was the most northern point that a large ship could sail to on the Hudson.

"Look Pa, we got beds to sleep in tonight," Charles said at the tavern, and he jumped on one and rolled over, looking up at the natural orange-colored beams supporting the ceiling.

"Well, you better enjoy them, boys," David said; "they may be the last you'll sleep in for quite some time."

In the morning after breakfast Dave and the boys drove the animals down to the horse-boat to cross the Hudson.

As Dave stood on the dock on the eastern shore, while Raiphe and Cy were taking some of the animals across, he heard a voice behind him yell out, "Dave, Dave Hotchkiss, is that you?"

Dave looked around and, seeing a familiar face said, "Clyde, what are you doing here?"

Clyde, along with one of his brothers, approached Dave. "I'm going back to Columbia. I moved to Ohio with my family and my brothers to an area near the town of Marietta. We bought some land there, but the Indians kept coming after us. They'd burn our crops and scare my wife half to death. The final thing was when they killed my brother Henry. They even scalped him. The next day we packed up and headed back east."

"I'm sorry to hear about Henry," Dave said.

"Thank you," Clyde said. "Where are you headed?"

Dave told Clyde where he was going.

"Tell me about this place, Dave. What's it like? Are there Indians there?"

Dave told him how they battled Ezra and the Indians at Ononaquaga. "As far as I know, there are no Indians in the Oquago Valley at this time, and I did visit there two years ago right after we captured Ezra." Then Dave explained what the land was like. "We've got a large patent of land, and I'm going to sell off lots; so if you know of anyone who wants to resettle, have them come see me."

Oh, oh, Dave mused, *maybe I should have kept my mouth closed.*

The boat having just landed, Dave said good-bye to Clyde, and he and the boys herded the rest of the animals onto the crowded boat. Dave, Charles and Gil enjoyed the ride across. It was a beautiful morning with the sun warming them. They could see several miles down the river. Men were rowing boats in various directions. They also had a pleasant view of the town of Athens on the western shore.

After landing, they enjoyed the ride along the Hudson as the road gradually rose several hundred feet, giving them an excellent view of the river. "Look how wide the river is here, Pa," Raiphe said. "There's even islands out there."

After crossing the Kats Kill Creek they headed west, and after a short distance the road disappeared. It became just a path through heavy woods with large blaze marks on the trees to guide them.

It was almost dark when they reached the small town of Acra where there were only a few houses and a tavern. Dave was able to find a barn for the horses, but they had to leave the other animals unfenced. "The cattle and sheep have to graze anyway," Dave said. "We'll just have to round them up in the morning."

Dave and his children went to sleep early on the floor of the tavern.

In the morning, when they went out, though, Raiphe yelled, "Pa, something's wrong with the cattle."

Dave looked at his small herd. They were all lying down and looked sick. "They must have gotten into some laurel or some other poisonous plant. I hate to do it, but I believe we must just stay here till they recover. I don't dare leave them behind, and they're too sick to climb the mountain."

After inquiring at the tavern about a place to enclose his animals, Dave was told to see a nearby farmer named Joseph Shaw. When Dave and the boys went to Shaw's place, Dave thought, *This is no doubt one of the poorest families I've ever seen.*

Dave and his sons went back to the tavern. "Pa," Raiphe said, as Dave and the four boys sat down at a table, "what are we gonna do here in this little wilderness town while we're waiting for the cows to recover?"

"Well, we've got my books you boys can be studying," Dave said. "Then, I think I'd like to ride to the top of Kats Kill Mountain up ahead to see the condition of the trail."

"Well," Raiphe said, "I'd rather be observing the trail ahead too. I don't think I need more book learning."

"No, I'll go ahead tomorrow on the trail," Dave replied. "You stay here and watch your brothers and tend to the sick cattle."

Later, Raiphe wrote about what happened that day and then wrote, "As we sat at a table, the door of the tavern flew open, and a huge young man entered. He looks about my age but is taller than me. After ordering a rum, he came over to our table and introduced himself as Joshua Whitney. He wears a white hunting shirt and breeches and carries a long hunting rifle.

"'Where are you traveling from here, Mr. Hotchkiss?' he asked as he sat down at our table.

"When Pa told him where we were going, Josh said, 'My father and our family located in that area last year, but further west, where the Chenango River flows into the Susquehanna.'

"'I'm pleased to hear that,' Pa said. 'We could use some neighbors. Tell me, does anyone live on top of this Kats Kill Mountain?'

"'Yes, there's one man in a cabin.'

"Pa said he'd take the sheep and pigs tomorrow and that he'd take Charles with him.

"I then asked Josh many questions about the area we were going to, which he answered enthusiastically. If I have to spend some time in this tiny tavern, it's great to have someone my own age to talk to, especially someone as cheerful and knowledgeable as Josh."

In the morning, Dave and Charles started out. After several miles, as they neared the top, the drop-off on the right side of the trail became a precipice. "Look, Pa," Charles said. Gazing straight out, both north and east, Dave had never been so high or been able to see so far.

At the very top of the mountain they found the log cabin of an old Dutch man and were able to confine the animals in a small field surrounded by a split rail fence.

"When our cattle are healthy, we'll be back." Dave said.

After going back down the mountain to the tavern at Acra, Dave found the cattle slightly improved. Five days later, the night before they were to start traveling again, Dave and his boys were having a light supper at the tavern. Suddenly the door banged open, and there was Clyde along with his wife and children.

"Hah! Dave, you're still here?" Clyde said. "What happened?" It was raining out, and Clyde and his family stomped their feet and removed their oilcloths.

Dave explained about the problem with the sick cows. "Are you going to follow us to Oquago Valley, Clyde?" Dave asked.

"That's our intent," Clyde replied. "But we have to wait a few days. Some of my older boys are behind us driving our cows."

Clyde's wife came over to Dave and said, "You sure there's no Indians on your land?"

"The only Indian I know of who might be there is the one that escaped two years ago, Squire Antonio."

"Hmm," Clyde said, as he rubbed his chin and took a swig of the rum he'd ordered, "after Ohio, I guess we can hold off one Indian."

After an almost sleepless night in the overcrowded little tavern, Dave and his sons rounded up the now healthy herd of cattle and proceeded to drive them up Kats Kill Mountain. Reaching the top after the long climb, they were greeted by the old Dutch man, who yelled, "My God! You got to get these pigs out of here! They eat everything."

"Thank you for watching the animals, sir; we'll be moving on. How far is it to Pataron?"

"Maybe five or six miles," the old man replied.

When they arrived in Pataron, Dave was surprised to see some fairly new cabins and several more under construction. They stopped at a log cabin that was built against a large rock about twenty feet high with a steep hill rising behind it. Dave introduced himself and his sons to the occupant, a man named George Stimpson, who claimed to be the founder of the town.

In the evening Raiphe finished writing about their progress while lying on the Stimpson's floor on a blanket. He wrote, "A thunderstorm just came up; the wind is howling outside. Pa and my brothers are awake now and the room is lit up by bolts of lightening. Mr. Stimpson is struggling to barricade the door, as it's rattling in the wind."

The crashing noise of the thunder kept them awake for over an hour.

As they started out in the morning, Dave and Raiphe had to use their axes in some places to clear out the downed trees and branches from the trail. The trail soon started downhill and ran along a wide stream. They saw a few Indian females washing their children in a pond in the stream.

After reaching the bottom of the mountain they crossed the head of the Delaware River, which was shallow. Finally they came to the small town of Harpersfield where there were just five houses and no tavern.

"How far is it to Franklin?" Dave asked the first man he saw, a fat man who was resting beside the trail. He had been plowing with his ox which was now eyeing Dave's ox.

"Hello stranger," the man said. "Moving into New York, huh? Franklin must be about 35 miles. You want to put up here for the night?"

When Dave said yes, the man pointed to a field nearby. "You can pitch your tent right there and keep an eye on your animals." The field had a rather low stone wall around it, with rails used to make the fence higher.

In the morning Dave awoke to the yell of Cy, "Pa, Pa, Handsome's gone!"

"Oh, no," Raiphe said. "We'll have to chase him. How'd he get out?"

"There's a hole in the wall over on the other side," Cy replied.

"All right, Raiphe," Dave said. "You, Charles, and Cy go round up Handsome. Gil and I will fix breakfast."

After the tough chore of rounding up the boisterous bull and traveling a long way, they reached the town of Franklin. As they set up camp, Raiphe said, "Pa, where will we cross the river?"

"Just before the spot where the Unadilla River flows into the Susquehanna," Dave answered. That evening Raiphe was too tired to write in his journal.

In the morning, after a few miles, they came to the Susquehanna and then followed a trail along the east side of the river, which went up and up, giving them a grand view of the river and valley below. Finally they began the descent and soon arrived at the point on the river for crossing that Dave had heard of. Dave paid a man named Slu Wattles to ferry them across the Susquehanna.

After they all crossed the Susquehanna, they forded the shallow Unadilla River and followed the Susquehanna southwest until dark, whereupon they set up camp again.

About noon the next day, after crossing a stream in a pouring rain, they came to a cabin set back from the river. "Is this the place where you and Fred captured Ezra, Pa?" Raiphe asked.

"No, we're not there yet," Dave said.

"Can we go in the cabin and get dry, Pa?" Charles asked. "What with the rain and going through that stream, I'm soaked through."

"All right, Charles, we'll see how friendly they are," Dave said. He dismounted and was about to knock on the door when the door opened.

Dave said, "John! John Doolittle, what a surprise! Good to see you," and he shook hands vigorously with the serious, rugged man.

"It's a pleasure to see you, too, David," Doolittle said, a black curl hanging over his sunburned forehead. "Come on in and bring your boys. You can put the animals in the field here. Look, Ma, it's Dave Hotchkiss and his boys." Mrs. Doolittle came forward with her three children and greeted her guests.

After drying off, Dave and the boys sat down to a good dinner with the Doolittles. They caught up with each other on what had happened to them in the last two years. After finishing, Dave asked Raiphe and Cy to go out and check on the animals.

"Do you have any neighbors?" Dave asked.

"When we first got here our only neighbors were John Lamphere and the Badger brothers about six miles north, but now Captain Knox and his wife, Lydia, returned. They're right across the river."

"Then there's Doc Guernsey," Mrs. Doolittle said.

"Yeah, that's right," John said. "Are you headed for the Allison patent?"

"No," Dave said, "we're going to... ."

"Pa, Pa!" The door burst open and Charles stood there. "Two Indians stole Bubbles."

"What?" Dave said as he stood up from the table.

"Yeah, they shot an arrow into her. Then one of them picked up the sheep carcass, put it on his shoulders, and they ran off into the woods. Raiphe ran after them."

"He did? Charles, get Cy!" Dave yelled. "We got to go after Raiphe!"

"I'll come with you," Doolittle said, and he grabbed a musket and ran out the door after Dave. The rain had stopped.

Dave saw Gil sitting on the wet ground crying. When he saw his father coming he shouted, "Pa, the Indian shot my Bubbles."

When Raiphe saw Bubbles fall and an Indian pick her up, he was at the full length of the field away from the Indian. *Those damn Indians ain't gonna get away with this,* Raiphe said to himself.

"Charles, go get Pa! I'm going after them," he yelled, and he picked up his musket and ran the length of the field. He quickly climbed the fence. The path ahead was very narrow, and it twisted and turned through the woods. He wondered, *Are they up ahead, or did they turn off somewhere?*

Raiphe ran as silently as possible, stopping occasionally to listen for any sound ahead. After about 500 yards he came around a curve and suddenly saw a clearing ahead, and there they were on the far side about a hundred feet away.

He stopped and stared across the clearing. It appeared that the Indians had stopped a moment so that the older Indian could catch his breath. He was sitting on a rock. Both he and the younger Indian, who was still carrying the sheep on his shoulders, looked back at Raiphe.

"Stop," Raiphe yelled, "put that sheep down, or I'll shoot!" and he aimed his musket in their direction.

Dave heard a shot from the woods and shouted, "Hurry, John!" *Oh, my God. Lord, protect Raiphe from harm,* Dave prayed as he ran to the end of the field in the direction they had heard the shot.

Charles yelled, "Raiphe went in here, Pa," and he pointed at a path at the far corner that went into the woods. Dave led the others running on the path, yelling out Raiphe's name.

"Pa, Pa, I'm right here," Raiphe shouted, and a few yards later there he was, walking on the path toward them smiling, with the dead Bubbles on his shoulders.

"What happened, Raiphe?" Dave asked. "Are you all right?"

"Yes, yes, Pa; I'm fine. When I saw that Indian pick up Bubbles, I grabbed my musket and ran after the two of them." Then he told them what happened. "I just fired over their heads."

They returned to Doolittle's field. "Well, Pa," Raiphe said, as he put Bubbles down, "looks like we're gonna be eating mutton for a while."

"Yeah," Dave said, "we'll leave a leg for Doolittle."

Gil walked up, wiping tears on his sleeve, "My Bubbles is dead. Those mean Indians!"

"Gil," Dave said, as he picked up the youngster, "Bubbles was getting old. She might not have lived much longer anyway."

"John," Dave said, "you certainly have a beautiful farm here. Was it difficult to cut all the trees down to clear the land?"

"It wasn't too difficult, 'cause the Indians originally cleared some of the land," John said. "Look, David, it's getting late. Why don't you stay here tonight. Then you can get an early start tomorrow. It's only about another five or six miles."

The next day, Dave along with his sons and the menagerie started out again. They soon came to a large house-like fort.

"This must be the place where you had the battle with Ezra," Raiphe said.

"Yes, this is it. Looks like no one is here," Dave said. It was now overgrown.

They dismounted and cautiously entered the house and noticed that one of the doors was knocked down. "Looks like it's being used as a lodge for hunting by Indians," Dave said. Dave told the boys just how they attempted to capture Ezra two years ago.

"And this is the room Ezra lived in," Dave said. It was latched, but Dave lifted the bar and flung open the door.

"Is that Aunt Anna?" Gil asked, and he pointed to the drawings on the wall.

"Yeah," Dave replied, as he put his hand on Gil's head to turn him around. "You boys shouldn't be looking at these. Come on! We have to move on."

The river now flowed directly south, and as they continued along the western riverbank, Cy said, "Pa, look at the fish in the river!"

Dave took a look and realized the shad were running. "When we get to our land, we'll get the nets out and catch some."

Finally, they came to a fairly large field which was still covered with brush and small trees. Dave looked at the blazes on the trees made by the surveyors the year before and studied the land maps.

"Our property is right here, boys!" Dave said, pointing southwest.

"It looks like good farm land, Pa," Raiphe said while he shielded his eyes with his hand and looked off in the distance.

"It is," Dave said. "Now you fellows got to help me pick a sight for our home."

"How about right by the river," Cy said. "Then we could fish any time we want."

"No, no," Dave said, "we want to be back a ways and on ground that won't be flooded."

They soon found a site about a hundred yards back from the river. "We'll camp here for the night, boys. Tomorrow we start cutting timbers for the cabin."

That night Raiphe finished off his journal entry with, "There's apple blossoms all over, just like on Doolittle's property. Gil and Charles gathered stones to make a fireplace for cooking while Cy, Pa, and I walked around the borders of the lot that Pa is keeping for himself. The land slopes up gradually from the river, and the further west we went the more timber there is.

"It appears Indians must have cleared the land years ago for growing corn, Pa says. We're all excited by what we see. Some of the trees are giants and can be turned in to excellent lumber once we have the logs cut."

The next morning they began cutting down trees for the cabin.

Chapter 36

Return

"Pa, Pa," Charles cried out, as Dave, ax in hand, was about to begin notching a log for the cabin, "Mr. Barrow is coming, see?" and he pointed north.

Dave brought out his map and showed Clyde the lots. "These lots are all two hundred acres each," Dave said. "I'm keeping ten of the seventeen for myself and my partners; so these are the ones available."

After looking around, Clyde picked out a lot north of Dave's.

A week later, when Dave woke up in the morning, he looked around at the construction from where he lay and was pleased with the progress they had made. The foundation for the cabin was taking shape. They had also made a rough stone boat to pull the stones from the field using the ox. A small enclosure was completed to corral the animals into at night, and they had even managed to net some shad, which they discovered were good eating.

But I need to bring other things, Dave thought. *Lumber for the floor and inside walls in the cabin. We need so many things.*

"Raiphe," Dave said, as he stood up and stretched, "I think I'll start back to Judd's Meadow today. Do you think you and your brothers can raise the log cabin, at least to make it a shelter for Penny and the girls by the time I get back?"

"Yeah, I remember how we built that shed a few years ago. I think we can raise it, though we may get some help from what neighbors we can find."

"All right, I'll take Gil with me."

As he started out, Dave pondered, *I wonder how Clyde's doing?*

When he arrived at Clyde's property, he found that Clyde and his boys had cleared a spot for their cabin. They were just laying down the first logs.

Clyde walked up to Dave's horse, and Dave told him he was going back to bring his family. Clyde said, "Dave, there are Indians around here. Yesterday, one of them came right over there," and he pointed to some large apple trees nearby. "The Indian was alone, and he began girdling that big apple tree with his tomahawk. He looked angry. I ran over to him and yelled, 'What in hell are you doing?' He didn't even look at me; just kept chopping.

"So I yelled at him again, 'Stop that!'

"Then he looks at me and says, 'Sullivan, Sullivan,' and he keeps on chopping.

"I had my musket with me; so I aimed it at him, but he kept cutting. If he didn't stop right away, he'd kill the tree. So I fired the musket over his head. That stopped him, and he ran off. But what did he mean by 'Sullivan?'"

"That's peculiar all right," Dave said. "Maybe he was drunk or just crazy. He was probably referring to the Sullivan expedition during the war. In 1779, mayhaps you heard about it, General Sullivan, with several thousand troops, floated down this river on rafts and barges from Otsego Lake and burned every Indian Village they came to."

Five days later, when Dave arrived back at his home in Judd's Meadow, Penny rushed out of the house and said, "I'm so happy to see you, Dave. And my Gil; hey, how are you little fellow?" and she picked him up and hugged him. Gil's sisters all greeted their father and their little brother with kisses and hugs and a million questions about their new home.

"I'm a pioneer, Ma," Gil said, smiling from ear to ear. "And I read some of Pa's books at night."

"What books did you read?" Penny asked.

"I studied Pa's spelling book and read some tracts."

At the meeting house on Sunday the sermon was titled, "Our Destiny." The minister explained his belief that the new lands in the West were put there by the Lord for the settlement of good white Christians, and that it was "our destiny to do so," a belief that was becoming more popular at this time.

After the service, Dave stood up and told the congregation what the land was like in Oquago Valley.

Upon leaving the meeting, Penny said, "Do you believe as our minister does that it's our destiny to settle in the West?"

Dave said, "No, I believe the Indians should give up their land for supporting the enemy in both the French and Indian war and the Revolution. Even so, there's plenty of land left for them."

Later Dave met with all his brothers and sisters, as well as Captain Gideon. Gideon said, "Do you have to go so soon, Dave? Seems like you just got back here."

"Yeah," Anna said. "We miss you. Can't you and Penny come to our house tomorrow night for supper?"

"That would please me very much, Anna, but we're leaving early Tuesday morning. Also, I have to talk to my partners and make certain arrangements. Why don't you and Reuben come to our house for supper tomorrow night. You can help our children pack up.

"Also, Eben, would you accompany us on this journey? I believe I'll need a strong hand to help me, considering all the goods we're taking with us."

"All right," Eben responded, "if my good wife can spare me and you'll make it worth my time."

Thursday, Anna and Reuben, as well as Titus, Eben and their wives came to Dave and Penny's house for supper. Also, Dave's two oldest daughters, Sarah and Asenath arrived with their husbands. After the children had eaten, the adults all sat down, crowded around the table, and enjoyed each other's company.

"This is certainly a wonderful pie you brought, Anna," Dave said.

"Thank you," Anna replied. "We still have hundreds of apples left over from last fall; so I wanted to use some up."

"Can you believe it, we have apple trees on our new place," Dave said.

"I understand Fred's going to stay home and look after your farm here, Dave," Titus said.

"That's correct," Fred replied. "I may work out some purchase plan with Pa later, but now I just want to pursue the law, and I'll try to keep up the place."

The guests all asked Dave a number of questions about the new land.

"It certainly sounds interesting," Reuben said, "but after Anna's experience there, I don't think we'll ever return."

"Now, of course, you'll be taking little Penny and Abby," Anna said, and then turning her head, "but how about you, Lavinia? How old are you now?"

"I turned eighteen in January, Aunt Anna. I've decided to stay here and mind the house for Fred. I'd never find a husband in the wilderness."

"How about the rest of you?" Dave said. "It's beautiful farm land there and timber too, just as I told everyone at the meeting house."

None of Dave's siblings wanted to leave their friends and relatives behind to take their chances in the wilderness, except for Sarah's husband, Justus Beecher, who said, "I think I'd like to go there some day, but we have the baby now, and Sarah's with child; so we need to wait a few years. Also, I want to be assured that we'll have no problems with Indians."

"Did our carpenter bring over those windows for you?" Titus asked.

"Yeah," Dave said, "our good brother, Gideon, brought me two doors as well.

"Now that we've eaten, will you fellows help old Dave load up our wagon and our cart?"

"Don't give me that old stuff, Dave," Eben said. "Come on, though, we'll help." The men began loading the wagon and cart with the lumber, windows, doors, a few pieces of furniture and as much of the household necessities as they could carry, and of course, their clothes.

Chapter 37

Three Boys in The Wilderness

"Raiphe, what's that noise?" the eleven-year-old Charles asked. It was in the middle of the night, and the three boys were sleeping on the dirt floor of the unfinished cabin. Outside the wind was blowing hard, whipping the tree branches.

"You woke me up. What's it sound like?" Raiphe asked.

"I think a storm's coming, but what I heard sounded like one of the sheep," Charles said. "Do you suppose an Indian killed one again?"

"Let's look. Cy, wake up!" Raiphe said, nudging the thirteen-year-old.

"What's going on?" Cy asked, as he opened his eyes and yawned.

"One of the sheep cried out," Raiphe said. "Light a pine stick, Cy. I'll get the musket."

The three boys crept out with Cy holding the torch up and Raiphe carrying the musket in front of him. They slowly approached the rail fence enclosure. All the animals seemed to be huddled at the end nearest the house, except Handsome, who was at the other end staring at something.

"What is it?" Charles asked, as a pair of eye-balls glared at them from the far end of the enclosure.

"Hold the torch up high, Cy," Raiphe ordered.

"Holy Hallelujah!" Raiphe cried out. "Looks like a panther." The huge cat was crouched over a dead sheep he had dragged to the far side of the fenced-in field. The three boys walked cautiously along the outside of the fence toward the panther. It's eyes followed them, and as they reached the end it snarled. Handsome had lowered his head and was snorting and pawing the ground.

"Careful, Raiphe, don't hit Handsome," Charles said.

Raiphe raised the musket up and rested the barrel on the top of the fence. "Hold still, now," Raiphe said, and he fired.

The loud noise plus the force of the musketball made the panther leap into the air. Its front claws caught on the top of the fence, but only momentarily. Then it flopped backward on top of the dead sheep. As the cat fell, Handsome charged forward and hooked the dead cat on his horns and threw him up in the air.

"My God, he's big!" Raiphe said.

As they hung the two carcasses up where other predators couldn't easily reach them, it began to rain. As they walked back, Charles said, "I wonder when Pa and Ma are coming?"

Chapter 38

A Chance Meeting

At Willard's tavern in Albany, a short time later, Eben, Dave, and Dave's family had just finished breakfast and were leaving to hitch up their cart and wagon. Penny looked off a ways and said, "Dave, that man over there on crutches, isn't that your friend and his niece?"

"You're right," Dave said and then shouted, "Hey Pres, what are you doing here?"

Pres Redway, who was some distance away, raised a crutch and waved it. "Dave, is that you?"

The two friends shouted greetings and approached each other. The children and Eben also heartily greeted Pres and Aza.

"Where are you going, Pres?" Dave asked.

"My sister Mehty and her husband live in Ballston," Pres said. "It's about 25 miles north of here."

"Are you two married now?" Dave said.

"No, no, not yet, but we plan to after I sell my land in Killingly and buy some in Ballston."

Dave leaned against the side of his wagon, and while Penny and Aza chatted he told Pres about the land available at Oquago Valley. "How many children do you have now, Dave, altogether?"

"You've met most of them before," Dave said, "but there's ten of them, not counting Penny's three by her first husband, who are all grown now."

"Ten, hmm, where are the rest of them?" Pres asked.

"Well, the two oldest girls are already married. We left Fred and Lavinia behind to watch our property in Judd's Meadow. The three boys, Raiphe, Cyrus, and Charles are at Oquago Valley, building our home. Then there's the three young ones here."

They chatted some more and then said their good-byes. Dave said, "All right, children, we're heading west now; so hop aboard."

A few days later, after driving the cart and wagon from Cherry Valley on the new road to Otsego Lake, they arrived at Cooperstown.

Dave went to see Will Cooper and explained where they were going. "I need a scow and a raft to take my things down the river. Also, I need a couple of men to help guide the boat and the raft and another to bring my horses down."

Will suggested that Dave hire Ship and young Whitney to help guide him and another man to lead the horses.

Dave spent the rest of the day trading his wagon for a scow and a raft suitable for floating down the Susquehanna. He decided to keep the cart, after removing the wheels, and mount it right on the raft.

The next morning Shipman showed up with one other man, a fat farmer. "This is Seth Morgan," Ship said, as he chewed on a twig. "Seth can guide your horses down along the river."

With the raft and scow tied to a dock near the start of the river, the men spent some time loading up the goods they'd taken off the wagon and cart.

The Hotchkiss boys at Oquago Valley had been spending most of their time notching logs for the new house.

One day Raiphe took a break from the work on the house to go down the river a way. He soon found a stream to fish. He had just thrown his line in and was thinking about how good the trout would taste when he noticed a man on the other side of the stream up about 50 yards who was also fishing.

Raiphe yelled, "Hello stranger," noticing the man looked to be about 60 years old. As Raiphe approached, he saw that the man had a brown horse tethered to a tree and a large dog. The man was wiry, had gray hair, was rather stooped over, and had a red, round face, though his wide-brimmed hat covered part of his face.

"Mr. Macclure, is that you?" Raiphe said, recognizing his old schoolteacher.

"Yes, yes," Macclure replied smiling, "and you must be one of the Hotchkiss boys I had in school. I heard your family might be here."

"That's right, sir. I'm Raiphe."

"Ah, Raiphe, of course," Macclure answered. "You may be aware I was hoping for an alliance with Penny Todd, but your father appealed to her more than an old schoolteacher. Are your parents here now?"

"Not yet, though they should arrive soon." Raiphe sat down on a boulder near Macclure.

"Where do you live, sir?"

"I live about nine miles east of here, three hours by my horse Hio. This is one of my favorite fishing streams."

"Did you come nine miles through the bush to fish?"

"No, I've been doing some surveying near here."

"When did you move from Connecticut to your home?" Raiphe asked.

"Last year. After surveying much of this land, I decided to purchase some for myself."

After they had talked some, Raiphe said, "Do you have a family, Mr. Macclure?"

"Not yet, young man, though I have written a lady who recently severed her treaty with another man, and I offered myself as a candidate for an alliance."

"You mean you've never married?"

"No."

Raiphe said, "Aren't you lonely?"

"Yes, I get lonely at times, but I have the satisfaction in seeing myself rewarded immediately for every hour's work. If I cut down trees for an hour, I see the sun come in to salute me."

"How about the winters, Mr. Macclure?"

"Ah, it can be severe, the winters. This winter was exceedingly cold, and the snow was deep. I was used to some society, but the weeks and months living alone began to drag on me heavily. Then the lack of bread and vegetables, due to the drought the previous summer, I keenly felt. I became weak, yet the deep snow prevented me from leaving. I became feverish, and finally I was so weak I couldn't even go to the brook for water.

"I was stretched out on my couch of hemlock boughs and unable to rise. It seemed to me that death was my only relief."

"My God! what did you do?" Raiphe asked.

"I didn't do anything. For some days my dog Beau here stayed by my side, but one morning he left, and when he returned Cornelius Hynback entered my cabin with him. Hynback lives about four miles from me in Kookhouse on the Delaware River. He said Beau appeared there, and by his actions and whining induced him to suspect something was wrong at Castle William; that's what I call my place.

"Hynback grabbed some stimulants and followed Beau. The dog wagged his tail, jumped up and down and barked while he hastily led the way back to me. Hynback stayed and nursed me back to health. He even returned several times to his home for supplies."

"Well, I'm pleased you recovered."

When Raiphe returned to the unfinished house, he was carrying seven good size trout.

"When will Mr. Barrow and Mr. Doolittle come, Raiphe?" Cy asked.

"Tuesday morning," Raiphe said. "I also just ran into my old schoolteacher, Mr. Macclure. He's a surveyor now, and he's coming too."

"Ah, good," Cy replied. "The more hands we have the quicker the raising should go."

Just then Charles put down his ax and said, "Raiphe, look! Here comes an Indian."

"Shall I shoot him, Raiphe?" Cy asked as he picked up a musket.

Oh, my God, Raiphe thought. *What does he want? Wish Pa was here.* Two other Indians stepped out of the woods behind the first one and just stood there.

Raiphe said, "No, Cy, but we can't show any fear."

The first Indian, who was still some distance away near the forest, said, "I come in peace;" he still had his gun strapped to his back.

"Put the musket down, Cy," Raiphe said in a low voice to his brother. "Let's see what he wants," and then looking at the Indian, shouted, "Come forward."

As the Indian walked up, Raiphe whispered, "I think he's the Indian who killed Bubbles." When the Indian was about ten yards away, Raiphe said, "Sir, stop there. State your business."

The Indian, whose face was covered with streaks of paint and who wore his long black hair in a messy, wavy mass down his back, stopped. He then spread his legs apart and said in a stern voice, "Why you young men build here? This Indian land."

Raiphe looked at his brothers and said, "Charles, get the deed." Then, turning back to the Indian, he said, "Our name is Hotchkiss. Who are you, sir?"

"Hotchkiss, huh; our tribe is Onondaga. This is Onondaga land. You must stop building and go."

Raiphe picked up the musket which Cy had been holding and said, "My father is not here now, but we have a deed here for this land signed by the governor of New York State."

"Hah, you say. Is your father named David? Is he a whip man from Columbia in land east of Hudson's River?"

"Why yes," Raiphe said, surprised at this change in their conversation. "Do you know him?"

"Met him once at Hartford."

Charles came up to Raiphe and handed him the deed. Raiphe said, "Here, see the deed! Can you read it?"

Raiphe walked up to the Indian with their deed. When Raiphe attempted to show him the document, the Indian brushed it aside with the back of his hand and said angrily, "Yes, I read. Your paper means nothing to me. This Onondaga land. You go!"

"Wait; my father is coming back here," Raiphe said. "You must talk to him."

"Uh, you got rum?" the Indian asked, attempting to look over Raiphe's shoulder at the provisions inside the house foundation.

"Yes," Raiphe said, surprised again by the sudden change in their talk. "You want a drink?"

"Yeah, my friends want some too."

"Bring me the crock, Cy," Raiphe said.

After Raiphe handed the rum to the demanding Indian, he took a swig and then walked back to his friends by the woods. He turned back toward Raiphe and shouted, "You must leave Onondaga land! You hear me?" and he and the other two Indians walked back into the woods and disappeared, taking the rum with them.

"What'll we do now, Raiphe?" Charles asked. "Should we go north to Doolittle's?"

"Let me think," Raiphe said. "We've got three men coming Tuesday to help raise the house. In the meantime, one of us will stand watch while the rest of us work. We have to keep the muskets loaded."

"Ship, I need your opinion," Dave said early in the morning as they were making their final preparations to start down the river. "Should my wife and children ride the horses through the wilderness, or should they come on the raft or scow?"

Ship tightened the rope holding some boxes secure on the raft and said, "No doubt they would be more comfortable on the water. But it is more dangerous if we have an accident."

Dave said, "Penny, put little Penny up in the saddle with you on one of the horses. Gil and Abby can ride on the other one. Seth will lead you."

When Dave began the floatation down the river with Eben, Ship, and young Whitney, they'd no sooner gone a few hundred yards, poling around logs and debris in the narrow, winding river, when they came to where a tree had fallen so far out into the water that they couldn't pass.

"Eben, grab the ax," Dave yelled.

Though the raft and scow were caught up in the branches of the downed maple tree, fortunately the trunk was slightly above the water line. Dave and Eben took turns with the ax, and soon there was a loud crack, as the trunk broke, and the river pulled the top of the tree around. Josh, poling hard, pushed them out, allowing the raft to swing around and float down the river. Ship followed right behind with the scow.

"Watch out for the shoals here," Ship yelled

After some time they arrived near Doolittle's. As Dave helped guide the raft toward shore, he yelled to Penny, "We'll stop for a meal here with Doolittle. Go tell them we're coming!"

The raft almost reached the shore when Penny rode toward the river near Dave and shouted, "Dave, there's a note on the door. It says, 'Gone to Hotchkiss house.'"

"I wonder why they chose now to visit our boys?" Dave replied.

Chapter 39

The Raising

When William Macclure arrived at the Hotchkisses' construction, Clyde along with Mr. and Mrs Doolittle were already there, and the two men were giving advice to Raiphe about doing the raising.

"Good morning, gentlemen," Macclure said, as he dismounted from his horse. "Is everyone here for the raising of your castle?"

"I'm pleased you came, sir," Raiphe said to the older man. "Yes, I'm afraid I have few neighbors; this is it."

The three men and three boys began lifting the heavy logs and putting them in place for walls. After about an hour, Macclure said, "Hey, let's take a rest," and he sat down on a log. Mrs. Doolittle brought out some cider and cornbread. The others all sat down on the log with Macclure on the north side of the house foundation.

"Here, try this, Mr. Macclure," Mrs. Doolittle said, and she handed him a crock.

Macclure tipped the half-empty crock way up to take a swig. Just then a shot was heard. The crock flew apart in pieces. "Oh, my God!" Macclure yelled, as the cider soaked his shirt and trousers.

Doolittle yelled, "Ma, get behind the walls, quick!"

"Come, Charles, Cy!" Raiphe shouted.

They all scrambled back to the other side of the partial log wall as two more shots rang out, throwing wooden chips up in the air.

Raiphe saw blood coming from Macclure's forehead, though he didn't seem to be hurt seriously. "Get the muskets!" Clyde yelled.

"Who the hell is out there?" Doolittle cried out.

"It must be those damn Indians who threatened us," Raiphe said. "I wonder how many there are?"

"I can see at least four," Clyde answered as he peeked through a crack between the logs.

"Well, if we don't fire back, they'll charge us," Macclure said, and he took out a handkerchief and wiped the blood and cider off his face.

Raiphe picked up his musket and aimed it just below some feathers he could see on the edge of the woods to the north. When he fired, there was a high-pitched scream, and an Indian fell forward out of the woods onto the ground. Immediately after this Raiphe yelled in pain, "Ah! I'm hit in the arm. Keep loading and firing while I bandage this."

As the raft and scow rounded a bend in the river, Dave said, "Eben, we're getting close now. Can't be more than a half a mile."

"What's that noise?" Eben asked.

"Sounds like shots to me," Ship said, "somewhere up ahead."

Dave yelled, "Pole in toward shore. We've got to stop Penny!"

"It might be just some hunters," Ship replied from the scow.

"Mayhaps," Dave said. "But I hear too many shots. Penny! Penny!" he shouted from the raft. "Where are you?"

"We're over here," Seth hollered from the shore.

Dave called out, "Penny, I want you to stay right here with Seth and the children till I find out what's going on up ahead."

Shipman said, "Why don't you let Eben and me go ashore up a short ways and reconnoiter."

After they floated for a few hundred yards, Ship and Eben got off the scow and waded ashore, while Dave and Whitney tied the scow and the raft to a tree.

"If we're not back in an hour, don't wait for us," Ship said.

As Dave and Whitney waited, they could hear more shots. After half an hour, though it seemed longer to Dave, Ship and Eben returned and waded out to the raft. Climbing aboard, Ship whispered, "They're Indians all right, about three dozen, I reckon, though I don't think they're the same ones Ezra was leading in Ononaquaga."

"Where are they?" Dave asked.

"They're all on the north side of your new house," Eben said. "They're firing muskets and arrows at your place."

The color drained from Dave's face. "Are my boys all right?"

"Can't tell, Dave, but they are firing back at the Indians," Ship said. "Why don't I take Eben and Josh and sneak up behind them and fire at them from their rear. With bullets coming from two directions it might be enough to scare 'em off. You can take the scow down stream. Keep it close to shore so that the bank will hide you."

"All right," Dave said. Then Ship, Eben, and Josh Whitney pushed Dave in the scow out into the current.

Oh, God, keep my boys safe, Dave prayed silently as he steered the scow close to the shore down the river. When he came closer to his house, he heard more shots and ducked down in the boat. As soon as he passed his house and reached the woods on the other side of the clearing that adjoined the house, he steered into shore and tied up the scow. After climbing the bank and penetrating the thick forest to a point opposite his home site, he peered out of the foliage at his cabin.

The scene before him frightened him. *My God, it's on fire!*

Because the south wall was not as high as the other walls, Dave could clearly see the inside of the partially completed cabin. The north wall was about four feet high, and beyond it, through the smoke and flames on the walls, he could see some Indians at the edge of the woods. With his musket strapped to his back, he ran toward the cabin and vaulted over the three-foot wall into the cabin, landing so hard on the dirt floor that he fell down.

"Pa, Pa!" Charles yelled, as he turned and saw his father lying on his side; "look Raiphe! Pa's here!"

Dave slowly rose to a crouched position while his sons surrounded him and slapped him on the back, welcoming him.

"Thank God, you're here," Mrs. Doolittle said. She was sitting down on the ground, her back against the west wall in the northwest corner, loading a musket.

"Pa, we're so pleased you're here to help us," Raiphe said, "but who's that firing at the Indians on the other side of them?"

"The damn Indians are starting to move toward the west," Clyde said. "Hey, I think I just got one."

Dave said, "I brought Eben, Shipman, and Josh Whitney with me. I see you got hit in the left arm, Raiphe. How's it feel?"

"Not too bad, Pa," Raiphe replied.

"Now is anyone else hurt?" Dave asked.

The Indians stopped firing and appeared to be moving west to avoid the crossfire.

"John burned his hand some trying to remove a burning arrow from the wall," Mrs. Doolittle said.

"Clyde, is your family all right?" Dave asked.

"I hope so," Clyde replied. "All my sons are there at our home site with their muskets. Damn, this is like Ohio all over again."

"How long have you been holding off these Indians?" Dave asked.

"About three hours," Macclure said. "I hope they don't attack."

Charles used a cloth to smother the remaining burning arrow.

"Look!" Cy yelled. "Here comes Uncle Eben." Dave turned and looked toward the river and saw Eben, Ship and Whitney, bending forward to keep low, running toward them.

"What started this Indian attack, anyway?" Dave asked, as the three new arrivals quickly climbed over the east wall.

Raiphe explained what had happened. "I think he is the same Indian that killed Bubbles. Also, he said he met you at Hartford."

"What?" Dave shouted in astonishment. "Then he is most likely Abraham Antonio, the damn murderer!"

"Hmm," Whitney said, "I heard of him. Colonel Rose said Abraham Antonio is the only Indian he was ever afraid of."

"Is he the murderer of your wife and sister?" Macclure asked.

"Yes," Dave replied. "Curse his dirty hide!"

Ship spoke up, "Are you saying then he's the son of the Indian who is chief of the Onondaga tribe, Squire Antonio, the one that escaped us at Ononaquaga?"

"Yes; do you think, Ship, that the leader of this battle is the Squire himself?" Dave asked.

"No, more likely it's that rum-crazy Abraham himself," Ship said. "Let me yell to him."

With that, Ship stood up behind the west wall. He took off his fox skin cap and waved it. "Abraham, Abraham!" and then shouted out some Indian words.

"English, English," was the reply from the woods. "Who are you?"

"I'm David Shipman. Who are you?"

"My name Abraham Antonio."

"I met your father. Why are you attacking these people?"

"This Onondaga land," Abraham replied. "I told them to go. David Hotchkiss killed our old chief. We attack in one hour if you don't go."

"If you attack us, many braves will die," Ship yelled. "You know that when the treaty was made the Onondaga gave up this land to the State of New York. Before you attack I want to talk to the Squire."

"No, no," Antonio hollered. "Squire not here."

"Where is he?" Ship yelled back.

"He not here," Abraham repeated.

"I will tell your braves in your language what will happen to them if they attack us," Ship said.

"No, no," Abraham shouted, and he stepped out of the woods with his hands in the air and walked about ten steps forward. Then he stood with his legs apart and his arms folded. "Is Dave Hotchkiss with you?"

"Yes," Dave replied. "I just got here."

"I fight Dave Hotchkiss. If I win, you all go away. If he win, you stay." Abraham had no shirt on, his face was streaked with paint, and he had some red feathers in his hair.

"No, Pa, no!" Raiphe cried out. "He killed Ma. He'll kill you, too!"

"But if I don't fight, they'll charge us, and we could all get killed," Dave said, as he kept his eyes on the Indian.

"We could just leave," Doolittle said. "I won't leave my wife here on any account."

"I'm not leaving," Dave replied, "especially since I've been looking forward to capturing this man ever since I learned it was he who killed Hulley and my Abby. Also, I've got too much invested; this land is mine."

Dave climbed over the west wall and, facing Abraham, said, "I'll fight you, you murderer; this land is mine, and I won't leave."

"Good! David Hotchkiss. We fight," Abraham said.

"What makes you believe I killed your chief?" Dave asked.

"I saw you whip him around the neck at Ticonderoga. I was hiding in the woods. After you left, I went to him, but the father of my father was dead."

"Abraham, we were at war. Your grandfather attacked me. I had to defend myself."

"My grandfather close to me. When you kill him I vow to kill two people close to you. Now kill you too, Hotchkiss. I use tomahawk. What weapon you fight with?"

"A whip," Dave said.

"Yes, that's what I think," Abraham said, and his face turned even more serious. "I not afraid!"

"Raiphe, throw me the Long Distance Reaper," Dave said. Raiphe quickly picked up Dave's long, rolled-up whip, and tossed it to him.

Dave slowly uncoiled the long whip and cracked it about ten feet in front of the now cautious Indian. Abraham just backed up a few feet, took out his tomahawk and said, "Just noise!"

Dave stepped forward a few feet and gave the Reaper a couple more cracks, the lasher getting closer and closer to Abraham.

Maybe I can just back him down completely, Dave thought, *but he doesn't seem frightened.*

After the fourth crack, as Dave was bringing his whip back, the Indian rushed Dave with his tomahawk raised high. *Oh, oh, here he comes.* Dave just had time to back up a few steps and using a side arm motion, brought the whip around to catch Abraham by the ankles. Dave stepped to one side and pulled tight on the whip, and Abraham fell ten feet in front of him.

"Good going, Pa," Raiphe yelled. "Get his tomahawk!"

But before Dave could maneuver to retrieve the tomahawk, Abraham reached down to unravel the binding whip. Seeing that he couldn't do it, but holding Dave at bay with the tomahawk he chopped at the whip, and after two blows he had cut through it and stood up, leaving Dave defenseless. Abraham stood in one spot, as if undecided just where his tomahawk attack should take place and gloated over Dave's lack of a weapon other than the very short whip. "Now you die!"

"Throw me your whip Clyde!" Dave called out while keeping his eyes on the Indian. Clyde hastily removed his whip from his shoulder and threw it to Dave, who caught it in his right hand while still holding his own short whip in his left hand.

Now, seeing Dave with another whip, Abraham paused, trying to decide what to do. After a moment the Indian suddenly rushed Dave again. This time Dave had the whip behind him, and as Abraham charged forward Dave stepped back a few paces and let fly with Clyde's long whip, catching the handle of the tomahawk and jerking it right out of the Indian's hand. After the weapon fell to the ground, Dave began pulling in the tomahawk. Abraham bent over and chased the tomahawk to retrieve his weapon, but as he came close, Dave stepped forward and, using the whip handle in his left hand as a club, hit Abraham on the back of the head a tremendous blow, knocking the Indian momentarily unconscious.

As Abraham went down, Dave dropped the whip and grabbed the tomahawk. Then, putting his foot on the Indian's back, he held the tomahawk over Abraham's head.

Dave yelled out, "I can kill you now, but if your braves leave, never to return, I'll not kill you, but you must go to trial for murder."

There is a pause for a minute, and Dave wasn't sure what to do. Abraham is now conscious and pleaded, "Don't kill me, Hotchkiss."

Just then, an older Indian stepped out of the woods wearing a chief's head-dress of red feathers.

Dave recognized him immediately and yelled, "Squire, I don't want to kill your son, but I will if you don't withdraw your braves."

The older Indian walked forward to within ten yards and said, "Do not kill my son, Hotchkiss. You can take him to your people for trial. I just get here. I am chief of Onondaga. We know this land not Onondaga land now after treaty. We can not fight the whole New York State, like Ezra wanted to do."

Abraham was looking up at Dave, fear in his eyes. Dave said, "Squire, your people promised before at Ononaquaga to return to Canada. Why did they come back?"

"I did not make that promise. Those braves at Ononaquaga two years ago not of Onondaga tribe. I not bring these braves here. Abraham did this."

"Do you and your men promise to stay off my land?" Dave asked, as he continued to hold the tomahawk over Abraham's head.

"Yes, yes, we go west over to Otsiningo on Chenango River," the Squire replied.

Dave said, "All right, but Abraham must go to trial for murdering the two ladies!" As Squire Antonio retreated, Dave turned and looked back at the house.

"Raiphe, get some rope so we can tie him up." After Raiphe and Ship tied up Abraham, Dave took his foot off the Indian and backed up.

Just then, as Abraham stood up, a high voice yelled out, "Dave, Dave, are you and the boys all right?"

Dave looked around to see Penny with little Penny riding toward him at a fast trot, their blond hair flying behind them. "Yeah," Dave said, "How about you and the children?"

"We all hid until the shots stopped. Where are the Indians?" Dave helped little Penny off the horse. She hugged her father. While Penny greeted everyone, Seth led a horse up with Gil and Abby mounted on it.

"The Indians are leaving for good," Dave said. "They shouldn't bother us anymore. Look, we captured Abraham. We'll take him to Kookhouse soon for trial."

The few braves who died or were severely wounded in the battle were carried off by the others in the tribe.

Penny removed the cloth around Raiphe's arm to inspect the wound. After the settlers had all greeted each other, rested, and refreshed themselves, Dave said, "All right, fellows, let's get back to the raising. Here, grab this log!"

"I better go home and be sure my family ain't hurt," Clyde said. "I'll be back soon."

Abraham was tied to a tree nearby.

Macclure stood up, his old back aching, and said, "Welcome to the frontier, Mrs. Hotchkiss." He looked around at the clearing and said, "I've done a heap of surveying, and this is the best land I've seen anywhere, in the old country or this country."

"Raiphe, where does this log go?" Eben asked.

"Yeah, let's get going," Macclure said, as he grabbed the end of the log. "I still got to go to Kookhouse tomorrow to find my cow. That'll be a wearisome job bringing her home."

As the men hoisted the huge log and put it in place, Penny looked around at her surroundings and said, "Dave, Mr. Macclure is right; this is a beautiful place for our new home."

Just then Cy walked up carrying a rifle, "See what I found over on the edge of the woods, Pa?"

Dave examined the rifle. "It looks like a Henry rifle to me."

"Look, Pa, there's something carved on the stock."

Dave said, "It says, 'Brutis.'"

The End

How Much of the Book Is True

Authors have a number of ways to find out what happened in history, but they can't learn everything. In writing this book, the author has attempted to not change history; so, of the people and events portrayed in this book, what is real and what's fiction?

The real characters are Captain Gideon Hotchkiss, Dave Hotchkiss, Preserved Redway, Azubah Jones, Polly Hall, William Macclure and all their family members, except Aunt Burt. Dates of family births, deaths, and marriages are accurate to the best of the author's knowledge. Also Aaron Burr is portrayed as accurately as possible, including the fact that he and Alexander Hamilton represented the opposing sides in the controversy over Will Cooper's patent. William Cooper was the father of James Fenimore Cooper.

David Shipman was real, and he along with Captain John are believed to be the men whom James Fenimore Cooper based his famous characters on: Natty Bumpo or "Hawkeye" and Chingachgook, the Mohican. Also, Squire Antonio and Abraham Antonio were real Indians living at the time. So many characters in the book were real people, including Chauncey Judd, Joshua Whitney, and John Doolittle that is easier to list those that are fictional. These are: Torch Morley, Clyde Barrow, Captain Blake, Constable Radcliff, Ezra Hopkins, and Squire Everett. All the towns are real, though many of the names are now changed. For instance, Columbia is now Prospect.

The events that are real are: The Lexington-Concord battle, the battle of Fort Ticonderoga, the robbery of Captain Dayton and the kidnaping and recovery of Chauncey Judd, Cooper's frontier auction and his selling lots, as well as the fact that Doolittle and David Hotchkiss were the first and second settlers of the town of Windsor, N.Y.

The story of the real people, Gideon and David Hotchkiss and his family, Pres Redway and Azubah Jones are largely fictional, though where they lived and the experiences of Titus, David, Eben, Captain Gideon, Pres, and Asa in the service of their country are based on factual information.

As to what happened to David after 1788, he managed to sell off lots and prospered.

David's wife Penny died on May 14th, 1817, at the age of 77, and the following year he married Jane Campbell. David died 5/8/1826 at the age of 86.

At one time in the 1800s Windsor was the second highest producer of whips in the country.